Praise for *Eve...*

'This is a story about lack of c...
lies and bottling things up. ...
fully written with plenty of ...
lifestyle detail. But at its cen...
and Angelico's great achievement is to create sympathy for
him'   *Daily Mail*

'A dark and addictive novel about marriage and friendship, love and sex, desire and betrayal . . . you almost
read through your fingers as they head on an unstoppable
course of self-destruction'   *Stylist*

'A dark novel that we couldn't put down'   *Bella*

'This book should come with a warning – don't start
reading if you need an early night . . . Unnerving and
exhilarating, it's a compelling and forensic exploration of
love, marriage and happy ever after'
            Marianne Levy, author of *Don't Forget to Scream*

'What a read. Dark and addictive, *Everything We Are* is
a brilliant exploration of broken people and destructive
relationships. I loved it'
            Nikki Smith, author of *Look What You Made Me Do*

'Darkly and steadily absorbing – the cool, even tone perfectly matched with the intimate, implosive subject matter.
The characters are so plausibly and skilfully drawn . . . I
loved it'
            Kate Murray-Browne, author of *The Upstairs Room*

'Totally addictive. An insightful and intriguing look into the minds of good or damaged characters who can't help behaving badly' Matt Cain, author of *Becoming Ted*

'A masterpiece . . . . Here is a writer who really sees and understands the mechanics of human nature, who writes beautifully about love, but not the shiny, happy kind – more the difficult and resilient kind that comes after many years together. It's almost painful at times in its accuracy. It's sharp as knives'

Laura Pearson, author of *Nobody's Wife*

'Addictive . . . Very readable, beautiful writing'

Kate Sawyer, author of *The Stranding*

Everything We Are

Karen Angelico

PHOENIX

First published in Great Britain in 2022 by Phoenix Books
This paperback edition first published in Great Britain in 2023
by Phoenix Books,
an imprint of The Orion Publishing Group Ltd
Carmelite House, 50 Victoria Embankment
London EC4Y 0DZ

An Hachette UK Company

1 3 5 7 9 10 8 6 4 2

A CIP catalogue record for this book is
available from the British Library.

ISBN (Mass Market Paperback) 978 1 3996 0034 7
ISBN (eBook) 978 1 3996 0035 4
ISBN (Audio) 978 1 3996 0036 1

Typeset by Input Data Services Ltd, Somerset

Printed in Great Britain by Clays Ltd, Elcograf S.p.A.

MIX
Paper from
responsible sources
FSC® C104740

www.phoenix-books.co.uk
www.orionbooks.co.uk

Karen Angelico was born in Coventry and grew up in the West Midlands. After moving between Surrey, Kent, Bahrain and Essex, she now lives in Suffolk with her four sons and works as a marketing content writer. She has a degree in Literature & Art History and an MA in Creative Writing from UEA.

Before

The ring must have cost a small fortune. Three diamonds – a larger one, the size of a plump green pea, flanked by two redcurrant-sized gems. Not a hint of colour, though; clear and sparkling. Under the bright lights of the kitchen, the pastry chef inserted the platinum band into the side of an almond cake square. It had lines of vanilla cream and blackberry mint jam, and he was conscious of not spoiling the aesthetic of his creation.

'You can't leave it hanging out like that,' one of the servers said. Everyone agreed. There was quite a gathering now.

'For fuck's sake,' the chef said. He pulled the ring out and shoved the ruined cake to one side. 'Plate,' he barked.

He sliced a fresh piece horizontally, making sure the line of cream was left undisturbed.

'Do people still do this?' he said, pressing the ring into the top layer. 'Really?'

'It's romantic,' someone said.

'Don't be fucking soft.'

The cake was dusted with almond sugar. He dipped a pointed spoon into a jug of blackberry coulis, considered drawing a question mark, and instead made a curling loop.

At the hob, the kitchen assistant was stirring the contents of a saucepan. The chef took the pan, looked into it with a frown and said, 'Good.' Everyone remained quiet.

I

Using a tablespoon, he drizzled the hot caramel sauce in a zigzag design over the back of a ladle, and after a brief cooling instant, placed the sugar cage over the cake.

He nodded. 'Service.'

At the table, there was laughter. Another bottle of wine had been finished and the volume of conversation between the four of them had steadily increased throughout the meal.

Luke wiped his mouth with his napkin. They had a round table in the middle of the room, one that Luke wouldn't ordinarily have booked. He preferred to watch rather than be watched, but this evening he wanted everyone to see.

'What did I order again?' he said to Sarah, who sat to the right of him. She was perfect tonight, her pale hair pinned up.

'The fig leaf ice cream, same as Daniel,' Kate replied, before Sarah could speak.

A waiter appeared and placed the cake down.

'I didn't order this,' Sarah said, looking up at the waiter, perplexed.

Luke grinned. 'I did – a surprise. It's almond cake.'

'You remembered.' Her eyes lit up and she gave him a coy smile.

Luke was pleased it was going to plan.

'And what did you have?' Daniel said, leaning towards his wife. He placed a hand on her thigh.

'The chocolate mousse, same as usual. No surprise for me.' Kate mock-frowned and put her hand over his. He gave her leg a gentle squeeze.

'Can I get you anything else?' the waiter asked.

'No, that's all,' Luke said.

'Bon appétit.' The waiter gave a little bow and Luke nodded a silent *thank you*.

They all picked up their cutlery.

'I don't even know where to start.' Sarah looked at the sugar cage as if it might bite.

Luke smiled in a kind way. 'Just give it a tap, like a crème brûlée.'

Kate tasted her mousse. 'This is divine,' she said to Sarah. 'Better than sex.'

'Bloody hope not.'

Kate pretended to ignore her husband and took another spoonful. 'You should have it next time, you really should.'

'I will,' Sarah said, still contemplating what was in front of her. 'But I always choose the chocolate.'

'You can never have too much of it.' Kate remained deadpan, as Daniel rolled his eyes. Sarah laughed along with them, more so from the comfort of being accepted than humour.

Daniel moved his hand up his wife's leg, his fingers soft, making her cheeks flush. They had discussed the possibility of another baby, but she was enjoying the flirtation and lightness of their relationship again, now their daughter had turned four. Just a while longer, she thought. Please.

'Enough of that,' Luke said. 'We're in the presence of culinary *art*, and Sarah needs a moment.' He experienced a brief agitation. 'Go on, darling.'

Sarah broke the cage with her fork, and they all cheered.

Daniel wasn't entirely sure what the fuss was about, but he had an idea. This was the third time they had been out for a meal with Sarah, and they never usually met Luke's girlfriends more than once. Sarah was young, a little naive perhaps, but he was glad for his friend. Luke seemed

3

happier, calmer somehow.

Sarah ate a tiny corner of the cake. It was delicious. She went to slice off a larger section and the ring fell out.

'Oh Luke,' she squealed. 'Is this . . . I can't believe . . .' She blinked and tried not to cry. Technically, they were already engaged – Luke had proposed two weeks ago on the balcony of their hotel suite, overlooking Lake Como – but he hadn't presented her with a ring. She had been worrying that he regretted his spur-of-the-moment gesture. But there it was, shining bright on her plate.

Luke was already down on one knee. There were oohs and aahs from the surrounding tables.

'Say yes,' someone shouted from the other side of the room.

'I haven't asked her yet,' Luke shouted back.

The whole restaurant was watching.

Luke took the ring. It was sticky with jam, and cake crumbs fell away. He put it in his mouth and licked it clean.

'Dear God,' Kate said, and handed him her napkin. 'With this spat-upon ring . . .'

Sarah smiled, nervously.

Luke wiped the ring, composing himself. 'Sarah,' he said. 'I knew the minute I saw you that you were everything I ever wanted. Will you marry me?'

'Yes,' Sarah said in a loud voice.

Applause erupted. Someone whistled. Luke slipped the ring onto her finger and pulled her towards him. 'I love you,' he managed to whisper. And there it was – in that moment, nothing was bearing down on him.

In the kitchen, after crowding around the doorway to watch, everyone filtered back to their stations. 'How the other half live, hey,' the chef said. He was thinking about his partner and the troubles they had been having. He wondered what it would be like to have a life like those rich people out there. He was sure they never had to endure tough times. Not in the same way. People like that wouldn't understand how love was sometimes not enough.

He put the used ladle in the sink and told his assistant to clear up the sugar mixture, now solid and stuck to the bottom of the pan.

I

Twelve Years Later

Luke is dressed in his favourite suit, with the new shirt he bought the other day, and a blue dotted silk tie. His father used to say the mark of a man was in the knot of his tie. As a boy, he spent hours practising. The simple four-in-hand, the double-knotted Prince Albert. He even knows how to tie a criss-crossing fishbone, although he would never wear anything as pretentious as that. Today, he decided on a full Windsor.

The en suite is fuggy. He wipes the mirror with a towel and gives his reflection a final once-over, smooths an errant tuft of hair. As much as he tries to focus his thoughts on the usual morning routine, the date keeps sounding in his head. A siren: March the sixth, March the sixth.

In the mirror, he sees his father, as if he is actually there, looping and tucking the end of his tie so quickly it is impossible to follow. For a moment, Luke is a boy again, copying his father's movements, noticing the new pinstriped suit that makes him seem even taller, more important. His father bends down and smiles, tells him he'll get it right if he practises. All it takes is perseverance. His brother Seb is there, watching from the doorway, waiting until their father leaves before he comes over and ruffles Luke's sticking-up patch, runs a finger along his jawline, half affectionate and half something else.

Luke turns from the mirror and goes back into the bedroom. Sarah is still asleep. She stirs, although she won't fully wake until after he has gone. He can just make out the lines of her face in the early morning light, the curve of her nose, the high cheekbones. Such a beautiful woman, his wife. Makes him think of that film where the man wakes up on Christmas Day and finds himself in the life he would have had if he had stayed with his sweetheart from college. *You've really grown into a beautiful woman*. Sarah loves that film.

She throws out an arm and pulls it back under the covers. Always this fidgeting routine. One of the good things about being married for so long – their eleven-year-old daughter a barometer – is the predictability, the unbending structure. He knows that without it, everything else would be meaningless. Only on days like today, its rigidity feels more of a curse than a blessing.

On his way downstairs, he goes over his schedule. Most of his recent investments have brought decent results, but the fund is not doing as well as he had hoped. Geoff is now laying down unnecessary operational procedures. 'We're running a hedge fund, not a fucking Economics department,' Luke joked in their meeting the other week. Geoff hadn't laughed. The old bastard is losing his edge.

In the hall, he hears movement behind him.

'Daddy?'

Zac is on the bottom step in his dressing gown, rubbing his eyes with his fists, hair sticking up in the same way Luke's does.

'What are you doing out of bed?'

'I wanted to say goodbye.'

He rushes over and puts his arms around Luke's waist, squashes his head into the bottom of Luke's ribs, exuding a sweet fusty smell.

'Come on now, back to bed. You won't do well in your maths test if you're tired.' He gently pats his son's head.

Zac frowns and steps back, folds his arms across his chest. 'I'm not tired. I always wake up at this time.' There's an edge to his voice like a prodding finger. Luke would normally try and cajole him out of his bad mood, only everything else is pressing in.

He straightens his jacket. Zac stands there, defiant, his small feet naked on the glossy tiles. For a split second, Luke isn't standing in the hall with his son, he is at the river's edge with his own father, looking down at his own bare feet. He is eighteen. His father is saying he will never be forgiven for what he has done. The river hurries past regardless, gurgling over the stones.

'Up those stairs,' Luke says. The annoyance is building now, is harder to contain. 'Mummy won't be happy if she finds you down here.'

Zac walks with an exaggerated gait, purposefully delaying every step. 'And anyway,' he says, not turning around, 'I had my maths test yesterday.' He runs up the last few stairs, two at a time. There is the sound of a closing door.

Luke releases a breath.

When his children were born, first Lucy, then Zac two years later, it seemed unthinkable that he would ever feel anything but joy. It was so simple: his wife, his children. Only, it hasn't been at all how he imagined. Sometimes,

8

the discord he feels is so powerful he's afraid he will crush them. Other times, he is the one being suffocated.

He picks up his laptop bag and goes outside, pulling the front door shut with the smooth ring of the door knocker. It is cold this morning and his breath steams. He looks down at his hands, expects to see them shaking, but they are still.

Steve is already there, the tick-tack rattle of the diesel engine echoing against the tall white buildings. Luke pauses before getting in, looks up at his house. He got everything back, didn't he? Home. Money. Family. He got it all back.

He grips the top edge of the car door and stares at the darkened windows.

'You okay, Mr Linton?' Steve says from inside the car.

'Yes, yes.'

He gets in, feeling his phone vibrate in his pocket. It is the latest release, ahead of its launch date, a gift from Geoff. Geoff likes to show off his connections.

'Usual coffee run?' Steve asks.

Steve has been his driver for the past six years. They rarely converse, but they have an understanding, a mutual respect. Steve's wife chucked him out of his house last year, threw his clothes into the garden, not even the decency of a suitcase. It was the only day he has ever been late for work. Luke gave him some cash, an early bonus. He knows what it is like to be at the mercy of other people's decisions, to have your life ripped away. Steve's back on his feet now, has a flat in Balham.

'Not today,' Luke says. He needs a coffee, but there is still this endless fucking game with Geoff. Who can get in the earliest, who has the greatest unyielding stamina?

9

His phone vibrates again, and he pulls it out of his pocket. He knows who the text is from, even before seeing her number.

Can't wait to see you

'Remind me,' Luke says, leaning forward and projecting his voice. 'The best route to Surrey? Kingston, down that way.'

Steve looks in the rear-view mirror and says there's a couple of options, depending on roadworks, and taking into account the traffic that's usually bad over the bridge. 'Is that where we're going, Mr Linton?'

'No, no. Straight to the office.'

Luke sits back and taps the end of his phone against his chin. The car stops at a junction. He types a reply, confirming he will be there at seven thirty tonight, and deletes the conversation thread. He looks out of the window. They are on the Bayswater Road now. He settles back, watching the familiar buildings, the fellow early risers.

2

Sarah is in the office. She doesn't usually work on Fridays, not unless there is a deadline panic on one of the ad campaigns, but she had a weak moment of obligation this morning and decided to come in.

While her computer fires up, she cranes her neck over the monitor to see who else is there; Harriet's jacket the only sign of life. She rushed to get in early as well, asked Magda, their housekeeper, to take the children to school and sacrificed her usual walk through Lincoln's Inn. She likes to pause beneath the vaulted stone ceilings of the undercroft and contemplate: the permanence, the brief sense that the world is exactly the way it should be. Silly really, but that is how she feels when she stands there, looking up. A moment of respite.

She puts her head back down. Her notebook has a few incoherent lines about the new campaign she is meant to be working on. Groundbreaking and clever were the directives from the meeting last week. She doesn't feel very clever today.

The truth is, she's lost her urgency. She always planned to be a creative director by the time she turned thirty-five

– she'll be thirty-five next year. That's why she went for the promotion, to keep herself on track. Although she isn't sure what she will do if she actually gets the job.

Chatter at the far end of the office. A few others have arrived and are settling at their desks. She twists her wedding band around, straightens the diamond trio of her engagement ring. All she can think about is Luke. It's the anniversary of his parents' deaths today and he is going out for a client dinner later. That will mean drinking.

She pushes the notebook to one side and opens her emails. A meeting request for Monday. She gets out her phone.

Think I'll find out about the promotion on Monday

She pauses before pressing send. Deletes the message. Puts her phone down. What she really wants to say to her husband is that she knows what he was doing in his study last night – what he has been doing most nights for some time – and she can't cope with it any longer. She wonders what he would do if she admitted that.

Perhaps quitting her job would be the answer. It wouldn't mean she had failed, would it? When she was at school, at university, she had such an inner force driving her forward. Her teachers used to praise her 'singular focus' and she was voted 'most likely to succeed'. Now, she isn't entirely sure what she was ever trying to prove.

Zac didn't say goodbye when she left this morning.

'Magda will take you to school, so that's a nice treat,' she had said.

He stood looking down at his scrunched-up toes. She knew she was talking to him like he was five, but she was trying to hold it together.

Luke doesn't understand what she has to contend with, how his distance makes everything feel unbearable at home, how it undermines her ability to cope with her own children.

Her daughter is going through a difficult stage. The other day, when Sarah came home from work, she heard a murmur of voices coming from Lucy's room. As she opened the door, Magda was holding Lucy's hand, patting it.

'Is nothing,' Magda explained later, chopping carrots. 'Not yet teenager, not feel like girl.'

When the children were babies, they'd hired a nanny. Luke said everyone had nannies – his friends, colleagues. But to Sarah, it felt like cheating. She shouldn't need any help. Of course, she is grateful for Magda, and feels justified because she works, but her old friends managed without nannies and housekeepers; they went back to work and juggled everything.

Her new friends, the ones she met through Luke, said they were secretly jealous of her ambition. They said her resolve to keep her career was admirable and she shouldn't have to give up anything. Money brought choice, they said.

But there are times when she imagines what it would be like to be a stay-at-home mum. Making a life out of organising ballet and football, getting involved with the school fundraising. She looks at those other mothers, the ones who take their children to a million clubs, the ones who make spectacular cupcakes and chair the PTA. She wonders if their children love them more.

She gets up and goes past the salmon-coloured sofas to the small office kitchen. Harriet is there, leaning against the sink with a steaming mug in her hand. They both joke about how they can't think until they've had their morning coffee.

'Have you heard yet?' Harriet says.

Sarah fills the kettle. The gush of water is loud.

'Thought I would have done by now. Richard wants to see me Monday.'

Harriet gives a sort of grimace and looks away.

'What is it? Have you heard something?'

Harriet is Richard's PA and knows all the gossip.

'I shouldn't really say anything.'

'Oh, go on, please. I can't stand the thought of waiting another weekend.'

Harriet drinks before speaking, as if she is considering what to say, and then lowers her voice. The kettle is noisily coming to the boil, making Sarah move closer.

'Amit stayed late yesterday. Richard asked me to do him a favour and type up those minutes from the meeting. I heard him on the phone.'

'Who? Richard?'

'No, Amit.'

Harriet pauses, but Sarah already knows what she's going to say. Her stomach somersaults.

'He was talking about when he starts as creative director,' Harriet says with a sad look. 'But don't say I told you. I just think it's a bit mean to make you wait.' She reaches out and touches Sarah's arm. 'I'm really sorry.'

Sarah focuses on her new mug. It looks pristine next to the limescale-crusted kettle. She bought it from Liberty the other day, imagined how it would look sitting on her new creative director desk in her new creative director office. It reminded her of the wallpaper in the bedroom when they had first bought their house. A sprawl of blue flowers – she loved that wallpaper.

'Don't take it personally,' Harriet says. 'Amit was here before you and he's been vying for that job for years.'

Steam clouds as the kettle clicks itself off.

'It doesn't matter. I'd been thinking I wouldn't accept the job anyway. The children . . .'

Sarah swallows. Stupid to feel upset over something she knows she doesn't want.

'If I had your life, you wouldn't see me for dust,' Harriet says.

Sarah spoons coffee into her mug, pours the boiling water and stirs. Keeps stirring, can't look up or else the tears will fall. Blinking and stirring. Blinking and stirring.

'Anyway, I'd better get back to it,' Harriet says, moving towards the doorway. 'Do you fancy lunch at that new place?'

Sarah drops the spoon into the sink and takes a sip. It scorches her throat.

'I think I'll just grab a sandwich.'

Harriet pauses. 'Are you okay?'

'Just tired.' She puts her mug down and takes the cloth from the side, wipes the worktop with concentrated attention.

Harriet comes back in and stands close, lowers her voice again. 'You've been looking peaky recently. A bit thin, if you don't mind me saying. Is everything all right?'

'I'm fine, honestly.' Sarah manages a smile. 'Time of the month.'

Harriet makes noises of consolation and agreement. Sarah leans against the worktop. There is a splinter in her throat, a fault line that might give way any second. She can't break down at work, they'll never take her seriously again. She considers Harriet's lipstick – always so perfect, no bleed lines. She must use a lip pencil.

'We should go out again, one weekend,' Harriet says, moving towards the door.

Sarah unclenches, the panic receding. 'Yes, definitely. Let's put something in the diary.'

'How about this Saturday? Tim's fishing.'

'I'd love to, but I can't. Our friends are coming over. I think you met them once, at a party.'

Harriet frowns and shakes her head.

'They're Luke's friends really, from his student days. Daniel's nice, you know, sincere. And Kate is too, but when we talk it's like there's something there, under the surface. Do you know what I mean? I've known her for all these years and yet I don't know her at all. I think she hates me.'

'She's just jealous. They're all older and you're—'

'Only eleven years. He's not as old as you . . . God, I didn't mean—'

'Don't worry,' Harriet says, shrugging it off. 'I know I'm an ancient cow.'

'I really didn't mean—'

'I know you didn't. You need to stop being so bloody serious.' Harriet gives a generous smile which creases up around her eyes.

Sarah had a thumb push puppet when she was a girl, a cheap wooden thing. Her brothers had one too. Hers was a dog and when she pressed the base, it collapsed. That's how she feels right now, like that dog – wired and ready to collapse with one push.

'I shouldn't have come in. I'm sorry. I don't know what's wrong with me.'

'You go home,' Harriet says. 'No one's expecting you to be here.'

Sarah nods.

'And have a good weekend. Get drunk. Give that Kate something to talk about.'

They both laugh and Sarah apologises again. Harriet waves a forgiving hand as she goes back to her desk.

The tap drips into the sink.

Sarah watches a bead of water appear, as if from nowhere, growing fuller until it falls. Plink. And then again. She thinks of Luke. His study. She has tried to make a special point of being more obliging with him in bed, but that only seems to highlight everything she is doing wrong.

She remembers when he took her to the hotel with beautiful sheets. Their room overlooked Lake Como and the sun made white sparks on the water. Lying in those sheets and making love. No fears, no swerving away. And on their last night, he asked her. He said he'd been planning it for weeks, although she sensed it was done with wild spontaneity – he didn't even have a ring. 'Say yes, or I'll throw myself into the lake.' That's what she had adored about him, his all-consuming ferociousness, his ability to make everything else seem insignificant. It didn't matter that he was older, or that they'd only been seeing each other for a few months. None of it mattered.

Last week when they made love, he said, 'Am I hurting you?'

She moved her hips to make him come as quickly as possible. It was like having a plaster pulled off a wound not properly healed. She blames her period or tiredness or preoccupation with the children. Everyone's sex life lulls after so many years, doesn't it? She tells herself these things and pretends to be reassured.

Sometimes, when she is in bed alone, she touches herself. Rolls over onto her hand and buries her face in the pillow. Once, she imagined Luke fucking another woman, imagined his pleasure at being inside someone else. It made her orgasm. And then she cried until she was breathless.

She devours articles about sex in magazines, as if the words will somehow change her. If she is feeling brave, she looks things up online. Sex problems, painful sex, loss of libido. She reads about the symptoms, the causes, the psychology. Until she is numb. Then she tries to forget, thinks instead about the new cushions she might buy for the sitting room, or the curtains that aren't quite the right shade.

She wants to be able to talk to him. Each night, they kiss and say, *I love you*, before shuffling into their usual positions. She could say something then, but it never feels right. When he gets out of bed, disappears downstairs, she could say something on his return, but by then she can smell the musky bleach of his semen.

Does he do it because she's gone off sex? Or has she gone off it because of the things he does in his study? The questions are an endless unanswerable loop.

Amit is in front of her, his smug face, grinning.

'Morning. You in today?'

'So it would seem,' she says.

She picks up her coffee, now tepid, and goes back to her desk.

3

The traffic from New Kings Road towards Putney is heavy, the continual stop-start of brake lights. Luke checks the clock on the dashboard. It is six fifty-two and he is meeting Jill at seven thirty. No need to hurry, although he wants to be the first one to arrive.

Over the bridge and along the High Street. The music needs to be loud, and he turns it up. Has to be Radiohead when he's driving, when he's feeling like this. There's still an echo of a buzz from the line he has done, but he could do with another.

All day he's been seeing his mother everywhere. It happens sometimes, not just today, although today is often the worst. At lunch, she was the woman who queued ahead of him. It was the way she kept touching her fingers to her nape, checking her hair was still in place. Later, she was the woman who stood in front of a shop window, elegant in her long camel coat. When he walked past, she smiled, as if seeing him had brightened her day. And in the pub just now, as he waited to buy his supplies for the night, she was the woman at the bar, smoothing down her skirt. She stood with a man and had her hand on his arm, her fingers in the crook of his elbow. Luke couldn't tear his eyes off them. It brought back memories of summers in Italy. Everything had slowed there. Even Seb was peaceful. All of them together on the terrace, Seb catching crickets in the grass. His mother would rest her hand on his father's arm. That simple gesture, something so familiar and yet so compelling. It made him feel safe.

The phone cuts in, ringing urgently. He forgot to turn it off. He never normally forgets.

'Hello?' he says. 'I'm driving.'

'Darling, I know. I saw your car was gone. Why are you taking your car?'

He cannot stand to hear Sarah's voice. She doesn't belong in the place he is in.

'Do I need permission?'

'Don't be silly.' She laughs, although he can tell she isn't sure if he is joking. 'Are you okay? You sound—'

'I'm fine. Fine. Concentrating on driving.'

'Don't be too late, will you? Dan and Kate are coming tomorrow. You haven't forgotten, have you? I've made a lamb cassoulet. But I can't remember, do they like lamb? I should have checked before now and—'

He knows the lamb is an excuse. She knows what Dan and Kate like to eat.

'Look, I have to go. The traffic's a nightmare.'

'Please drive carefully, darling . . . and don't drink, will you? Luke, please don't drink and drive.'

He tells her he won't, and they say goodbye. I love you, she says, and he says it back. There is a cold snap as soon as she is gone. He turns the music back up and thinks about Jill. Everything else needs to disappear.

★

The restaurant is easy to find. A short walk from the car park. A trendy place, a vision of dark leather, dark wood, chrome. He pulls up a stool and orders a single shot of bourbon. There are a few couples eating, a group of women laughing and two other lone men. The couple at the nearest table are young. They look no more than eighteen, but everyone looks like a teenager now he's the wrong side of forty-five. The boy is fawning over the girl, his body language apologetic, submissive. The girl tells him she wants to *pig out* after her shitty week. 'Let's get smashed tonight,' she says, and laughs brashly. She holds the menu in front of her face. The boy's eyes are searching, eager for her to look at him, and when she does, the boy reaches his hand across the table to take hers. 'I love you,' she says. Luke turns away, unable to watch them any more.

He sees Jill a moment before she spots him. She looks different out of her work suit. Her legs are slim in tight blue jeans, her body unusually trim for a woman of her age. She wears the sort of outfit that tells him she is trying hard to be sexy but wants to make it look as if she's not bothered. He likes that.

They reach towards each other, although he notices she doesn't let herself get too close. They politely shake hands. He feels familiarity in this routine and yet at the same time a frisson of newness.

'Did you find it okay?' she says. 'It's so easy coming from town. That's why I moved out here.'

He nods in agreement and tells her he parked in the car park she recommended. He asks what she would like to drink and waves at the barman, orders two small glasses of Sauvignon Blanc. She perches on a bar stool. He can see how nervous she is, twisting her earrings around then touching the buttons on her top.

'You look lovely,' he says, and makes sure to hold her gaze for just long enough. 'Shall we go and sit down? Get something to eat?'

They take their glasses to a small booth with high-backed seats. She puts her bag next to the wall. He takes his time and remains standing, looks around the bar. With some women, he understands how he needs to be overly attentive, to make them feel safe; others prefer a little distance at first. Jill, he guesses, wants him to go slow, although he doesn't want to put her off entirely by seeming too distracted. This part is a delicate balance.

He sits and fingers the stem of his glass, smiles at her. She smiles back and leans into the table.

'I thought it would be nice to meet away from town,' she says.

'It's perfect,' he says. 'I came to the racecourse once. And years ago, a colleague lived out this way. Oxshott, I think. It's a lovely area.'

'Yes,' she says. 'Lots of big houses.'

He looks to the bar where a waitress is putting drinks onto a tray.

'We should order,' he says. 'What do you recommend?'

'Oh,' she says, blushing a little. 'I haven't been here before. A friend said their seafood is very good.'

'Seafood it is!' He gives her a warm smile and he can tell she is pleased.

The waitress walks to a neighbouring table, and he catches her eye. As they wait for her to come over, Jill checks her bag. Luke notices a flash of diamond on her wedding finger. He remembers the mention of a husband, how she spoke about him in a sentimental way. He recalls her saying they had recently separated, but it is even more of a thrill to think that she is taking a risk in being here with him.

'Shall we order a bottle?' he says.

She closes her bag and runs her fingers through her hair. 'I shouldn't really have any more. I'm driving.'

'Don't worry, I'll look after you,' he says. 'We have plenty of time and the food will soak it up.'

He is about to tell her that he's nervous as well, to put her at ease, but the waitress arrives and places a pot of breadsticks on the table, hands them each a menu.

'Can I get you anything to drink first?' the waitress says. He can't help noticing her slim wrists, the precision of the fine bones.

For a moment Luke considers them both. He imagines Jill's jealousy. And afterwards Jill would suck him off. She'd do it willingly.

'If you can bring a bottle of white,' he says. 'The Sauvignon.'

The waitress smiles, and they have a brief moment of connection. She bends over the table and touches his empty glass.

'Have you finished?' she says.

'Oh yes.'

She picks up his glass and leaves.

Jill puts the tip of her finger in between her teeth, as if she is deciding something. That gives him an unexpected rush.

'Just think,' she says, shifting in her seat. 'We wouldn't be here if Geoff had come to that meeting instead. It's funny how coincidences happen, isn't it? But I knew the minute you sent me that message. We've already gone over those points, I thought to myself. It's just a straightforward contract.' She looks at him, to see his reaction, and when he gives her a shy smile, she visibly relaxes and continues. 'I never thought I'd be back on the dating scene. I couldn't stand to do that online thing. So tacky . . . and you don't know who the hell you'll be meeting, do you?'

She picks up a breadstick, snaps it in half and nibbles at one of the pieces.

'I'm not a serial killer, I promise.'

She laughs and relaxes further, as if she is relieved to have the first awkward moments over. He laughs with her when she recounts a funny anecdote about speed dating.

'I wonder what you'd have thought about me?' he says.

'I'd have tried to impress you.'

She blushes, keeps talking, relaxed enough now to hold his gaze for longer. He watches the opening and closing of her lips, sees the wet of her tongue.

Once they have ordered – him the seafood platter, her the seared tuna salad – they talk about holidays and places they would like to visit. She tells him she wants to walk along the Great Wall of China one day and that she once saw the Berlin Wall, before it came down.

'Did you know they rebuilt it in the eighties and made it fourteen feet taller? With murals and graffiti all over. But it was art, you know, not real graffiti.'

Her face lights up as she talks, and he tells her he would have liked to see it.

'You should have been there when it was pulled down,' she says. 'The way people greeted each other. It makes me want to cry thinking about it. The army was there, handing out cups of tea.'

'You have a thing for walls, don't you?'

'I've never really thought about it. I suppose I do.'

He likes teasing her and making her laugh.

This anticipation is to be savoured. He watches how she takes her hair in her hand and flicks it over her shoulder as she talks. The delicate pulse in her neck, the flush of colour in her cheeks each time he smiles. He can sense what she is going to be like when she lets herself go.

When the meal is over, they sit for a while, talking some more, until she checks her watch and says they'd better be going. 'I've got to get back for the babysitter.' The way she looks at him as she says this – confident, yet an undercurrent of self-consciousness – is very satisfying. He pays the bill, and they walk back to the car park.

They stand next to his car. The light from the over-hanging streetlamp casts a deep shadow across her face. She fiddles with her earrings and then points at the bonnet of the Porsche.

'Is this yours?' she says.

He nods.

'It's really nice. We nearly got a second-hand one years ago but didn't in the end. You know, with the children and everything.'

'Do you want a drive?'

'I need to get back,' she says, stepping away.

'I thought we were going to spend some time together.'

'Everywhere's shutting now. And I really have to get home.'

'Clubs are always open. Or a hotel. We could get a room for a while. Unwind.'

He hates how she is making him say it outright like this.

'Oh, no. I don't think so.'

25

She pulls at the strap of her shoulder bag, moves it in front of her body.

'Really? What about your messages? You said—'

'No, I don't think I . . .'

'So, you've got me down here for what?' He laughs to make sure she knows he is only joking. He feels a little out of breath. 'Come on. Just a quick spin, I'll bring you straight back, I promise.' He goes to the passenger side and opens the door. 'I don't want the evening to end, Jill. Do you?'

He signals for her to get in, but she shakes her head, laughs with a nervous trill. He can't believe he read her so wrong.

'I'm sorry, but I really must be going,' she says. 'Thank you. It's been such a lovely evening.' She pulls a bunch of keys from her bag, stands there expectantly. What is she waiting for? Does she expect him to kiss her now, after rejecting him?

He shuts the door and goes to the front of the car, purposefully not looking at her as he makes his way to the driver's side. He should drive off, not drag it out any longer, only he has to feel her skin under his lips, has to know how it tastes. In fact, the craving is too much to bear. He goes to her, and she doesn't stop him as he cradles her head in his hand, threads his fingers through her hair. Her kiss is lingering, albeit chaste.

In his car, he watches her drive off. Spots of rain appear on the windscreen. The noise of the seat belt clicking into place is loud, so grating he could rip it out of its socket. His hand shakes as he opens the packet of coke he bought earlier at the pub. Then it becomes steady again, controlled.

26

He starts the engine and turns the music up loud. Before driving away, he sends a message to Eloise to say he will be calling in on her within the hour. All he will think about is the beat of the song, the roar of the engine.

4

It is after midnight. The tick tick of the clock, the thump thump of his heart. Daniel rolls over and rams his fist under the pillow. Another week. If he doesn't get a job soon, they will lose everything. They would be forced to move in with his parents, and he can imagine what that would be like. Endless talk about the beans from his dad's vegetable patch, nobody daring to mention their situation. Kate would leave him. She'd take the girls. It would be one of those angry drawn-out divorces. They'd argue over kitchen utensils and old CDs. She'd blame him for all the wrong decisions they ever made, dragging up old wounds. That one decision she was forced into, all those years ago.

He scrambles to sit and grabs the glass of water from his bedside table. Gulps it down. His skin is clammy, his T-shirt stuck to his back. Thoughts are insidious in the night, like bindweed. He needs to get a grip. He knows Kate made her choice freely. She had been the one to persuade him, not the other way around. When she was scared at the hospital, he knew it wasn't anything to do with their decision. He had known that.

It was during their final year at university. They had been together two years and were meant to be going out to celebrate. She said she didn't feel like it. She said she needed to tell him something.

He went with her to the doctor's. A week later they caught the bus to the hospital. She had to wear one of those papery gowns. The nurse said reassuring things, but Kate was clearly terrified. Her eyes kept flitting around, taking in the metal bed frame, the blue-green privacy curtain hanging from a wonky rail, the cardboard sick bowl. It was as if she was looking for something she had lost, something she wouldn't be able to live without.

When the doctor arrived, Kate asked if there was another way. He explained that she could have the tablets instead, two taken twenty-four hours apart. It would be like a painful period, he said, with prolonged cramping. The bleeding could last for some hours. He sighed and said that if she wanted to do that, she would have to be discharged and booked in for another appointment. Perhaps she ought to go home and think about it some more? He stood at the end of the bed, remained there while she deliberated. A pair of stupid kids, the look on his face said.

Daniel had sat on a chair covered with blue plastic, pulled as close to the bed as possible. He hadn't known what to say for the best. They held hands and he tried to ignore the dragging sensation in his legs, his wrists. He wanted to stand and look the doctor in the eye, wanted to say the only reason Kate was wavering was because of the needle. She hadn't had an anaesthetic before.

They had spent several days going over it. The kind of discussion that felt like a fight. She reminded him about their finals – only six months away. They had a plan, she said. After they graduated, they were going to get a flat together. She would study for a PhD, and he would get his career started. They'd regret it for ever, she said. A baby was meant to come later, once they were married, once they'd had those indulgent years of spending whole weekends in bed, only getting up to grab something to eat, feeding each other chicken slices from a packet, spooning peanut butter straight from the jar, laughing when they realised they didn't have a clue whether it was breakfast or dinner.

But still. The suspicion that she blames him rears up every now and again, like the pain in his shoulder from an old rugby injury. Their argument earlier hasn't helped, either.

It was after dinner and the girls had already gone up to their rooms. He got a couple of wine glasses from the cupboard and went over to the fridge.

'You look like you need one of these.' He held up an opened bottle of white.

'God, yes,' she said.

He handed her a glass and raised his in a toast. 'Here's to getting through another day.'

She didn't smile.

'So?' she said.

Her head gave an impatient wobble, like she was waiting for him to respond to something she had already said.

'I'm sorry?' He looked down at the fruit bowl on the counter, toyed with one of the waxy apples.

'So, what's your plan? You don't tell me anything these days.'

'My plan?' He knew exactly what she meant.

'Daniel, you need a realistic plan.'

She swigged her wine aggressively, as if that would somehow upset him.

He had already told her about the endless emails, the hours on the phone, the spreadsheets with every permutation, every conceivable forecast for how long their savings would last. The banks weren't recruiting, but he was looking into all sorts of other jobs. She knew this. They had even discussed the possibility of him teaching, only he would have to do a course. It wasn't like he'd been sitting around doing nothing.

He should have cut through it, should have gone over to her, held her in his arms, should have told her he was sorry for being a miserable bugger – *Please don't worry, we're going to be okay*.

But he didn't. That's what he needed to hear from her.

Instead, he had stared out of the window above the sink. The wind was up, dashing the skeleton heads of the old hydrangea blooms against the sill.

'I can't fucking go on like this,' she said. 'You don't tell me anything and it's all on me. It doesn't take much, does it? To make the wrong decision.' She was so angry she threw her glass into the sink. It broke like an egg and the remainder of her wine glugged down the plughole. He felt like shouting: *What the hell do you mean?* But he let her storm off. He was afraid of what she might say.

A dog barks outside and he is pulled back to the bedroom, aware now of the gap in the curtains. A slice of moon piercing the dark. One more burst of barks and the dog will stop. He has deduced it belongs to Mrs Thompson, the woman who chairs the village neighbourhood watch programme. She lives three houses down and walks her black and brown Yorkshire terrier every day after lunch. Remarkable the things he knows after six months at home.

He tries to get comfortable, pulls the duvet up. His hand reaches out, feeling the cool expanse of sheet, seeking the warmth of her body, even though he knows she isn't there. It's unbearable when they argue.

A line of light shines beneath the bedroom door. He imagines her asleep in the armchair, half-marked school-books slipping from her lap, her drink knocked over. She'll be cold down there, wake with a crick in her neck, like she did the other week. Another stupid row. He'd forgotten to put on a load of washing. *What's wrong with you?* she'd shouted. The next morning, she said she hadn't intentionally slept downstairs, but it was obvious she was trying to make him feel terrible. And he does – she's having to work so hard, juggling two teaching jobs.

He could tell her that he forgets things because most days he only manages to draft a few emails before he real-ises the girls need picking up from school. That he can't sleep and even when he does, he wakes with a leaden body. He has this unaccountable anger. Even though he's proud of how hard she's working to support them, he also resents it. Makes him feel like a failure. She said the other week she was going to write a book. How can she manage that, on top of everything else? How can he tell her that the more she does, the more useless he feels?

The other day, she reminded him about how they used to enjoy brainstorming ideas, how he had once been such an integral part of her research and studies. She kept on about it like she wanted him to admit they had drifted apart. That their marriage was in trouble.

Then there are the other times, when she appears happy and relaxed, when she flashes him a teasing look. It is confusing. These moments should bring reassurance, not anxiety. Even with the burn of desire, he still can't make his body respond properly. It has been going on for months now. He is a complete failure.

He throws off the duvet and leaps out of bed. He won't sleep until she is beside him.

Downstairs in the living room, the fire in the wood burner has dwindled to an ashy pile. The smoky smell of it lingers. Kate is curled up asleep in the wingback chair, her head resting on the arm, her feet poking out. A sweep of hair lays across her cheek. He resists the urge to tuck it behind her ear. Perhaps he could scoop her up and take her back to bed. They could make love and this awful feeling would be gone. Most of all, he wishes for that.

He stands back and looks around. There is an empty wine glass on the coffee table. The essays she was staying up to mark are also there, neatly stacked, although he doesn't see any evidence of the usual biro-penned notes in the margins. Her laptop is on the floor and next to it, a half-empty bottle of white, leaning against a fallen cushion. It isn't the bottle he took from the fridge earlier but the cheap one he bought the other day. He sets it straight, accidentally knocking her laptop with his foot. The screen comes to life. He picks it up, puts it on the table. There is an open window on the screen. A chat with lines of messages. A blinking cursor.

Do you know how many times I've thought about you today?

He scrolls.

When are we meeting then?

Who says we're going to meet? Don't be so presumptuous.

The room contracts. She sleeps, her big toe poking through a hole in her tights. The nail bright pink, like those overly manicured women he used to see on his morning train to work.

He leaves everything where it is and takes the stairs at a silent run, finds himself outside his youngest daughter's room. Can't move. Just stands there, enveloped by the rhythmic sounds of her sleep.

Kate was fearless. The sort of person who didn't blindly follow the crowd. He immediately sensed that about her when he saw her for the first time. They were at a pre-going-out party in the communal lounge in one of the halls. It was the second term of their first year at university. Everyone had settled into their social set by then, although there was often a prolonged feeling of hesitation at those parties. He had arrived late, with Luke, by which time most people were already drunk. There were plastic cups of cheap cider, four packs of discount lager. Luke spotted Isla, who he had been sleeping with for a few weeks. They went over.

'This is Kate,' Isla said, introducing them to the girl she was standing with. 'She's doing anthropology.'

'Hi,' Kate said. She had hair the colour of autumn conkers. She waved, as if they were stood at a distance, and Daniel found himself waving back.

He couldn't have explained it properly at the time, but she didn't impose any uncomfortable expectations. She emboldened him. Other girls he had met made him feel awkward, as if he was already a disappointment, but he forced himself to talk to them because he thought that was how it was meant to feel when you liked someone.

Of course, he had been obsessing about sex for months before he went to university. Throughout the previous year at school, he told his friends he lost his virginity to a girl he met on holiday. Either that, or he avoided the subject entirely. It was something he definitely should have done by the time he turned eighteen, or else he was a complete loser. Cherry prick, limp dick. Gay. Life would have been hell if any of his classmates had found out. That's why he slept with the first girl he kissed during freshers' week. He couldn't remember her name and doubted she remembered his. It had probably been her first time too. They were both very drunk. She gripped his penis and yanked it up and down with determined intensity. He endured it for as long as he could, before distracting her with a kiss. She lay back on the bed. He was anxious about his glasses – should he take them off or not? Surely, once he was inside her, it would feel how he had imagined. And then, there he was, finally doing it. He suspected she only allowed the ordeal to continue so she could say she had done it too.

But with Kate, it wasn't about sex. Not in the way it had been with those other girls. That first night, when everyone else went on to a club, Kate said she wanted to go for a walk. She said she needed to get away from the rabble. 'Do you ever feel like that? When you have to just

35

walk?' He told her he did, and she smiled. They went to Regent's Park, and went around the rose garden, even though it was February. He didn't want to admit that he was cold.

Kate talked the whole time. She said sex had undergone an altered emphasis due to changing social constructs. He smiled and told her she'd definitely get a first if she wrote that in an essay. She pushed him playfully, and said it was actually something that interested her. She wanted to write a book about it. Sex had been commodified in the capitalist expansion, she said. And now it was a goal to attain, along with a shiny new car and a detached house. He knew exactly what she meant. And although he was desperate to pull her close, to taste her lips, her neck, her breasts, he didn't want her to think he was a hypocrite. It remained that way for many agonising months – nothing happening, everything happening.

Flo murmurs in her sleep, a jumble of incoherent words. Daniel opens his eyes, aware that he is still on the landing. He isn't sure how long he has been standing there.

Do you know how many times I've thought about you today?

The pain is so overwhelming, he can barely put one foot in front of the other. He rubs his hands over his face and forces himself across the landing to the bedroom.

Across the bed, a shaft of moonlight. He goes to the window and looks through the gap in the curtains. The road is empty, still. On their driveway, Kate's car is squeezed behind his, bonnet to boot. It reminds him of another time when they had looked out of the window together. The estate agent had been waiting for them downstairs and they had made their decision, right here in this very

36

spot. Kate held his hand and they had imagined the cars they might have one day, parked on the driveway of the house they might own.

When are we meeting then?

He shuts the curtains properly and crawls into bed, pulls the duvet over his ears.

5

The fire has burnt out, not even a hint of orange in the ashes at the bottom. Kate lifts her head from the arm of the chair and uncurls her legs. She must have dozed off. Her left foot feels sparkly, all pins and needles. She flexes it up and down, noticing the hole in her tights. It's very late now, nearly three, and she ought to go to bed. Instead, she blows warmth over her fingers and reaches for her laptop.

There is nothing more from Alec, but she has a message from someone new.

I think we have a lot in common. Do you have a photo?

She clicks onto the profile. ArabianNights is a London-based professional, married, looking for passion and adventure. She could send him her standard reply – *it would be good to chat and get to know you* – but she has been thinking of coming off the site altogether. Perhaps she will send Alec a final message and let him know the truth. She doesn't know why she hasn't already told him.

Alec – probably not his real name – contacted her three weeks ago, when she first joined. His messages are often long and rambling, as if he needs someone to sound off to.

His views about relationships are intriguing. He believes dissatisfaction is a necessity that fuels desire. She isn't sure if she agrees.

Earlier, after a particularly flirtatious exchange, he broached the subject of meeting. He's getting tired of their word games, of the extended online foreplay – it was inevitable, she knew that. These men aren't there for a late-night philosophical chat. **Don't be so presumptuous**, she wrote back, hoping to deflect his suggestion with humour. He hasn't replied. There's a realness to it now, and that scares her. It was never meant to be real.

It started a month ago, with the article in the paper. She was on her way home from the university. A week where she had been reminded of everything she hadn't achieved. She had been filling a bag for years, not noticing the things she was putting in, and now that bag was broken, spilling its contents on the floor, forcing her to look and realise: Oh yes, that's what I set out to accomplish, that's what I planned to do. Here she is, still lecturing 'Being Human' every Friday to first years – it was only meant to be a temporary post, until she got a proper position. And now she has taken the teaching job at the school as well.

As she waited for the train to pull out of the station, she had picked up a discarded newspaper from the seat next to her. *Married women join cheat website for sexy romps.* It was a typical tabloid article, but she read it as she would an archival document.

'I use the website regularly and tell my husband I'm meeting colleagues after work. Our sex life has been terrible for years, but now our marriage is better than ever. I just meet someone from the site whenever I feel the need.' Linda from Hertfordshire

Kate was shocked. Not by the candour of the women in admitting their affairs, or even how remorseless they were. No, it wasn't that. As she sat on the train, the crowded buildings giving way to houses and patchwork fields, she felt something inside slowly unwinding. She realised she understood exactly what the women were saying.

That evening, she delved into the cupboard under the stairs with a surge of energy she hadn't felt for a while. She got everything out: suitcases, their old computer, toys from when the girls were little, crates of plastic food jumbled up with horses and unicorns. Her box was right at the back – the see-through plastic storage kind with a flip-open lid. She slid it into the living room. Inside were her notebooks with scribbled ideas, dense books with cracked spines, various drafts of her thesis, and the final bound copy: *An ethnographic study of divorce and polygamy in Tanzania after the 1971 marriage act.*

It came to her then – the concept for a book. She had wanted to write something before, but ideas had never been forthcoming. Now, it felt like an urgent need. She had to write it. Not a stuffy article, but something for ordinary people. A book that was relevant to the men and women she saw pushing trolleys around the super-market, the blank faces on the tube. Something about desire, relationships, marriage. That's why she went onto the website. That's why she started chatting to the men. She wanted to do research for her book. That was the reason, wasn't it? Research. She told herself she was nothing like those women she had read about in the newspaper.

Bob69 messaged first and sent a photo of himself in the shower: a middle-aged balding man with a pot belly and a grub of a penis. Days_By_The_River asked if she would like to see a picture of his enormous trout. That one made her laugh out loud. But then she got the serious messages, the ones that felt like a bright torch was shining at the end of a long tunnel.

Last week, she told Daniel about her book idea.

'A book?' he said.

'Yes. You know I've always wanted to.'

He had stood with his arms folded. The look on his face implied that her writing a book was the most absurd thing he'd ever heard.

'But that was such a long time ago. How are you going to write a book now you're back at the school?' he said.

'I don't want to be doing that, do I?'

She couldn't understand why he was being obstructive.

'You were so happy when they offered you the job. You said it was perfect. You said it might lead somewhere.' He looked genuinely perplexed. She wanted to shake him.

'Daniel, for God's sake. I'm only at the school because you lost your job.'

He walked off.

And she knew she shouldn't have said it, but it came out twisted. She also knew that if she tried to explain, it would have been like the time they had painted over the purple in the bedroom. No matter how many coats of ecru they put on, the purple still showed through. How could she say that when he lost his job it made her realise all the things she hadn't done, all the years she had wasted? That for some reason she felt pulled down, an invisible hand at her back. He would have assumed she was saying that she regretted their life together, regretted having the girls. It

41

wasn't what she meant at all, but she knew he would only see the purple.

As a girl, she used to curl up on her bed and imagine her future. The wall under her window had a patch of black mould, and she would close her eyes, pretend it was a magic portal. Every night she wished for it to open. By the time she was sixteen she had stopped imagining such childish things. She studied hard, did all the right things to get away from that place. She wasn't going to end up trapped, like everyone else on the estate.

So why is it going wrong now? Why does it feel like she's falling?

Earlier tonight, she told Daniel she needed to talk. 'I want us to be like we were before.' She thought he would understand.

All he said was, 'Before what?'

She felt confused, couldn't say what was in her head, accused him of not having a plan. She wanted to make him feel bad about his redundancy and told him they'd lose the house. Why did she do that? Their conversations used to fill her with a sense of expansion, like they were moving towards something better. Now, she has this force inside, a wrecking ball, making her say things she doesn't mean.

A noise. The dark garden presses against the window. The house creaks as it settles into the night. Go to bed, it says. Go to bed.

She shuts her laptop, making sure her history is deleted and the messages are gone. Everything else can wait – the wine glass and half-empty bottle, the cushion. She wants to leave the mess so that in the morning it will be a re-minder. Maybe it will make her stop.

The stairs are steep, and she pulls herself up the bannister rail. The wall is lined with pictures – boxy canvas prints of family photos. She pauses at the one they paid to have taken in a professional studio, eight years ago. Maisie was seven and Flo had just started to crawl. They were in town, and someone thrust a leaflet into her hand – half-price special offer. She remembers afterwards wishing she had worn something else because her dress clashed horribly with Daniel's shirt. The photographer said it was best if they stood away from one another.

Posing for the photo had been different to how she had imagined it would be. The brightness of the lights, the way she felt like a spare part, pushed aside as the photographer fussed over Daniel, getting him to stand behind and then to the side. In the end, the woman made him sit on a chair because he was too tall. *Such beautiful girls*, she kept saying, moving in to take a few close-up shots. Maisie twirled in front of the spotlight. Daniel pulled Flo onto his lap, crumbs of rice cake scattering on the shiny floor. 'A model father,' the woman said, 'Such a natural.' It should have made Kate feel proud, but the way the woman said it was cloying. She wanted to grab Daniel and the girls, hold them close. She wanted to tell the woman they would stand exactly how they liked.

Kate turns away from the pictures and carries on up the stairs. Across the landing, her bedroom door is ajar. There isn't a sound, not even Daniel's heavy breathing. Perhaps he will stir when she gets into bed. Perhaps he will touch her. It comes over her regularly now, an acute longing.

Earlier, when she said she was going to stay up late to finish her marking, Daniel didn't even look at her. He just muttered something, turned away. She wanted to tell him how sorry she was for getting upset and breaking the wine glass. She wanted to explain what was going on inside her. An explosion.

'What did you say?' she asked.

'It wasn't anything important.'

'Go on, it's okay, you can tell me.'

'It's nothing . . . just a lot on my mind.'

'Why do you do that?' she said.

'Do what?'

'That dismissive thing you do.'

He looked at her then. Only it wasn't Daniel. It was her mum telling her she was being difficult. Her dad, when she said she wanted to go to university. The woman at the supermarket, sighing while she counted the mound of copper coins. The man at the chemist, who dispensed her mum's prescription. The teachers at school. Their eyes summing her up with one look.

It reminded her of the time she had started sneaking out for walks. She must have been eight, maybe nine, when she went off for the first time. Her mum's bad weeks had got really bad by then, and her dad was either on the sofa with a joint, or else he would have disappeared for a few days. To begin with, she would only go around the block. Just to get away from the flat. Then, when she liked how it made her feel, she went further. Down the road to the traffic lights, across the park to the old railway track. *Who am I who am I who am I?* She would say it until her head buzzed. Over and over, until the words bunched together, becoming meaningless. *WhoamIwhoamIwhoamI?* And she realised that when her mum and dad looked at her, the teachers at school, her friends, none of them could see

44

the truth. All they saw were their own assumptions, and the more they looked at her, the more she felt like a song being sung off-key.

That's how Daniel looked at her tonight.

6

Sarah remembers the first time Luke didn't come home. They had only been married a year and he hadn't done anything like that before. As the hours went by, her anger had turned to dread and then to panic. She left several voicemails, sent dozens of messages, which left her cringing with embarrassment when she reread them.

Last night, he did at least come home, even if it was nearly morning.

She finishes dressing and goes into the en suite. The hand towels hang unevenly, and she adjusts them to make a perfect line. She wipes a stray hair from the sink and as she brushes her teeth, she tells herself that his excessive drinking comes and goes in cycles. He needs to let off steam every now and again. After all, he's been under such enormous pressure, being so stressed about work. And this time of year is never easy for him.

As she turns to go out, she almost collides with Luke, who is out of bed now and rushing towards the toilet. He kneels, retching and vomiting. After flushing, he drops the lid and sits on it, holding a length of toilet roll. He looks tired and pale. He says it's food poisoning.

'You should check with Geoff, see if any of the others got ill,' she says, leaning against the door frame. She knows he is sick from too much drink, but she wants to see what he will say. He doesn't respond.

'And you should call the restaurant to let them know. They can shut places down. Where did you say you went?'

'I can't remember what it's called,' he says. 'Some place out Clapham way.'

He blows his nose.

'I thought you said you weren't going to drink. You were driving, Luke . . .' She mustn't say anything more. He got really cross with her last time.

'I didn't drink,' he says.

He goes over to the sink and splashes cold water on his face, pats it dry on a towel, ruining the neat line. There's an acrid waft of him as he goes back into the bedroom. Stale alcohol. Cigarettes. She imagines a dark place with sofas, thumping music, girls wearing miniskirts, bare legs without a blemish.

'So, the fact that you stink of booze is my imagination, is it?' She follows him. 'I'm not stupid, you know.'

He climbs into bed, drags the duvet right up, covering his head completely. She stands beside him, her hands on her hips. There's a fist in her chest.

'You could've been pulled over, or worse, and did you even think about today and the fact that I'll have to lie to your friends, cancel the weekend because you . . .' She swallows. 'God Luke, this has to stop.'

He pokes his head out and tucks the duvet under his chin. 'I only had a couple when I got back, to settle my stomach.'

47

She can't listen to his lies a minute longer. 'I've got to go,' she says. 'The children are waiting.'

'I'm sorry,' he says, quickly. 'I really am. Please don't go. I've ruined our weekend, haven't I?' His hand reaches out from under the duvet. 'Don't be mad at me, darling. I can't bear it.'

She sits on the bed, lets him take her hand.

'I'm not mad,' she says. 'But I should be. I'm just sad.'

He tells her how much he loves her, promises he didn't drink and drive. It was the seafood, he says, he should never have had seafood. He sits up and cups her face in his hands.

'My darling, I'm so sorry,' he says.

And despite the fact that he's the one apologising, he's the one reaching out, she still has that awful feeling. Like he's a balloon in the wind and she's gripping the string.

Downstairs in the hall, Zac and Lucy already have their shoes on. They are glaring at each other as if they have been arguing. Sarah grabs her bag and tells them to get in the car, says they both have to sit in the back, and she doesn't want any bickering.

In the car, Zac pinches his sister. Lucy punches him in the arm.

'You're wrong,' he hisses. 'She said Jammie Dodgers.'

'No, she didn't.'

'Yes, she did.'

'She won't buy you anything if you keep behaving like a baby,' Lucy says.

'*She* said it was my turn to choose,' Zac says. He pinches his sister again.

'Ow.'

Sarah reaches back, the seat belt cutting into her neck. 'Are you talking about Grandma?' she says, yanking Zac's hand away.

Brown and green eyes stare back, unblinking.

'Do you remember what I told you both? Do you? Now stop arguing.'

'Sorry,' Zac says. He looks just like his father when he says sorry.

Sarah turns to the front, ignoring the urge to return to the house. Why does it feel as if something bad is happening?

She starts the car and turns the radio on, searches for an upbeat song.

7

When Daniel wakes and feels Kate's toes rub across his foot, it is confusing. A provocative stroke rather than an accidental nudge. He's in the middle of the bed, his head jammed between the pillows. As he turns over, she smiles at him. He must have been in a deep sleep when she came to bed.

'Hello you,' she says.

He instinctively pulls her close, squashing her body down the length of him. He was going to confront her immediately, but now he can't. He keeps holding her.

'I've missed you,' she says.

'I haven't gone anywhere. I'm right here.' He kisses the top of her head.

'You know what I mean.' She kisses his shoulder, and her mouth is warm through his T-shirt.

'I know,' he says.

They remain motionless, holding each other, and he wants so much to believe that nothing has been ruined.

He knows she won't mention their argument. She doesn't talk about their rows, as if she can't stand to dissect them. Or maybe she no longer cares. Whenever they argued before, they were able to talk it through afterwards. Sometimes, they would talk themselves into knots and the argument would start up again, but there was always a point where they would laugh about how ridiculous they were being. Then they would make love. Passionate sex that cleared away the jagged energy. Talking and sex fixed everything. Now they don't seem to be able to do either.

She puts her hand on his boxers and touches him. 'Take these off,' she whispers.

He finds himself throwing them onto the floor. She burrows under the duvet, her mouth on him. Electric shocks, spasms of sensitivity. He wants her, but he is too conscious of his thoughts, of his breathing, of how his penis keeps going soft. Why is he going soft? He keeps asking himself if she's been doing it with anyone else. Has it gone that far?

She comes up for air and lies on top of him, her weight pressing on his chest.

'Are you okay?' she says. 'Do you want me to stop?'

'No. Just a lot on my mind.'

She kisses him on the lips, then moves off and puts her head next to his on the pillow. He can feel her fingers, can feel his penis grow hard again in her hand.

'I want you,' she says.

He rolls on top of her, and she grinds herself against him. All he wants is for her to be his. That's all he wants. She reaches for his penis.

'I really want you,' she says in his ear. 'Fuck me.'

It's just so hot and the duvet is wound around his foot and his T-shirt is sticking to his back. Her hand is gripping him too tight. The more he tries to focus on staying hard, the softer he gets. He can't even make love to his wife. No wonder she's talking to other men.

She looks up at him. Those eyes. It usually makes everything disappear, strips his thoughts. But he can't get to that place. They are too separate.

He falls back onto the bed.

'Are you okay?' she says again, and he can hear the hurt.

He can't speak. Kicks off the duvet.

'Is it me?' she says.

He could leave. Get in the car, drive and never stop. Anything to stop this pressure. He pushes himself up and sits on the edge of the bed, holds his head in his hands.

'Is it?' she says again.

'Of course it isn't.' He turns back around, ready to ask what he is afraid to ask, but she is off the bed and putting on her dressing gown. She busies herself, the way she does when she's upset. Plumping her pillow, straightening her side of the duvet, moving things around on her bedside table. She goes to the door.

'I'll have a shower first, if that's okay?'

'Sure,' he says, but she is already gone.

It's like he's trapped behind one of those two-way mirrors. He's on this side, waiting for her to notice, but all she can see is the usual reflection. He hears the swish of the curtains in one of the girls' rooms, a low murmur of voices. The white noise as the shower is turned on, a tinny echo against the porcelain bath.

He lets out a breath and looks up at the painting above the chest of drawers. It was a gift he bought for Kate from Covent Garden market, the summer they graduated. Kate explained it wasn't meant to be of anything in particular.

Abstracts were about emotions, about how the colours made you feel. He stares at it now.

There used to be a big group of them. They would go to Covent Garden each Saturday, sit on the cobbles outside St Paul's church and clap for the man who could squeeze himself through a tennis racket. Kate liked the bed of nails trick best. She was always the one to put up a hand when the man asked for a volunteer. Then they would go to the pub for lunch. 'I'll get this for you,' he used to say, and he loved to see the look on her face, even if it meant he was short for the rest of the week. He wanted to give her everything.

It was on one of those Saturdays when Kate saw the painting. She kept going back to the stall, kept picking it up. 'It reminds me of how it feels right now,' she said. 'Before the rest of it starts.'

He lived in Primrose Hill for his second and third years, sharing a flat with Luke and the others. They had been friends since their first year and, although Luke never bragged about it, everyone knew how wealthy his family was. The others would borrow cash off him all the time. Loans that were never repaid. Luke didn't seem to care but Daniel never asked for anything. When he told Luke about the painting, he was just talking, he wasn't expecting any help. The next day he found an envelope of cash on his bed, a note from Luke saying *Anytime you need help, just ask*.

Daniel looks away from the painting and slams his fist onto the bed. They'll go to Luke's this weekend, and everything will be righted. They'll get drunk, play some poker. He'll talk to Luke about the investment idea he has, about the commission job he's been considering. Luke will help. He feels buoyed by this.

A rush of water through the pipes. Kate comes into the bedroom, a towel wrapped around her body. Her hair is slicked back, dark and wet, her cheeks flushed. She has her mobile in her hand.

'Luke's got food poisoning. They've postponed,' she says with a sigh.

She turns away and puts her phone down on the chest of drawers. The painting is above her, the colours a fiery halo around her head. He watches the drips from the ends of her hair run between her shoulder blades. And just like that, the promise of restoration is snatched away.

8

Arriving in the cul-de-sac, Sarah can already see her mum at the window of the bungalow. Lucy and Zac rush out, slamming the doors. Sarah waits. It's difficult with her parents. Especially now, the way her dad is.

Her mum opens the door, looking carefully put together, as she always does. Navy trousers, a sensible blouse. Pearls. That line of coral lipstick.

'My angels,' Janet says and pulls the children into a squashing hug. 'Say hello to Grandpa first, then go and look in the spare room. I put some magazines in there for you both. And a DVD.'

Sarah slips off her shoes and waits for the invisible barrier to lift. She can't remember a time when it wasn't there, although there are flashes of warmth, a brief moment.

Her mum says, 'I'll put the kettle on. Luke not coming?'

'He went out last night and had seafood. He's been really sick. We had to cancel Dan and Kate, so I can stay longer if you like?' Sarah follows her mum into the kitchen.

'You should complain,' her mum says. 'They can shut restaurants down for that, you know.'

Janet bustles about with mugs and plates. She's had her

hair cut and coloured and Sarah is about to tell her it looks nice, when Janet says, 'You look tired.'

Sarah forces a smile, says she's fine, just been working hard. 'How's Dad?'

Her mum gives a grunt.

'Still the same. No visitors this week, although someone from the golf club dropped in last week. I don't expect it will last. What can they say?' She shrugs. 'He just sits there, doesn't even try. And people have their own troubles, don't they?'

Sarah knows she should say something consoling. She nods and says 'hmm', pushes her hands into the pockets of her jeans.

'And the couple from the social club came the other week. That man from the council, a while back. But I told you that, didn't I? You know who I mean . . . I can't remember his name. He came with *her*. She had a bloody nerve. I thought I'd made it quite clear she wasn't welcome.'

Opening cupboards, shutting cupboards. Never making eye contact, but Sarah feels it all the same, like her mum is lashing out with a hot poker. What her dad did is never mentioned openly, but her mum always finds ways to refer to it. Sarah cannot watch any longer, cannot stand the stifling atmosphere.

In the conservatory, her dad sits on a small wickerwork sofa, incongruent with the green and red chintz cushions, his hands in his lap, staring out at the garden. Cards with words written in big letters are in a pile on the coffee table. The brass reading lamp has *lamp* sellotaped to the slim stem, the bookcase has *books* stuck to a shelf, and one of the panes of glass looking out onto the patio has a small card with *window* on it. She sits next to him.

'How are you, Dad? Luke's sick and couldn't come.'

She waits for a response, like the speech therapist said, but he only makes indistinguishable noises, as if he is clearing his throat. Some weeks are worse than others.

'Shall we have a practice?' She reaches for the pile of cards. The first word is *chair*. She holds it up for him to see. He looks away and waves his hand, like shooing a fly.

'No. I cuppen graf. I'm goin graffen . . .'

His face goes red.

'Here we are,' Janet says, putting a tray onto the coffee table. 'Let it stew for a bit. I've put some biscuits out as well. If you want any more, the packet's in the tin.'

Janet huffs and blows. She hovers next to the table, doesn't ask what is wrong. Sarah's sure she doesn't bother to practise the words with him. And then she wonders if her mum interacts with him at all. Does she ever hold his hand?

'I'll take the children to the shops now,' Janet says. 'You can have a nice chat, can't you? Go for a nice walk. He hasn't been out for a few days.'

'We can go to the Water Gardens,' Sarah suggests.

A pause as her mum's face hardens. Sarah knows what she has said. She did it on purpose, can't help herself, hates the way her mum talks to her dad like he is a child.

Janet picks up her handbag from beside the coffee table. It looks new, although it is the same style, the same navy blue she always has – her Thatcher bag, Sarah calls it, much to her mum's annoyance. Not a real Launer of course. She won't let Sarah buy one for her, says they are far too expensive.

'See you later then,' Janet says, giving an upward nod. Sarah notices the tight mouth, the forced arrangement of the bag on her arm. She suspects she is the only one to notice these things about her mum, the sudden changes of expression, the suppressed words.

When she was younger, she used to ask her dad why her mum was like that. Sarah could never understand why he stood up for her, never a single bad word. But then her dad was someone who said *yes* to the world. Her mum was the one who said *no*.

'You wish you'd chosen her, don't you?' Sarah said to him once. It had been freeing to finally say it out loud. She had wanted to punish him, although at the same time she had known why he had done it. Her mum never made anyone's life easy.

The children's voices filter through from the hall. The front door bangs and it is quiet. Sarah lets out a breath and picks up the spoon to poke at the teabags in the pot. Her dad has already resumed his window staring. The clump of yellow daffodil heads nod in unison as the wind picks up.

'I didn't get the promotion, Dad. They gave it to Amit.'

'Oh . . . oh no,' he says and then mumbles something else she cannot understand.

She pours their tea. They both look out at the bird table. It is hypnotic, watching the birds come down to peck at seeds then fly away.

'Shall we go to the Water Gardens then?' she says.

'Y-yeah,' he says. 'Why not.'

She used to love going there when she was young, the canal like a serpent. She would run from the top end by the lake with the fountain, all the way down to Coombe

Street, where she imagined sliding off the wet tip of its tail. Her dad would take her, just the two of them, as a special treat, then buy her an ice cream from the van. He always made sure she had an extra Flake. When she was older, in the sixth form, she'd go with friends, and they would eat their lunch on a bench before going to the shops. The place was never the same, not after she saw her dad and Elaine that day.

'Do you remember Will?' she says. 'He moved to America. He's married with three girls now.'

Her dad reaches with his good hand to put his mug back on the tray. She doesn't know what made her think of her first boyfriend. Sometimes she finds herself looking at the photos he posts on his Facebook page, of him and his wife. They look happy.

'Do you remember when you had to drive down to rescue us from that camping trip in the New Forest? His car broke down and we'd run out of money.' She laughs, not because it is funny, but because she feels a kind of hysteria rising up inside.

'Yeah,' her dad says. 'L-long time.'

'Do you ever think about Elaine?' The question falls out.

He grips his hand into a fist. 'Sh-she's purpiten . . .' he says. 'No, not . . . purtiten . . . fuck . . . whattim say.' He bangs his fist against his head.

'Stop. Don't do that, Dad. Please.' She holds onto his arm to steady him. 'I'm sorry.' She wants to tell him about Luke, how frightened she is, how she has no one to talk to, how she has days when the sadness is so overwhelming, she feels as if she will break.

'Oh, Dad!' she says. A wedge in her throat.

59

He puts his hand over hers and gives it a squeeze. Outside, a small brown bird pecks at the seed before flying away.

9

Later that morning, Daniel sits in his parents' kitchen extension. His mum asks if he would like a piece of cake. The sun breaks from a cloud and shines through the windows making bright rectangles on the floor. Marian, his mum's friend, is on the opposite side of the table, talking about her son, who has just bought himself a new car.

'Here you are,' his dad says, putting two mugs down on the table. 'It was one sugar, wasn't it, Marian?'

Flo sits beside him, quietly waiting for her cake. Kate isn't there. She said she would stay at home, to make sure Maisie got on with her revision. It isn't unusual – Kate doesn't always come for visits, and he knows his mum can be overbearing – but her decision today feels significant.

'There you are, poppet,' his mum says to Flo, giving her a plate. 'Daniel? Large or small?'

'Just a small piece, thanks, Mum.'

The cake has buttercream spread over the top and strawberry jam in the middle. Daniel has grown up with his mum's cakes. Every weekend she would make one, and he would be allowed a piece after he finished his lunch.

He was never allowed a second piece. It was put back in the tin for the following day. Sometimes, he would sneak down in the night, once he heard his parents go to bed. He would shave off the thinnest of slivers. Before he knew it, he had taken so many wafer slices, a whole chunk was missing.

Flo has finished already and pulls at his sleeve. 'Can I go in the garden?' she whispers. She is often shy in company these days, even with her grandparents. He worries she is being affected by his job problems. The tension between him and Kate.

'I'll take her,' his dad says, brushing crumbs from his jumper. 'I've got to get back at it and Flo can help.'

Daniel watches them go. He feels helpless all of a sudden and panicked. A vision of Kate on her laptop, sending messages, while he's here, listening to Marian telling his mum that they might not have enough chairs for the event next week at the library. He is about to get up, make some excuse, when his mum says, 'It's so good to see you. A lovely surprise. Any news?' She places her hand lightly on his arm and when she takes it away, her eyes have that sickened look.

'Did I tell you about the interview?' he says. He cannot help the lie. The discomfort of his mother's disappointment is overwhelming.

'Oh, that *is* good news,' she says.

'Yes, with Sabre. It's a small fund, but good prospects.'

She smiles and he feels a rush of relief. 'Well, that does sound promising.'

'I've been shortlisted for final interview.'

'See, I told you something would come up.'

She pats him on the arm and smiles at Marian. He

absently eats another piece of cake. The buttercream clogs his throat.

'And I was thinking,' his mum continues. 'You could always go back to your other job, you know, before the bank? You were doing so well there. I don't know why you left.'

He puts his fork down and pushes his plate away. She's talking about the first job he had after he graduated, and he wishes she wouldn't keep bringing it up. If she wants to tell him he has made a string of bad judgements, he would rather she just came out with it.

'God, that was years ago, Mum.'

'I'm sure you could at least contact them. That was a job for life. I hope Kate realises what she did?'

Hearing Kate's name makes his stomach lurch.

'I made the decision, Mum, not Kate.'

'Hmm, yes. I just wish you'd talked to me before making these decisions.'

He isn't sure if she's referring to him taking the job at the bank or marrying Kate. He can't sit there a minute longer.

'I'll go and see what Dad's doing,' he says, getting up.

'Okay dear. Marian's off soon, aren't you, Marian? Then I'll heat us up some soup for lunch.'

In the utility room, he slips on a faded green pair of wellies and takes an old wax jacket from the peg. His dad still has it – the dark brown Musto he wore for Sunday walks. Daniel remembers those trips to the woods, when they lived in Hertford. He puts it on, and the smell conjures memories of eating mints, tramping through bracken and wet fallen leaves, overcooked roast dinners in a smoky pub. The jacket is snug around his shoulders,

63

won't meet around his middle and the sleeves are too short. His dad always seemed so tall, so solid. In one of the pockets, he finds a half-eaten bar of Dairy Milk. The chocolate is old, powdery grey with pale blotches. He covers it over with the ripped wrapper and puts it back.

Flo is by the vegetable patch. There is a smell of rain, although the sky is clear, with high wispy cirrus clouds – he still knows the name from his school Geography lessons – like the stuff his mum used to put on the Christmas tree. Angel hair.

'Come to help?' his dad says, putting the wheelbarrow down on the soggy grass. His breath comes out in light huffs. 'I'm so behind, what with all that snow.'

'Yes,' Daniel says, pushing his glasses up with a knuckle. 'What do you want me to do?'

'Flo's doing a great job. Can you give her these? They're the carrots. Tell her not to put them in just yet, start with the seeds. I need to sort out the cloches.' He turns the wheelbarrow around and heads off towards the end of the garden.

Daniel takes the tray of seedlings to the vegetable patch. The raised bed is neatly edged with wooden boards and has a layer of dark compost, finely crumbled like coffee granules. Flo is engrossed at one end, with a trowel, spreading out the remains of a mound. She looks up as he puts the carrots down next to her.

'I've come to help,' he says. 'Grandad said don't put these in yet.'

'Daddy, we have to get it ready for the seeds, make sure there aren't any big lumps or stones and spread this all over the top.'

64

She puts her trowel down and gives him some lollipop sticks with black writing on.

'You do the spinach and broad beans and I'll do the kale and parsnips,' she says.

He gives her a salute. 'Yes, sir,' he says, picking up the spare trowel.

She giggles and pokes him in the side with her grubby finger. 'Be serious, Daddy. We've got to do it properly. Do you know what to do? You have to leave enough room for the greenhouse things.'

'The cloches,' he says, and she frowns at him. He laughs, but not to be unkind. She reminds him so much of Kate.

All those times when she would come to his room. Those times when he didn't know whether anything was happening between them, or if it was all in his head. She would sit cross-legged on his bed, and he would attempt to juggle a couple of tangerines. 'Be serious, Daniel,' she would say. 'I'm trying to tell you something important.' Her gorgeous, earnest face.

He feels sick.

Flo is staring at him like he's gone mad.

'Yes, it's okay,' he says, swallowing hard. 'Your grandad showed me when I was your age, and I probably used this very same trowel.' He waves it in the air and pulls one of his funny faces.

She giggles. 'Oh, Daddy.'

He goes to the other end of the bed and digs shallow furrows.

How is he going to check her laptop? He knows her password, but she rarely leaves it at home. Has she always taken it to work? Everything now is a question mark.

Flo is next to him. 'Daddy, what are you doing? You've

65

put those in the wrong place. I said the spinach has to go in this row. You're ruining the plan.'

He stands up. He shouldn't be doing this, not with his twinging shoulder.

'We can make it a row for the beans instead,' he says.

'You can't change the plan. Grandad said I have to follow the plan.'

'Sometimes you have to change the plan, Flo. Sometimes things don't go the way you expected.' He says this with unintended force.

'You've ruined it!' She stamps.

'You do it then.' He drops the trowel, is about to walk off, when he sees the look on her face. Her bottom lip is wobbling.

'Because you're so much better at it than me,' he says quickly, crouching down to her height. She sniffs and wipes at her face with her dirty sleeve. 'I tell you what, I'll go and get the cloches. What do you say? Come on now, you're okay.'

He hands her the trowel, remembers the old bar of chocolate in his pocket, breaks off a square and gives her one.

'Don't tell Granny,' he says, as she pops it in her mouth.

He walks across the lawn and snaps off a piece for himself, lets it melt on his tongue.

In the greenhouse, his dad is sweeping the floor. 'You all done?' he says, stopping and leaning on the broom.

'Just need the cloches now, Dad.'

His dad points to the side where they are neatly stacked. Daniel has a sudden rush of impatience. 'We really must be going soon. I've got to get back.'

66

'Oh, that's a shame,' his dad says. 'Your mum'll be disappointed. At least stay for something to eat.'

'We've just had . . . it doesn't matter.' Daniel sees the look on his dad's face. 'We need to be off by two at the latest.'

His dad nods, checks his watch. 'Plenty of time,' he says.

Daniel picks up a small stack of cloches and heads towards the vegetable patch.

'Oh, and Daniel,' his dad says, waving a hand. 'Can you take a look at my computer before you go? I can't get into my email properly, keep getting a message popping up. Something about a server. If you can't do it today, you could do that screen sharing thingy, like you did before.'

'No problem,' he shouts. And then it hits him. Why didn't he think of it before? He walks across the lawn, his boots making a trail of footprints across the wet grass.

10

Another working week has gone by, and it is Friday afternoon. Kate has managed to get a table by the window, in the far corner of the café. Each time the door opens, she turns around to see who it is. She isn't entirely sure what she is doing here.

Her table has an annoying wobble. The only other free table is by the door, but she doesn't want to be that exposed. She twists a piece of hair from behind her ear until it pulls at her scalp. There are snatches of conversation from the tables behind. Coughing, laughter, a baby grizzling. Noise from the cappuccino machine as the barista froths the milk.

Alec suggested this place. She hasn't been here before, even though it's near the university. She told him she finished at three on a Friday. He thinks she works in a bookshop on Euston Road.

An afternoon coffee, what's the harm in that?

She should have told him then, should have explained that she was doing research for her book. She should have thanked him for his help and said goodbye.

The door opens and a rush of cool air comes in. It's

not him. A woman with two girls. Cute things, not much older than five or six, wearing school uniform and matching hairbands, knee-high navy socks, scuffed shoes. Kate watches them and thinks of Maisie and Flo. The way they used to move in the world without the burden of self-consciousness.

A sudden image then, of Flo all alone in the playground. Kate grabs her phone from her bag.

'It's me, can you hear me? The reception isn't good. I've just seen the time and Flo needs picking up. Have you got her?'

Daniel's breath is in her ear. 'She's got dance club,' he says. He speaks slowly, a nasal voice, like he's been asleep, and she imagines him rubbing his hand over his face, the way he does when he's preoccupied, before putting on his glasses. A moment of vulnerability that usually plucks her insides.

'Yes, but it's been cancelled.'

'I'll leave now,' he says.

'Oh Daniel, she'll be waiting and wondering where you are.'

Kate moves the phone from ear to ear and slides her arms into the sleeves of her raincoat. 'Why didn't the school call me? The reception's bad, but I've got two bars.'

'Stop panicking. I'll call them now.'

She wants to cry. To tell him how sorry she is. She hasn't even done anything.

'It's all right,' he says. 'Let me get off the phone and I'll call them. Are you finished?'

'I'm with a student, but I can—'

'Okay. I'll message when I've got her,' he says. 'See you later.'

69

Kate hangs up and lets her raincoat fall onto the chair. Why didn't he demand that she come home? Say that he needs her to be with him. What is she doing? Alec is nearly half an hour late. An impossible force keeps her there, an inner defiance, pushing her to see what will happen if she stays.

The two girls in their matching hairbands squeal with delight. They are bored with waiting and are playing a game that involves getting on and off their chairs and going under the table. They keep knocking into people. The mother asks them to sit nicely; apologises to a man who is getting the brunt of it. She tries to distract the girls with a pen which she produces from her bag, draws something on a serviette with a suppressed sigh. Kate remembers that feeling. She is glad her girls are older, and she no longer has to lose herself completely. That is what we do, she thinks, we give ourselves away. Of course, the sacrifice is done willingly – she would do anything for her girls, anything. Even when they pull away, reject an offered hand, or roll their eyes, she still has an unfailing certainty. Their bond can never be broken. She used to feel that way about Daniel too.

She looks out of the window at the people walking past. She thinks back to last weekend, Daniel's penis, squashy in her hand. How she'd felt dirty for going down on him. How he'd looked at her before rolling off and turning away, like he was disgusted by her. He's never made her feel like that before.

'Mum and Dad asked after you,' he had said, when he got back from visiting his parents. He didn't mention anything about her puffy eyes. 'They've invited us over for lunch tomorrow. I stupidly said we'd go. You know how my mum can be.'

He put his arm around her. She thought he was going to say that he would make an excuse, that they didn't have to go. She used to be reassured that he understood how his mother made her feel. *Is your father still living in the flat, dear? Must have been so hard for you, growing up there, I can't imagine . . .* But he said nothing. Planted a dry kiss on her forehead. It was as if he was holding her so close because he didn't want to look at her.

They went for Sunday lunch. She sat opposite his mother, watched how she talked to Daniel, witnessed their similar gestures, the way Daniel made his mother laugh. She was reminded of something Alec had written in one of their late-night messaging sessions. It had become confessional, and he agreed that it always gets to a point in a marriage when the differences that never used to matter before suddenly become glaring beacons. Like choosing a piece in a jigsaw puzzle, finding that perfect bit of sky only to discover in the end that it isn't the right piece after all. Had Daniel realised that?

And later, after lunch, when they had sat in the velvety sitting room. Mother and son on the sofa, Kate on the armchair. Margaret had looked at her, smiling with her unsmiling eyes. Ordinarily, Kate would have sat properly, not with her feet pulled up, or holding onto the teacup with two hands like a mug. Normally, she would have made herself fit. But she realised that even if she acted how Margaret acted, said the same words, laughed at the same jokes, Margaret would never see her as an equal. No matter the fact that Daniel had chosen her. No matter her PhD, her intelligence, her hard work. None of that was important to Margaret. And perhaps underneath it all, it wasn't important to Daniel either. How had she not considered this before? As she had sat on one side of the room, them on the other, she was the girl from the estate again.

Another gust of cool air and Kate is suddenly aware of Alec at the door of the café. He stands looking around, unmistakable in his dark suit, perhaps a little older and stouter than expected, with greying hair at his temples. She could pretend she doesn't know who he is. She could grab her things and leave.

He sees her.

'So sorry I'm late,' he says, coming over. He grasps her shoulders with both hands, presses his cheek onto hers. He is much shorter than Daniel and their eyes are almost level.

'I had an emergency patient, a pre-op that needed to be seen. I'm afraid I don't have much time now.' He smiles and it makes her insides jolt. 'Would you like another?' he says, pointing at her empty coffee cup.

'I'm fine, really.'

'No, let me get you another.' He signals to one of the girls behind the counter.

Kate forces herself to appear calm, but her hands, what should she be doing with her hands?

'We meet finally,' he says.

They both sit down. He chooses the chair on the opposite side of the table. The way he looks at her is intense.

'Yes. I—'

He doesn't let her finish, as if he has a set format and she is spoiling it. 'So, tell me,' he says. 'How are your children? Your eldest has exams coming up, is that right?'

She pauses and tries to remember what she has told him – they have said so much to each other, and a lot of what

72

she has told him isn't true. 'Yes, that's right. She's bright, so she'll be okay. And she's at a good school. She won a scholarship.'

'A scholarship. You didn't mention that.' He smiles encouragingly.

They could be old friends who haven't met for years, reacquainting each other with their respective lives. When their coffee arrives, he pauses. He takes charge, without hesitation.

'And have you had any other offers? he says when the girl has gone.

'Offers?'

'Or am I the first?'

'Well, I haven't—'

She thinks of Daniel walking past, seeing her there with this man. Would he come in and make a scene? Cause a scuffle, punch Alec in the face and make his nose bleed. She looks out of the window.

'This is your first time, then? I wasn't sure.'

He leans forward slightly and lowers his voice, rests his hand on the table. Long fingers, a faint line of a scar across his knuckle. So different to Daniel's hands. She doesn't understand why she likes messaging him, why she looks forward to the uncertainty of what he is going to say.

'I don't know what I'm doing on there, to be honest. I'm writing a book.'

She focuses on her cup, the brown dribble down the sides. It's the only thing she can look at for any length of time without wanting to pass out.

'A book?' he says.

'Just the early stages, I'm researching some ideas.'

'I'd like to hear about that.'

She wants to say she loves her husband. They are happily married. What is she doing?

'So, we'll meet properly then, and you can tell me all about your book. Yes?' He takes a hurried gulp of coffee and puts his cup down on the table.

'Properly?' She knows exactly what he means.

'I have to go, I'm afraid.' He looks at his watch and becomes businesslike, brusque. 'Let's organise an evening. I'll send you some dates.'

And then it is over. He is gone. She sits at the table, letting the experience sink in. The mother and two girls have also gone, and someone else is sitting there now.

She puts on her raincoat and checks her phone. Daniel has sent a message.

Don't worry. Everything sorted, Flo safe

11

Friday afternoons are always a drag. Luke is at his desk, working through the figures. He can't stop his leg jiggling up and down. He asked the team for a full compilation of livestock and meat, but soybeans and coffee have also been included. Usually, he devours these reports, finds revealing insights, but today he cannot work the numbers. Perhaps he needs to do a quick line, something to keep him sharp. It's been a week since the fiasco with Jill, and it's left him feeling more jittery than usual.

A folded copy of today's *Daily Telegraph* sits on his desk. He never usually buys it, but there is an article on page nine. He turns to his computer and rereads Mr Beachcroft's email, informing him of his aunt's death. Mrs Lettice Linton-Beresford died two weeks ago on February the twenty-seventh. Her last will and testament has been read out. Mr B extends his sympathies. The estate – what's left of it, after she sold the farm – has been bequeathed to the National Trust. In the paper, there are photographs of the house, and the inevitable mention of his parents.

Luke closes the email. There's nothing he can do about it now. Mr B says as much, and even if he could, he won't face that ordeal again. He went through enough trying to dispute his parents' will.

A knock and Geoff's head appears at the door. 'Do you have a minute before you go?' He waves a manila folder in the air. Luke gestures for him to come in, but Geoff is already making his way to one of the small armchairs.

Geoff clears his throat and says, 'I'd like you to take a look. I'm meeting the sheikh. He did an MBA and thinks he knows it all.' He laughs at his own joke and takes a document from the folder, puts it down on the coffee table.

Luke goes over to join him, sits in the other armchair. He is pleased that Geoff is asking for his input because recently he's been feeling pushed out. A new client made a large investment last month, and Geoff had taken Tom along for the opening pitch. It shouldn't have bothered him – after all, they're a team, and Luke can't be everywhere doing everything – but he can sense something untoward going on in the shadows, as if he's being plotted against. He needs to keep a careful eye on Tom.

Luke scans the figures. 'These look right,' he says. 'I guess you could up the total by half a per cent, especially when I get confirmation of African Alliance.'

Geoff sucks in a breath. 'I thought we'd agreed we weren't going to touch the emerging markets. I specifically said I didn't want us going off on that tangent.'

'I don't recall you saying that.'

'We stick to our plan. I'm not having us going for anything, grabbing like kids in a sweet shop.' Geoff pauses to clear his throat again. 'The key is consistency, Luke. I'm not being stuck with illiquid assets. Carter and Prike went down that road and they never recovered.'

Geoff takes off his glasses and sits with them dangling in

his hand. Any minute now, he'll mention his capital input; that he invited Luke to join with specific aims; how he's built something from nothing; how his own assets are at risk. Luke's heard it all before. Thankfully, he knows how to deal with the old bastard.

Luke smiles and speaks slowly.

'If you recall, when you first approached me, you said I had a unique way of looking at the spread of assets, the interplay others often miss.' Geoff leans forward, tries to cut in, but Luke holds up his hand. 'It's what I'm good at.'

Geoff twirls his glasses. He isn't so easily reassured these days.

'You used to trust me,' Luke says.

'Where's the data? The evidence for these recent decisions you've been making?'

'Evidence? Come on, you never used to—' Luke coughs, stops himself from saying how retentive Geoff is being. He really should have had a line; he would be razor-sharp. He just needs to keep his focus.

'You never used to make mistakes.' Geoff looks properly angry, folds his glasses and slips them into his top pocket.

'Mistakes? What are you talking about?'

'Look.' Geoff is the one to hold up his hand now, and his voice changes gear, takes on a patronising tone. 'You're off your game. Tom's noticed as well.'

Luke can feel his heart hammering against his ribs. 'You've been talking to Tom?'

'He is a key member of the team.'

'That's fucking out of order, don't you think?' Luke struggles to keep his voice even. He can't let himself get too riled, show any sign of weakness. This is what Tom's been waiting for, an opportunity to make his move.

Geoff gathers the papers on the table and puts them back in the folder. Luke goes over to his desk and leans against it, gripping the edge.

'Maybe you need a holiday. How are things at home?' Geoff smiles as he looks up, like he's won a point.

'What?' He wasn't ready for this today.

There is a knock on the door and Geoff's secretary comes in to say that it's almost five o'clock.

'Thank you, Eleanor,' Geoff says, rising from the chair, tucking the manila folder under his arm. He comes over to Luke and says in a low voice, 'We all have times when we trip. I'm just making sure you don't fall.'

And it's as if Geoff has waltzed into his home, turned out every drawer, scrutinised every belonging, every achievement and walked away, nodding with the knowledge of what he has learned, pretending to give commendation but ultimately judging everything. Luke feels it in the pit of his stomach.

'Maybe you should take a long weekend,' Geoff says. 'Spend some time with that beautiful wife of yours.' He doesn't wait for Luke to respond and walks out, leaving the door open wide. 'Thanks for this,' he shouts, waving the folder in the air.

Luke pushes the door to, but not before noticing Tom staring at him from across the other side of the room. He leans his shoulder against the door, shuts it firmly, lets out a breath as if he'd been holding onto it the whole time.

His mobile buzzes. It's a message from Sarah.

When will you be home? I've bought us a nice bottle xx

He goes back to his desk and sits down, shoves the *Telegraph* into the wastepaper basket with an angry swipe. Perhaps they will move abroad, start again somewhere new, away from this fucking place. Sarah will save him. His wife and his children. He needs to hold onto the thought of them. He is being pulled between opposing forces.

He picks up his mobile and types: **Just have to finish off a few things**

It is best not to give exact timings, because then there are no expectations.

Outside, on the corner of the building opposite, two pigeons are preening, fluffing their feathers. One makes a show of walking up and down, like a tightrope walker. It goes over to the other pigeon and pecks its neck. They tussle but don't fight, more like they are at play. Their beaks fuse together, as if they want to swallow one another. They break apart and repeat this ritual a couple more times, both of them complicit in the dance, until one cowers down. The other one hops on top, balancing, stretching out its wings. The moment seems endless, yet it is over in a second.

Luke watches until they fly away.

A few hours later, he is home. He puts his laptop bag and a bottle of wine on the hall table. Perhaps he will take Sarah and the kids to the coast, find a nice hotel, a cottage to rent. If he can get far away, he will feel better. Something is pushing and prodding at him. Go on, it keeps saying. Go on.

His father used to arrange surprise weekend trips to the beach. Especially out of season. He would come home from work on a Friday and tell them to pack their overnight bags. It became a fun game for Luke and Seb, guessing when their father was going to surprise them again. This was during the years when both he and Seb were at the

79

local school, before Seb was sent away to board, before their father got too busy with work.

Luke remembers the cottage on the Suffolk coast. It wasn't their house, but it belonged to one of his parents' friends. A small place, with only two bedrooms. He shared with Seb and there was a big double bed. He remembers how the blankets were tucked in tight, that getting into bed was like sliding into an envelope. In the morning, he and Seb would go into their parents' room. Their bed seemed really tall, nearly up to his shoulders, and Seb would have to help him up. His mother would be very sleepy. She would yawn and push herself up onto her elbows, ask what time it was. She'd act really shocked, as if it was the middle of the night, and she'd tell them to go back to bed, to try and sleep for a little while longer. They never did, would sit and talk about how many crabs they were going to catch that day. Seb would ask things like: 'Can crabs smell?' and, 'Why don't they remember what happens when they smell the bacon?'

They'd have pastries for breakfast that made their fingers sticky. Luke liked to pick the raisins out and eat them first. Then they'd walk across the bridge and down to the section of river that smelt like the sea. Nobody else would be there so early. His parents didn't like crowds. Seb carried the buckets and Luke held the box of cut-up bacon pieces. His mother sat on a fold-out stool and watched. She'd guard the big bucket, squealing when one of the crabs tried to escape. 'Boys, it's getting out,' she'd say. And Seb would go over and pick it up, hold it out, saying, 'It won't hurt you Mummy.' She'd squeal again and leap off her stool, laughing in a way that was like crying. Then they'd all laugh. Luke would feel strangely exhilarated watching his mother get flustered. And when he caught one, he'd join in too, holding his crab in front of her face. The pincers would sometimes nip his hand, but he'd keep holding onto it because he wanted her to know he was as brave as Seb.

Sarah appears, and Luke is still standing in the hall.

'Oh, it is you,' she says, smiling at him. 'I thought I heard the door.'

Her gaze seems different to usual. She isn't looking at him as he is now, but as he once used to be, and he suddenly feels it is going to be all right. It is, he tells himself, and he decides he will surprise her with his idea for going away for the weekend. He takes the bottle from the side.

'I got this,' he says, holding it up.

'Another one? Oh Luke, didn't you get my message?'

'It's a ninety-nine Grand Cru Les Clos.'

She gives him a blank look.

'Don't you remember?' he says.

She frowns.

'That's the year we met. And at our first dinner, we had a bottle of this.'

'Oh darling, that's so thoughtful.' She comes towards him and wraps her arms around his neck, kisses his cheek, then his nose, then his lips. 'You're such a romantic.'

The smell of her is overwhelming. All flowery and light.

'Come on,' she says, taking his hand.

They go into the kitchen, where she puts the wine in the fridge. He tells her to put it in the freezer, so it will chill quickly.

'I've already opened this one,' she says, and she takes a bottle of white Bordeaux from the side, spilling a little as she pours him a glass. She wipes the drip with her finger then puts it in her mouth and gives a gentle suck, making him instantly hard. It is confusing, experiencing her like this, and he cannot fully appreciate her. He wants to ask her why she is being like this.

'Have you eaten?' he says.

'I ate with the children. You go up and say goodnight and I'll heat your supper. Zac's really tired, but he wanted to stay up until you got home.'

She looks at him through her eyelashes. Her usual seriousness is gone. If he didn't know better, he'd say she was being playful, coquettish even.

Upstairs, he takes a few breaths. He will take his family away for the weekend and the ground will feel solid again. How pathetic he is being. How weak.

He pauses before opening Zac's door. In his mind, he sees how it should be with his son, how he'd sit on the bed, brush the hair from his sleepy face, and listen as Zac talked about his day. There might be an incident that had bothered him, and Luke would be able to say something profound, something that would give reassurance. An intimate father and son moment, and with one look, Zac would know how loved he was.

He pokes his head around the door and whispers, 'Goodnight, son.' Zac is asleep. Luke turns off the light and goes to Lucy's room. She is on the phone, talking to one of her friends, and she flicks him a glance, returns his smile as he mouths *goodnight*. He finds his daughter a little easier, although nothing is easy when it comes to his children. Sometimes, it's like trying to punch through a brick wall.

As he stands there, he realises he has lost the feeling he

had when he was in the hall, the memory of climbing onto his parents' bed, his mother squealing at the crabs and all of them laughing – that feeling has turned into something else now, something sharp and painful.

He pulls the door closed.

When he goes back into the kitchen, Sarah is dishing carrots onto a plate with a thick stew.

'Are they okay?' she says.

'Zac was asleep.'

'They won their match the other day, did I tell you? Zac was thrilled.'

She takes his plate over to the table where they both sit.

'Aren't you having anything?' he says.

'I told you, I've eaten already.'

'Why don't you have something? You know I hate eating on my own.'

She goes to the kitchen and pulls open the fridge, comes back with a small plate of pre-cut melon cubes.

'There,' she says. 'Happy?' She sticks her tongue out, then blushes and prods a piece of melon with her fork, puts it in her mouth. She really is quite tipsy.

They continue like that – him picking out the cubes of beef, her spearing the melon – until she tells him that she might be working on the new Mercedes campaign. She talks about her work, and he talks about his. Naturally, he skims over the part about his conversation with Geoff, about Tom and how he feels like he's being edged out, and the email from Mr B. Conversations should be like paintings, revealing a particular version of reality.

'I'm going to take us away this weekend,' he says. 'I was thinking we could get a cottage, or how about a last-minute flight? We could go to Lake Como, show the children where I got down on one knee.'

She puts her fork on the plate and creases up her mouth as if she is about to cry.

'That's such a lovely idea,' she says. 'But not this weekend. Did you forget? Dan and Kate are coming. We can't cancel them again.'

'Oh Christ, yes.'

He can feel his leg jiggling up and down, like it's trying to tap out Morse code. He wants to see Daniel, of course he does, but even that feels oppressive, like it will push him over the edge. To see his old friend, who always made sure he got back to his room, and allowed him to carry on talking as he came down from a high. There is a connection with Daniel that he can't understand in himself. A feeling of being exposed and yet safe, the same way his brother made him feel – the same but entirely different. He doesn't need that right now.

'We could go away at Easter, or half-term,' she says. 'The weather will be warmer, then. So much better.'

'Yes,' he says, and he smiles so she doesn't think he is being difficult. He puts his knife and fork down, pushes the plate away.

'Are you okay?' she says. 'Do you want anything else?'

He shakes his head. Can't she see what is happening? They have to get away from here. If they leave, he can make it better, he will be able to stop feeling like this. Why can't she see that? Doesn't she know how hard he is trying to make everything go silent?

'You go and relax,' she says, taking his plate across to the kitchen. He watches her move, the way she rests her

84

fingers on her lips while she thinks about something, the way she arches her back to stretch, always at the end of the day.

Over on the sofa, she comes and curls up next to him, rests her head on his shoulder. He puts his arm around her, and she is warm.

'Oh,' she says. 'I forgot the wine.' She goes to get up, but he gently pulls her back. He wants to hold her so tight that he can forget where he ends and she begins.

'But it's in the freezer, Luke. Let me put it in the fridge.' And as she gets up, there is a wave of panic, something horrible is about to happen to him. He closes his eyes and forces it away.

'Are you tired?' she says.

He opens his eyes. 'Not really, just a long day.'

'I need to talk to you about something. It's . . . oh, I don't know how to say it.'

She sits down and looks at him in a way that makes his stomach turn over.

'What is it? God, you're not pregnant, are you?' He thinks she's laughing at his joke, but she is sobbing into her hands. He says, 'Come here. I can't hear you. What on earth's wrong?'

'We'll be okay, won't we?' She takes her hands away. Her face is flushed but there aren't any tears. For a second, he imagines what would happen if he told her. He can almost feel the relief of the unburdening, before the shame of it.

'I'm worried,' she says.

'What about?'

Her eyes search his face. It is confusing, the way she is looking at him.

'About us and how things . . . how they aren't quite . . .'

A crashing sense of doom. It rushes to his head this feeling, then spreads across his chest. She has never been like this, why is she being like this?

'It's getting worse, and I can't—' She shakes her head.

'Shh.' He puts his arm around her to make her quiet. She mustn't say any more.

'You won't leave me, will you?'

'Of course not. How could you think such a thing?'

'I've been worrying. Nothing has changed, has it?'

'Nothing has changed.'

'You go down to your study in the night. And I've been reading about—'

'Everything's okay.'

He kisses her hard. She tries to pull away; he can tell she wants to keep talking, but he needs her to stop. He keeps kissing her, holding her tight.

He holds her to his chest, puts his hand over the side of her head, over her ear, as if to shield her from a loud noise. When it feels safe, he takes his hand away and says, 'I need to shower. Why don't you choose a film for us to watch?'

She looks up at him and nods. He sees the flash of recognition in her eyes, the rise and dip of her swallow. The smile.

'I love you,' she says.

He usually tells her he loves her too, but right now, he can't.

'Luke?' she says, before he walks away. 'We understand each other, don't we?'

'Of course,' he says again, and he means it.

He goes out into the hall, up the stairs.

It should make him happy, his understanding wife. But he realises he doesn't want her to be understanding. He wants to make her feel like she is breaking too.

12

Daniel eases his foot off the accelerator. The roads are always busy at the end of the week. Stupid drivers, people braking for no reason. Flo is in the back, tired and sullen – how she usually is after school, until she decompresses. Maisie is in the passenger seat beside him, picking at her nails. She is usually the chatty one. Daniel normally listens to her stories of the day, the facts and information she regurgitates from her lessons. His daughter's interpretation of things. It is interesting to see how she questions in ways he wouldn't think of doing. Hypothetical what ifs. His mind doesn't work like that. He finds it is much safer to contain things within absolutes.

'So, what's the countdown this week?' he says. 'How many more days till there's no more maths? Is it forty or are we down to thirty now?'

'I don't know,' she says.

'I thought you'd been counting.'

She sighs, biting her nails, chewing her fingers.

'Don't do that, love,' he says. 'You'll make them bleed.'

She shoves her hands underneath her thighs just as the traffic comes to a sudden stop. They jolt forward, seat belts snapping tight. 'Idiot,' he shouts through the windscreen.

'You okay?' he says to Flo in the rear-view mirror, but she is oblivious.

'It's the traffic lights, Dad. Didn't you see they were on red?' Maisie rubs her neck as she says this.

He just wants to get home. He hasn't had the opportunity to look at Kate's laptop yet. He has been waiting all week. It is infuriating.

Maisie opens the window, allowing a gush of car fumes in.

'Not in this traffic,' he says. 'Shut it please.'

She closes the window and turns the music up, a song on the radio that she likes. *Never ever ever ever*, the girl sings. And the boy says, *only so many opportunities*. Op-por-tune-ni-ees.

Daniel indicates left and turns past The Chapel – Kate's favourite restaurant. He usually books a table for their anniversary, but they had to miss last year because of the redundancy. Kate had said, 'Don't worry, let's get a Chinese,' and they sat on the floor, eating out of the containers like they were students again. He spilled rice on his lap and Kate kissed him. They laughed. Nothing could touch them, not ever. That's what he'd thought.

The song finishes and there is a brief pause, a silence.

Then Maisie says, 'Are you and Mum getting divorced?'

A loud advert comes on the radio with a man talking about prawn sandwiches and car insurance.

'What? Of course not. Where on earth did you get that idea?'

'I'll have to leave school, won't I?' She doesn't say this directly to him but turns to look out of the passenger window.

'What are you talking about?'

'I'm not stupid.'

'I didn't say you were. Has something happened at school?'

'Huh!' She turns back around to face the front and crosses her arms, glaring out at the road.

'Has your mum said something?'

'No.' She pulls her feet up onto the seat, hugs her knees. 'Mum's always crying, always upset over something.'

'Take your feet off. Sit properly. And your mum isn't always crying.'

'She is. I'm not stupid. I am *there* in the house, you know.'

He takes a breath. The air dries his mouth. She's in one of those moods where nothing he says will appease. He doesn't know how to deal with her when she gets like this. Kate knows how to handle her better.

'Maisie, will you put your feet down.'

She sighs loudly and slams her feet into the footwell. He looks straight ahead and grips the steering wheel. All week he's managed to keep everything in order: take the girls to school, write emails, make phone calls, check spreadsheets, pick the girls up from school, eat dinner, watch TV. Everything the same as it was, no deviations, else it will all come crashing down.

He just needs to keep his eyes on the road. Ten more minutes and they will be home.

'So, will I have to leave school, then?' Maisie says. He can feel her eyes on him. 'Because you still don't have a job, do you?'

A simple yes or no is the way to deal with her. He

90

knows that she only wants to rile him. Speak calmly, yes, no. That's what Kate does when she gets like this.

'Why on earth would you have to leave school? Your scholarship runs to the end of the academic year. You know that. Your place has nothing to do with my job.'

'But I won't be able to stay for sixth form, will I? Whatever happens, you won't be able to pay for me to stay.'

The back of the car bangs down on a speed bump.

'For God's sake,' he says. She's pushing him. Pressing his buttons. Maisie's always been the one to press his buttons, even when she was little. She seems to know exactly what to say. He could really lose it and shout, but he sets his jaw, keeps his voice steady.

'It costs a lot of money, Maisie. Even if we get the bursary, it won't cover all the fees. Do you understand?'

'I'm not stupid, you know. You talk to me like I'm a baby. Mum said even if you got a new job, you wouldn't pay for me to stay.'

'I don't think she said that. Your mum doesn't know what's going to happen.'

He thinks he hears her say *for fuck's sake,* and that really provokes him.

'Do you know? Sometimes I wish we hadn't sent you to that school. I can't believe you're being so selfish. Your sister left all her friends without a single complaint.' He checks Flo in the rear-view mirror. She has her pencil case in her lap and is counting her pens. He looks back at the road. 'I never thought you'd be like this, so bloody arrogant. Like a spoilt . . . You know it wouldn't hurt to be—'

'No wonder Mum cries.' She snatches her bag from

the floor, the zip scratching along the dashboard making a loud scrape. 'She must hate being around you all the time.' And with an exaggerated jerk, she turns towards the window again, hugging her bag. He can see her back huffing in and out with each angry breath.

When they arrive home, he pulls up onto the driveway, turns off the ignition. He goes to make a joke about what he will cook for dinner – Maisie teases him about his bad cooking – but she is already out. She slams the door so hard the car shakes.

In the house, the air smells stale and fishy. He should have emptied the bin before he left. Flo talks to him while she takes off her shoes.

'. . . and so, she said I didn't know how to make one and I told her I'd got one at home but she didn't believe me, and then Megan said she did believe me so Leah just went off and now she's not talking to us. Megan said I should bring it in to show everyone.'

Daniel makes noises, to give the impression he is following what she has been saying, all the while watching Maisie kick off her shoes and race up the stairs. She bangs her bedroom door shut. The three of them usually sit at the kitchen table with a drink and a snack. Maisie asks for help with her maths. He shows her the best way to look at a problem, gets out a sheet of paper and writes down the steps. He realises she hasn't asked him for weeks.

'So, can I, Daddy?' Flo is patting his arm. 'Daddy, can I?'

'Can you what? Do you want a drink?'

'Can I bring it in?'

'I'm sure,' he says, walking towards the kitchen. 'Yes, I'm sure you can. We'll talk about it later. Do you want a drink?' But she has also gone, disappeared up the stairs.

He goes into the kitchen, where the fish smell is stronger, and opens the bin. It is packed down and full. As he lifts it out, the bag splits, ripping open along one side. The contents spill out onto the floor. Everything is wet and caked with a porridge-like sludge. Long rectangles of grey fish skins slip onto the tiles.

'SHIT.'

He looks at the mess.

'FUCKING SHIT.'

Florence appears at the doorway.

'Stay back. Just go back to your room. I've got to clear this up.'

He gets the roll of black sacks from the cupboard under the sink and rips one off. His fingers are clumsy as he tries to open it. He kneels down and scoops up a handful, drops it into the clean bag. Dark red-brown liquid drips down his arm and onto his jeans.

Flo is still there, staring at him.

'JUST GO UPSTAIRS.'

She runs off and he shovels the remaining crud into the bag with his hands, not caring now if it drips all over him. When he's finished, he ties the handles together in a tight knot and carries it into the garden. Before throwing it in the wheelie bin, he spots something. Two yellow Selfridges bags, folded up. He puts the black sack down and takes them out. Inside each one he finds a receipt.

Back in the kitchen, he lays the strips of paper on the worktop – a dress for £95 on one receipt; bra and knickers for £64.98 on the other. He stares at the numbers, a variety of images appearing: his wife wearing a new dress, admiring herself in the mirror; his wife lying on a hotel bed, slowly undoing her new lacy bra. He snatches the receipts up and shoves them in his pocket. Perhaps he will just whip them out when she gets home, confront her there and then. He is seething now, cannot think.

The floor is a mess. He gets the mop and bucket from the pantry cupboard. As he fills the bucket with hot water, his thoughts go back and forth. He should show her the receipts, tell her that he knows about the messages as well. No – he should wait until he's had a chance to look at her laptop. By the time he hears Kate's key in the door, he doesn't have a clue what he is going to do.

He takes a saucepan from the cupboard.

'Oh, what's happened?' She looks at his stained jeans and shirt.

'The bin bag split and went everywhere. I'm just going to change.'

She stands with her hands on her hips. Is she sharp or soft today?

'What's for dinner?' she says, still with her elbows jutting out. He thinks it might not be a good day.

'I'm not sure. I was just clearing up.'

'I'll do it. You get changed.'

She smiles at him, a proper smile. Such a relief to see that, even though he then remembers how angry he is, remembers what he has found.

'Daniel?' she says. 'What's wrong?' She takes the saucepan from him and kisses his cheek.

'Nothing,' he says.

'Don't be long if you're having a shower.' She is behaving normally, no hint of anything amiss. He puts his hands in his pockets as he walks away, feels the receipts. She continues to talk. 'I'll heat up that leftover Bolognese. I think we have some garlic bread in the freezer as well . . .'

In the bedroom, he puts the receipts in his bedside drawer, underneath the book Kate bought him for Christmas: *When You Are Engulfed in Flames*, by David Sedaris. He hasn't read it yet. She said she bought it as a joke and that reading about another man's midlife crisis might help him. He found it funny at the time, and they had laughed.

Then he finds himself standing in front of the wardrobe, going through her clothes, sliding each hanger in turn, as if he's checking off an inventory. There it is, right at the end. He pulls the dress out and sees that it still has the price tag attached to a plastic string. Ostentatious, he decides, and immediately hates it. Who was she thinking of when she bought it? Because she certainly wasn't thinking of him. He likes the soft colours she usually wears, the clothes that remind him of when she was happy to throw on a simple white T-shirt, a pair of jeans. Twist her hair up into a knot. Barefaced and beautiful. Sexier than any of the clothes she thinks she needs to wear now.

He puts the dress back and shuts the wardrobe door.

Downstairs, he looks in the living room first. She normally puts her laptop on the coffee table when she gets home, but it isn't there. He can hear her in the kitchen, singing along to the radio.

He goes into the hall and sees her laptop on the pine settle bench. He just has to look.

'What are you doing?'

Kate is behind him. He manages to quickly close it, then reaches across and rummages in the pocket of a jacket

95

that is draped over the arm of the bench. He is positive she hasn't seen him touch her laptop. His body is surely blocking her view.

'I had a phone number on a scrap piece of paper,' he says loudly. 'On the back of a receipt, I think. For a recruitment company.'

'Why are you looking in my jacket pocket?' she says.

'Is this yours? I was just going through everything. Where have I put the damn thing?' He goes to the coat rack and rifles through a few pockets.

'Why did you write it on the back of a receipt?'

'And that reminds me,' he says. He turns to face her, can feel it all brewing in him now. 'Have you spent a hundred and fifty pounds? From our account.'

She looks at him, a wooden spoon in one hand, a tea towel in the other. 'What are you talking about? I haven't done the shopping for weeks. You've been doing it.'

'Maybe you bought some clothes.' He wants to give her the opportunity to come clean. It would be better if it came from her. 'You know we don't have that kind of money spare.'

'Don't you think I don't know that?'

She looks to the side, as if she is thinking, as if she is trying to calm herself.

'I haven't bought anything,' she says finally.

'Are you sure?'

'Daniel, you're being really odd tonight. I think the stress is getting to you.' She laughs in a way he isn't sure how to interpret. And before he can say anything else, Flo appears at the bottom of the stairs.

'Perfect timing. You can set the table,' Kate says, ushering her into the kitchen. 'Oh, and Daniel, can you give

96

Maisie a shout. You'll have to go up there, she's got those headphones permanently attached to her head.'

A few minutes later, when he comes back downstairs, he notices her laptop has gone.

13

It is Saturday night, and they are at Luke and Sarah's house. The children have already eaten and are upstairs watching a film before bed. Sarah has organised a special meal for the four of them, as if to celebrate, although Kate isn't sure of the occasion.

She rearranges the napkin on her lap. Pristine white linen with decorative stitching around the edges. Sarah likes things to be done properly. Kate knows this, has known Sarah for over twelve years. So why does she still feel so awkward around her? She looks across at Daniel, who is busy talking to Luke, and then back down at her empty plate, realising something she has always known. Sarah isn't a real friend.

'That was lovely,' Kate says, as Sarah gets up to clear the table.

Sarah goes across to the kitchen, where she puts the plates down on the large centre island.

'And this wine's good too.' Kate swallows, wishing she was drunk.

Conversations with Sarah are always so polite. They skate around each other, never getting close. Over the years, she's gleaned snatches of details, enough to know that Sarah had the sort of life where she was bought a new pencil case for the start of every school year. New shoes and new bag. She would have come home every day to meals prepared by her mum. They would have sat at the table as a family. When Sarah went off to university, her parents bought her a car. They packed the boot with boxes of food and supplies, a new duvet cover for her room.

What would Sarah say if Kate told her that when she came home from school, her mum was more than likely still in bed. On a really bad week, her dad would have disappeared too. With nothing left in the fridge but half a pint of milk, a bag of carrots with black patches spreading on the orange, and a small rectangle of cheese. She had to decide whether to risk going to the shops on the parade, just down from the flats, or make do. If Trisha Price was working, she'd be in luck, because Trish also lived on the estate and would turn a blind eye when Kate slipped a tin of beans into her bag. Sometimes, she didn't need to go to the shop, and there'd be a packet of Smash in the cupboard. She would make it up in a saucepan and get the last bit of cheese from the fridge, cut the hard plasticky end away and make cheesy mash. When her dad finally came home, she would wait until he had smoked a few joints and was woozy and mellow, almost asleep on the sofa, before she asked for some grocery money.

When she went to university, her parents didn't buy her a car, or help pack her things, or getting any supplies. Her dad said, 'Who the fuck do you think you are? Upsetting your mum, thinking you're better than us with your posh friends.'

She can't tell Sarah any of this. They talk about the

children, their work. Safe topics. Kate keeps herself hidden, even though it creates in her an agitated sense of disquiet. A battle between trying to conform to a false image of who she imagines Sarah wants her to be and who she really is.

Sarah comes back to clear away the remaining dishes. 'I'm so sorry again for cancelling the other week.'

'You don't need to worry. It really wasn't a problem,' Kate says. She gets up to help, picks up the pepper grinder.

'I hate people who cancel last minute,' Sarah says.

Kate puts the things down on the side. *I don't hate you*, she wants to say, but Sarah has her head in the fridge. Kate returns to the table.

'Not sure why the hell you put up with him,' Daniel is saying, loudly. They seem to be talking about Geoff now, Luke's business partner. 'Can't you buy him out?'

'Not yet.'

'Pity.'

'We should've set up a fund all those years ago,' Luke says. 'Do you remember? You had that formula. You said if we invested in the emerging markets, we could be retired by the time we were forty.'

'Youthful naivety, my friend.'

'You were on to something, though. We should set something up now. Don't you think?'

Kate wants to interrupt, but they are on a roll. Daniel doesn't need to be led astray by Luke's impulsiveness. He needs to get a proper job.

'Anyway,' Daniel says. 'I don't know what you're talking about. You could retire right now, couldn't you?' He waves a hand at the room.

Luke gives a closed-lipped grin. Then, in a mock Yorkshire accent, says, 'But the key to success is in diversification.'

Daniel laughs and joins in with the impression of their old Economics professor, wagging his forefinger, pretending to be serious. 'Anticipating the anticipations of others.' They both fall about.

Daniel leans back in his chair, interlaces his hands behind his head. He's more content than Kate has seen him for a while, laughing like his redundancy never happened, his body language relaxed, confident. Why isn't he this happy when he's at home?

'You two,' Kate says, but they are still laughing.

Sarah says something from the kitchen about strawberries or grapes and Kate nods, although she didn't really hear what was being asked. A plate of profiteroles is placed in the middle of the table. As Sarah leans over to put a bowl of strawberries down, a tendril of hair falls from her chignon, a feathery wisp, which she tucks behind her ear. Always so beautiful, so perfect. Her cashmere jumper, her soft flowing trousers. Luke looks up as Sarah spoons strawberries onto his plate. The way they are together, so visceral, no need for words.

'I'll be back in a minute,' she says, getting up from the table. 'Too much of that pre-dinner cocktail thing you made, Sarah.'

She goes out into the hall and across to the cloakroom, where she stands for a few minutes, her hands on her hips, blinking back tears. *Get a grip,* she says and yanks her skirt straight. She should have worn her new dress. After all, that's why she bought it, to wear tonight, so she could feel nice. But as she was getting ready to come out, she remembered Daniel's weird question about her spending money on clothes. She had bought the dress from her own account, she was sure. Why was he asking her that? It made her feel strange inside, guilty, as if she had done something terrible. She had spent too much, but she wanted something nice for this weekend. Being with Sarah and Luke, surrounded by constant reminders of their wealth. She didn't want to be triggered; the horrible feeling of being less than. Then she had pictured herself wearing the dress to meet Alec, wondered what he would think of her. She took the dress off immediately then, put it back in the wardrobe and pulled on her old faithful skirt.

She tucks her hair behind her ears and goes back into the kitchen.

'. . . could lead to a position, couldn't it, Kate?' Daniel says as she approaches the table.

'I'm sorry, what?'

'I was telling Luke about the book you're writing. It might lead to something full-time at the university.'

All eyes are on her and her stomach lurches, as though she is in a lift, hurtling down.

'I don't know about that. I'm not really sure what I'm doing yet,' she says as she goes back to her chair.

Luke comes around the table with a bottle in his hands. He touches her shoulder. 'More wine?' he says, topping up her glass. One hand on the bottle, the other on her shoulder. His hand is warm. He looks right at her and smiles, as if he is noticing her reaction.

'Thanks,' she says quickly and turns away. 'Those straw-berries look perfect, Sarah.'

★

An hour later, the children are in bed, and they have moved across from the dining table to the sofas by the patio doors. Daniel is shuffling a deck of cards.

'Aces high or low?' Luke asks.

Daniel is on the other sofa, sitting next to Sarah, and he tells them aces are low. He deals the cards onto the square coffee table between them. They always play cards, each time they visit, and Kate usually enjoys the way they fall into the old dynamic of their student days. But tonight, something is different. Daniel is trying to make Sarah laugh in a way that is unnatural and he's drinking far too quickly. He's hyperactive, manic even, and it's making her uneasy. Luke leans across and says, 'I think we need more of what he's having.'

She laughs. She's in that space where she's drunk but not drunk.

As if he could read her thoughts, Luke points to the empty wine bottle and says, 'Actually, we should do it properly.' He puts his cards face down and goes over to the kitchen, returns with a bottle of Stoli and some shot glasses. The bottle is cloudy-cold.

'Not on the table, Luke,' Sarah says. 'Put it on a mat.' She gets up and fetches some coasters from the dining table.

'You shouldn't put it in the freezer, you know,' Daniel says. 'Spoils the flavour, or something.'

'When did you suddenly become the connoisseur?' Kate says, meaning it as a joke, but he seems to think she is being hostile. She smiles, to let him know she was only teasing, but he looks away, asks Luke if he remembers the mess they got into that time when they had a poker night with vodka jelly shots.

'You threw up over the speaker and we found you the next day trying to get the dried bits out of the grill with a needle,' Luke says, laughing.

Kate is about to ask if Luke remembers the time they got completely wasted on shots at another party, that summer after their first year, but she stops herself in time, not because of the awkwardness of mentioning Luke's parents or his old home, but because of what she did.

Luke had picked her up from the station in a battered old Land Rover. There were people on the terrace, in the house, sitting on the grass. Lots of people she didn't know, and she had looked for Daniel. They were only friends at that point and she wasn't sure what he really thought about her – that awkward feeling, where she wanted to say something, but was afraid he didn't feel the same way.

After looking everywhere, Luke told her Daniel couldn't make it. She spent most of the party with her girlfriends. It was only later that she ended up in the barn with Luke and Nils and the others, doing vodka shots. Luke put his arm around her. She enjoyed the feeling of him wanting her, even though she didn't want him. When it was dark, she followed him into the trees. He didn't kiss her, but he made her come with his hand. The next morning, even with the worst hangover, she knew what she had done. But then she told herself she didn't remember. Nothing is real if you don't remember.

Luke hands her a glass. 'Knock that back, girl,' he says.

She drinks the shot quickly, lets the cold–hot liquid slice into her chest.

The next few hours go by in an increasing haze, and when she realises they are no longer playing cards, Daniel is asleep, slumped on the sofa and Luke is sitting next to her, smoking. There's a cigarette between her fingers too, and she takes a drag. Luke nudges her arm and tells her she needs to dance to this one. The music is loud. She still has a sense of being part of what she can see, but also separate, like in a dream.

Sarah is at the patio doors, opening them wide. 'If you two want to smoke,' she says, 'you need to go outside.'

Luke leans forward and stubs his out and Kate takes another drag before doing the same. It claws at her throat and makes her cough, makes her want to apologise. She doesn't know why she's smoking. A sudden urge to hide under the weight of Sarah's scrutiny.

Sarah says, 'I'm going to leave you all to it. I'm going to bed.'

Luke blows her a kiss. 'We'll be quiet.'

Once Sarah has gone, Luke pulls Kate off the sofa. He turns the music up and makes her laugh doing stupid dance moves. She relaxes then, can feel herself coming back. It's been a while since she properly laughed. Luke lights another cigarette and holds the packet out, gesturing for her to take one. He blows smoke out of the side of his mouth.

'I shouldn't,' she says.

'Is that because of Sarah or because you don't want one?'

'Probably both.'

'You never used to be such a coward,' he says, taking a long drag, eyeing her up, as if he is deciding something. 'She doesn't mean to be like that, you know, she just likes everything to be in order. Go on,' he says, forcibly offering her the packet. 'You don't need to worry.'

Kate takes a cigarette, and he steps closer to light it. She can sense him studying her as she inhales. He flips the lid of his lighter shut.

A different song comes on now, something she hasn't heard before with a thumping bass beat. She is aware of her body and Luke's, the way they are standing so close. Although she is drunk, she is embarrassed and shy, as if they are strangers. She keeps catching Luke looking at her and recalls something a friend at university once said, that he was the sort of boy who made you relaxed and nervous all at the same time. An intoxicating feeling of being safe and also walking along a cliff edge. She had forgotten how Luke could be.

He wanders back over to the coffee table, nodding his head in time to the music and pours himself a vodka shot, knocks it back. 'Come on,' he says, beckoning. He goes to the open doors and stands blowing smoke into the garden. She joins him.

'Don't you ever feel like fucking off out of here?' he says.

She isn't sure what he means, whether he's talking about Sarah, so she doesn't say anything. The cold air makes her unsteady on her feet and she holds onto the door handle. Her thoughts are flitting from one fragment to another, and she can't concentrate entirely on what he is saying. He seems to notice her unease and puts his arm around her, gives her a squeeze. He becomes someone different then. Just a friend.

'So, how are you really?' he says. 'You seem . . .' He leans in and looks at her, makes a sad face. 'What's up?'

'Oh nothing,' she says. 'Probably a midlife crisis or something.'

'Do you remember what we agreed? That I was going

to buy us a place, that we'd meet up every summer. Where was it we said would be good? You were going to travel, and Daniel would work for the Foreign Office, get a post overseas. You'd be able to research your projects. Africa and South America. Where's that place you were always talking about? Ecuador?'

'That was years ago. Back when we were young and idealistic. Once you have children, you have to make sacrifices.'

She doesn't mean this. In fact, she has just repeated what Daniel said in an argument. She believes that children should be part of your dreams, not an excuse to never pursue them.

Luke smiles at her kindly, tells her nothing has to be sacrificed. 'There's plenty of time,' he says. She wishes he would stop being so nice.

'God, I need to sit down,' she says, swaying a little, going back to the sofa, where Daniel is still asleep.

He showed her a video the other day – something one of his friends had shared on Facebook. 'You'll find this really funny,' he said, and he'd turned his laptop screen round so she could see. It was a compilation of people falling over and hurting themselves. There was a middle-aged woman in a bikini trying to pole dance. The pole was set up in her bedroom and halfway through a spin, the whole thing collapsed, brought some of the ceiling down with it. Daniel laughed so hard, even though he said he'd watched it a dozen times. But it wasn't funny. It made her feel empty and sad. Daniel seemed to get annoyed with her because she hadn't reacted the way he'd expected. She tried – blew air out of her nose and made a noise in her throat that was like a 'ha!' – but it felt worse than an awkward silence. Such a minor thing, a stupid moment that should have meant nothing. They'd never needed to agree on everything before. It had struck her how they were completely out of alignment, and that was frightening. She'd thought they were fixed, like train tracks.

'We should get Daniel into bed,' Luke says. 'Look at him, absolutely wasted.'

Daniel's mouth is open, his head lolled to one side, glasses squashed against a cushion. She gets up and stands over him, tries to wake him by pressing on his shoulder, talking in his ear. 'Daniel,' she says. 'We need to go to bed. Can you hear me?'

'He'll be too heavy for you to move,' Luke says, and he comes up behind her. 'Here, let me help.'

Before she can do anything, Luke goes around to the other side and puts Daniel's arm around his neck, hoists him off the sofa. Daniel stirs.

'You're a heavy fucker,' Luke says. 'Kate, you take his other arm. Quick, I think we can get him to walk if you grab him.'

They steer around the coffee table and through the kitchen to the hall. At one point, she's sure they'll collapse, but they manage to get down the basement stairs and along the small corridor to the guest suite. They lay Daniel on the bed, and Kate takes off his glasses, folds them up and puts them on the bedside table.

'He'll have one mother of a hangover,' Luke says.

Kate climbs onto the bed.

'You not coming for a nightcap?'

'I'm done for,' she says. The room is swaying.

'Come on. I've got something that'll sober us up, give us a second wind.' He smiles at her as he goes out.

She gets off the bed and heads for the en suite, pulling her tights and knickers down on the way. And she doesn't think of anything but how nice it smells, all lavender and freshness. She concentrates on wiping herself with a balled-up bit of toilet roll, then washes her hands with the lavender soap. Her reflection glares. *What do you want?* She is trying so hard not to think of anything at all as she walks past the bed where Daniel is asleep and goes up the basement stairs.

In the kitchen, Luke is sitting on the far side, on one of the sofas.

'Thought you'd bailed on me,' he says. He's making two thick lines of coke on the coffee table.

'I can't believe you still do that.'

'Here,' he says, holding out a short metal straw.

'No thanks.'

'Come on. It'll be fun. And I've got this.' He holds up a small self-seal bag.

'What's that?'

'MDMA,' he says, opening the bag. 'Come on, sit down.' He licks the end of his finger and dips it in.

She finds herself sitting next to him, rubbing a couple of dabs across her gums. He holds out the metal straw.

'What about Sarah?' she says, pointing to the mess. Luke grins, as if she's said something else entirely.

The metal straw is in her hand. She leans over the coffee table, blocking off one nostril and snorting half a line. It stings. Luke does a line, plus the remaining half. He sits bolt upright, squeezes his eyes, pinches his nose with his thumb and forefinger.

'Tell me about this book, then,' he says.

She goes to speak but he gets up and goes over to the kitchen.

'Carry on,' he says, coming back with a bottle of wine and pouring them both a glass. As he hands one to her, he strokes her finger. She is sure that's what he just did, but she doesn't allow herself to look at him. She moves her hand away, takes a sip. Her legs don't know where to be and she crosses one over the other. She is small and yet too big, the space suddenly contorted. Luke stares at her thigh, where her skirt has ridden up.

'Oh,' she says, uncrossing her legs, tugging at her skirt. 'You don't want to be bored by my academic ramblings.'

'No, go on. I'm interested.' He looks right at her as she says this.

'You don't need to be polite,' she says, laughing.

'I'm always interested in what you're up to,' he says, and he settles back against the cushions.

Touch me, she wants to say. Just touch me again. And she tells him everything, about the research she's been doing, about her idea of putting together a collection of interviews with men and women. About desire and expectations. It all comes out in a rush. Luke listens. But she doesn't mention the website or the late-night messaging, or Alec, or the way she's been feeling recently, or how it's like she's hanging onto the edge of something. She isn't sure what will happen if she lets go.

He smiles and says, 'But what do *you* think about it all?'

She tips her glass up, drinks the last drop.

'I'm not sure,' she says. 'And anyway, it's not about me. I want to find out what other people think. There isn't just one way of looking at it, is there?'

He pauses before saying, 'No, there isn't.'

She is about to go on, to tell him that she used to know with absolute certainty what she wanted, what she believed, but now, for the first time in her life, she isn't sure who she's meant to be.

He leans towards her.

'You know,' he says, running his hand through his hair. 'I've always thought we were alike. That we have a kind of connection. Have you ever felt that?'

And then, as if she has silently given him her agreement, he grabs her hand and pulls her up. The music has changed, the tempo slowed. His hand is around her waist, the other hand under her chin, lifting her face to him.

Time shifts and she is next to Daniel, in the bed in the guest room, under the duvet. She slips out, her bare feet shaky on the cold wooden floor. Her head is thick. Pounding. It must still be early because the light is grainy. And it is quiet. Not a single sound as she makes her way across the room. The quietness makes her movements seem even noisier. She pulls down her skirt, her knickers, and empties her bladder in the toilet. The night before is a blur. There was a card game, drinking and dancing. She remembers that much. And they had a job to bring Daniel downstairs. She sniffs and pinches her nose, remembers the coke. Luke's finger in her mouth. Remembers him saying, 'You and me. We're the same, aren't we?'

She flushes and pulls up her knickers, feels a patch of dry skin on her stomach, just under her tummy button. She cannot look. What has she done? She strips off her clothes and gets in the shower. The water is cold at first, but she doesn't care. She rubs at the dry patch, which feels sticky on her fingers. She keeps rubbing and rubbing, the water getting hotter and hotter. Even when it is gone, she keeps rubbing until the skin is red.

The steam goes up to the ceiling and swirls around the lights. She stays under the hot water for as long as she can bear, until she could pass out, then dries herself with a towel. In the bedroom, she finds her cotton nightdress, neatly folded at the bottom of the small overnight case, along with Daniel's pyjama bottoms and a change of underwear. Nothing happened, she keeps telling herself. Nothing. Not if she can't remember.

She pulls the nightie over her head and crawls back into bed. Daniel is breathing heavily and does not stir as she threads her arm through his. 'I love you,' she says. 'I love you I love you I love you I love you.'

Sarah hooks open the patio doors. The room reeks of cigarettes. She could smell it even before she came into the kitchen, before she went over and saw the ash and mess all over the coffee table, fag-ends spilling out of a dish. Her dish. The one Luke bought her for their anniversary last year. Made her even angrier, seeing that. As she washed it up and put it away, she remembered the Waterford vase. Meeting Luke for the first time.

It was in a menswear shop in Jermyn Street. Twelve years ago. She was standing next to a display table, deciding between two ties. A voice behind her said, 'I think he'll probably love anything you choose.'

She turned to see a man with the greenest eyes. He smiled and ran his hand through his hair, apologised for bothering her, said the recipient of the tie was the luckiest man alive. She felt embarrassed but didn't walk away. Not like she usually did whenever anyone tried to chat her up. He seemed different to other men. They always wanted something in return for a compliment.

'My dad's birthday,' she said, quickly picking the blue one with cream dots.

The shop assistant came over and asked if she needed any help. Which was annoying, because when she turned back, the green-eyed man had gone.

She paid at the counter. It was twenty past two, and she made a conscious note of the time – a foolish thought that he might come back again next week. As she left the shop, she was still fantasising about how she could bump into him again. And there he was, standing by the window. He asked if she fancied a post-shopping drink and she said she would love to.

'Luke,' he said, holding out his hand, quite formally.

'Sarah,' she said. His hand was warm. She noticed they kept hold of each other for a few seconds longer than necessary.

'I'm supposed to be shopping for a wedding,' he said as they started to walk. 'There isn't a list, don't you just hate that? I never know what to get.'

She hadn't long graduated, none of her friends were married yet, but she agreed that not having a list was a real pain. He flagged down a black cab and it felt like the most natural thing to be with him. They went to Fenwick's on Bond Street, and she suggested he buy a Waterford vase. She had heard her mother talk about the brand, as if it was very expensive. Luke looked like the sort of man who only bought expensive things.

What she remembers most about that day was that there was no need to fill the space with chatter. When some of her friends spoke about falling in love, they said things like, *we talked all night*, or *I just knew he was the one when we couldn't stop talking*. With Luke, it wasn't like that at all. In fact, it was the opposite. It's what made her so certain. She had never felt so happily silent before.

The doors rattle in the wind. Sarah goes back into the kitchen and makes herself a camomile tea. As she is about to go and sit down, Daniel comes in and stands next to the fridge.

'I'm getting too old to be doing this,' he says, giving a weary smile.

She offers him toast and coffee. 'I'll bring it over,' she says, pointing across the room. 'I gave the kids breakfast. They're up in the TV room watching a film.'

'Thank God for the telly.' He goes over and collapses onto one of the sofas.

She butters Daniel's toast and walks across with it, precariously carrying both his coffee and her tea in the other hand.

'Thanks,' he says. 'I need this.'

She sits on the sofa facing him. His crunching fills the quiet. She relaxes back and sips her tea.

'I can't drink like that any more,' he says.

'I know,' she says. 'You were passed out on the sofa, do you remember? What time did you get to bed?'

'God knows.'

'It was almost four when Luke came up,' she says.

The patio doors rattle again.

'I wanted to let the air in,' she says, by way of explanation. 'It smelt disgusting when I came down this morning. But it's too cold, isn't it?'

'It's okay.' He stifles a belch. 'Leave them open if you like.'

A gust blows in and Daniel rubs his hand up and down his arm.

She goes over and unhooks the doors. The wind takes her breath. She shuts them, stares into the garden.

'I did tell him to smoke outside,' she says. 'Luke hasn't smoked for ages. I don't know what the hell he was doing.' And before she can stop herself, she is crying.

Daniel is in front of her. 'Come and sit down,' he says, guiding her back to the sofa.

The tears spill down her face. 'I'm sorry,' she says, pressing her cheeks with the heel of her hand. 'He just makes me so mad, the way he behaves . . . he thinks I don't notice.'

Daniel sits next to her.

'It's been a stressful time. But it'll be okay. He seemed really good when we talked last night.'

'I know,' she says, sniffing.

'And he gets carried away. He's always been like that. All the parties we had at uni. He'd be the one, still up all night, still going for it.' He laughs, warmly.

This makes her cry more, knowing her tears are really anger, all the while Daniel is sitting here being so lovely, supporting Luke like a brother.

'Come on, it'll be okay,' he says. He gives her an awkward hug, one arm around her shoulder.

She tells him she's fine, that she doesn't know what came over her. 'He's been going out a lot. That's all. It doesn't get easier, does it?' she says.

'No, I don't suppose it does.'

He removes his arm, and the conversation returns to safer things.

Later, after Dan and Kate have gone and the children are in bed, she is back on the same sofa with Luke. She lays her head on his chest.

'Excellent weekend,' he says.

'Yes.' She waits and then says, 'So what did you do after I went to bed?'

'Not much,' he says. His heartbeat is steady in her ear. 'Daniel was so wasted. We virtually had to carry him downstairs. He's never been good with vodka.'

'Did you go out?'

'Out? I came to bed.'

She sits up and looks at him. 'You shouldn't drink so much. And you promised you wouldn't smoke. You left mess all over the table.'

He strokes her face. 'We were having a good time.'

'And you shouldn't smoke. You weren't doing anything else, were you?'

He sighs.

'It makes me worry. It's dangerous when you drink too much.'

'Dangerous?'

He's getting annoyed but she can't stop. 'You're different with other people, especially Dan and Kate.'

He sighs again. 'So are you, my darling. So are you.' He keeps stroking her cheek. She wants to push his hand away but instead she lays her head back down on his chest.

'I didn't get the promotion,' she says.

'Didn't you? They're idiots.'

'They gave it to Amit.'

'Well, he has been there longer.'

'That's what Harriet said.'

He puts his hand around her shoulder and gives her a squeeze. She could tell him she has been thinking about giving up her job, that she didn't want the promotion in the first place, and she only applied to make herself feel less afraid of the future. But why should she tell him things if he can't be honest with her? She imagines confronting him about what he does in his study. Only, she knows he will say it's perfectly normal, and what does she expect, with how she is about sex?

How she is about sex.

She once walked in on her friend's brother, wanking in the bathroom. She must have been about thirteen and sex was something she didn't want to think about. The brother was straddling a magazine laid out on the floor, with a pull-out poster of a woman with big dark nipples. He was staring down at the woman as she opened the door, and she saw the poster, saw his penis, the look on his face. She couldn't imagine a boy ever looking at her like that.

She was eighteen when she lost her virginity. She had been going out with Will for almost a year, and they decided to do it after the sixth-form prom. She wasn't as drunk as she had hoped and undressed quickly. He scrambled to take off his clothes and climbed in beside her, his single mattress creaking. They kissed for a while, and he grabbed at her breasts. He kneeled over her as he rolled on a condom. All she could think about was her friend's brother and the poster. The look of violent urgency on his face.

How she is about sex.

Then there was Pete. They didn't go out for very long, barely a month. He told her she was frigid. A prick, her friends reassured. They didn't know what she saw in Pete. He was only after one thing.

Julian studied Medieval History and was quietly introspective. Quite the opposite of Pete. Sometimes, when they made love, she could almost imagine what it might be like to have an orgasm. But when the summer months

118

came, he wanted to do it on top of the duvet. The sun streaked through the open window across their naked bodies. 'I just want to look at you,' he said. She couldn't explain that it felt like he was going to take her apart.

How she is about sex.

When she slept with Luke for the first time, they were staying in Bath. He had booked one of the suites at the Royal Crescent. She remembers placing her overnight bag at the side of the room and looking out of the window, trying not to notice the king-sized bed. She was worried what he would think of her, whether he would be disappointed. He was much older, after all, and must have been with lots of confident women. She was never good at any of that sexy stuff – suspenders and lacy underwear. It made her feel indecent. He came and put his arm around her, cupped her face in his hands and kissed her gently. He told her she didn't have to worry, that he wouldn't do anything she felt uncomfortable with. He wanted to do things properly. When he pushed himself inside her, it wasn't like any of the times before. She didn't feel scrutinised. It wasn't just something he was doing to her, but something she was doing as well.

'Are you tired?' she says.

'A little.'

'Do you remember Bath?' she says.

'Rory's wedding?'

'No, before we were married. You know, that first night.'

'Oh yes,' he says. 'You were magnificent.'

She slaps his leg. 'I mean, do you remember how it was for you, really? Was it everything you wanted?'

'Of course. You were virginal and pure.'

'I wasn't a virgin.'

'You were in my mind,' he says.

'But it wasn't disappointing?'

'What's this about?' he says, and he lifts her up, looks at her. 'Sarah?'

'Nothing,' she says, struggling to be free of his grip. 'It's nothing.' And she almost retreats, but something pushes her forward.

She kisses him, touches the crotch of his jeans until she can feel him go hard, then unbuckles his belt. She kneels down on the floor.

Daniel sits on the sofa and opens Kate's laptop. She has finally left it at home. He logs onto her email and is glad to discover her password hasn't changed. They have always known each other's passwords – there has never been any reason to keep them a secret.

The email he just sent is there, in her inbox, along with the file attachment for the spy software he plans to install. He clicks. She won't be back from work for hours, but he is on high alert, straining for any noise.

An error window appears. Installation failed.

He tries once more, then picks up his laptop and sends a new email, attaches the file again. It fails. He pushes the laptop onto the sofa. 'Bloody hell,' he shouts. 'Bloody fucking hell.'

Upstairs in the bedroom, he swipes the nail clippers from the chest of drawers, where he left them earlier and yanks open the wardrobe doors. The dress she bought is still there, moved to the middle now, so that every time she opens her wardrobe, he sees it. He hates this fucking dress. He grabs a handful of the skirt, folds a small piece of the fabric into the nail clippers and snips.

Then again. Snip. He continues, until it is completely punctured.

Pulling it off the hanger, he sits with it on the bed. The hanger swings up and down, banging against the wall. He pokes his thumb through one of the nail-clippered slits. Then his fingers find other holes and he pokes the tips through, like he once did when he read *The Hungry Caterpillar* board book to the girls, making them laugh as his fingers devoured a slice of Swiss cheese, a piece of cherry pie, a sausage, a cupcake, a slice of watermelon. He can still remember the story and see their giggling faces. 'Again Daddy, again!' He removes his fingers and takes a deep breath. The dress is completely ruined. Despair now overrides the all too brief sense of triumph. What has he done?

Outside in the garden, he gets one of the rubbish-filled bags from the wheelie bin and undoes the knot. Using a cane from the shed, he pushes the balled-up dress down into the middle. The smell of rotting food is strangely satisfying. He makes sure it is completely hidden, then reties the bag and throws it back into the bin.

The black and white cat from next door scrabbles up the fence and appears at his head. It stares at him before walking to the fence post, where it sits with its tail curled in a question mark. Daniel considers shooing it away with the cane, but he is aware that the lady next door is likely to be in her kitchen, looking out. He returns to the house, rubbing his temples. A headache is forming in a tight band across his eyes. He should get on, sort it out. Ring the software company, that's what he should do. That's what he should have done in the first place, instead of behaving like a madman.

★

By the time Kate gets home, he has organised the right version of the software. It is too late to install it now, but he feels calmer, more in control. He is at the dining table, reading through his emails. The dinner is made, and Kate is upstairs having a shower. They have barely spoken. He realises they have said very little to one another since the weekend at Luke's.

A hum of voices from above makes him look at the ceiling. Toing and froing across the landing. Low shouts. Was that Kate or the girls? Then a creak directly above his head, the loose floorboard in their bedroom. Perhaps she is opening the wardrobe, noticing her missing dress. Will she be distressed that she can't wear it to go out as she had planned? She hasn't worn it yet, so she must be saving it for something. A vile image then, of her with a faceless man, his fingers fumbling to unhook her bra, tracing them down her back, over the knobs of her spine. He imagines her moaning.

He gets up. Everything is compressed: her face, the dress, another man.

The sound of water runs through the pipes as the toilet flushes. Footsteps down the stairs and noise from the kitchen.

'And you need to have a serious think about what you've done,' Kate says.

'I haven't done anything!' Maisie shouts.

A cupboard door is banged. He crosses the hallway to the kitchen. Maisie is standing at the fridge. Kate is dishing out the dinner.

'What's going on?' he says.

Nobody responds. Maisie pours a tall glass of orange juice and sits at the kitchen table.

'What is it?' he says to Kate, but she ignores him.

Over dinner, Flo talks about being Alice in Wonderland for World Book Day. Maisie prods at her broccoli and says, 'How original.'

'So, have you thought about it?' Kate says to her. 'Have you?'

Maisie puts her fork down in her half-eaten dinner and folds her arms.

'And you're grounded for two weeks,' Kate says. 'Banned from your phone as well. Do you hear me?'

Maisie gets up and runs out of the kitchen, saying something that sounds like *I hate this house.* Flo stares after her, then looks at Kate.

'What have I missed?' Daniel says. 'She was fine when I picked her up from school. What has she done? Shall I talk to her?'

'No,' Kate pushes her unfinished plate to the middle of the table. 'She has to know there are consequences. If we don't nip this in the bud now, God knows what else she'll steal.'

'What do you mean?'

'She's taken one of my dresses,' she says.

'She can't have,' he says quickly.

'Well, she has. I found one of my tops in her drawer as well.'

She looks right at him. He can't stand to hold her gaze. It's as if she's goading him into admitting what he has done.

'What did she say?'

'She said she asked if she could borrow my top, but she hasn't taken my dress. I know she's lying. She's hidden it somewhere.'

'So, she didn't take your top, she did actually ask?'

124

'Well yes, but—' She stops and looks at Flo, who is silently listening to them. Flo looks from Kate to Daniel as if she is watching a tennis match, waiting for one of them to make the next serve.

'Flo, why don't you go and get ready for bed?' Kate says.

'It's not bedtime.'

'Go on, do as you're told,' Daniel says.

He nods at her, pleads with his eyes. She goes off. It's just the two of them then, facing each other. For a while, neither of them speaks. Kate sniffs.

'Maybe you left it at Luke's,' he says, shrugging his shoulders. 'I'm sure I saw it in the case.' He isn't supposed to know which dress she is talking about, but she doesn't seem to notice his slip.

She shakes her head. 'I know I didn't take it.'

He looks down at his plate, scrapes his knife absently through the remaining gravy.

'They say it's a cry for help, don't they?' she goes on. 'Do you think it's drugs? Should we search her room?'

Dear God. He turns to the garden and sees the cat picking its way along the fence. Perhaps he could say the cat got in, that it was in the wardrobe and clawed her dress to shreds. He looks across at her – she has her elbows on the table, her head in her hands.

'Everything's falling apart,' she says.

'That's a bit dramatic. It's only a dress.'

'Only a dress?' Her eyes crease into slits.

'No need to get things out of proportion,' he says.

'Our daughter's stealing things and I'm getting things out of proportion,' she juts her chin out. 'And do you think I'm getting things out of proportion when I mention what a mess we're in? That you can't get a job, that we might end up—' Her voice pitches higher, louder.

'Ssh,' he says, looking towards the door.

She screws her face up. 'Don't shush me,' she says.

'All right.' He raises his hands.

'I can't stand this,' she says, getting up. 'I'm going to get some air.'

Upstairs, Maisie is lying on her bed listening to music, curled up as if she has been crying. He motions for her to take off the headphones.

'Are you okay?' he says. He wants to comfort her, like he did when she was little and fell off her bike.

She sits up and hugs her knees. 'And she says I'm being childish. Huh. Could she have slammed the door any harder?'

'I know. She's just upset, and she's worried about you.'

'Worried about me? Huh.'

'It's hard being a parent.'

'I don't know what you're talking about. She's accused me of stealing her fucking dress.'

She glares, challenging him.

'Maisie, please,' he says.

'Well, I haven't touched it. Why would I want that frumpy thing?'

'I know. I know. It's just a mistake, that's all.'

He isn't sure what else to say. He looks across the room, scanning for something to bring instant resolution. His eyes lock onto the framed photo on her drawers. It was taken on holiday last year, before he lost his job. They went down to the Dorset coast, fossil hunting on the beach. Maisie found a belemnite in a rock, protruding like a bullet. In the photo, she is holding the rock, delighted with her find. They are all laughing in the photo because the wind was blowing so hard, it felt like they might lift off. They went for chips afterwards and as they walked back to the hotel Kate had held his hand. 'I don't care if the weather's rubbish,' she said, 'as long as we're together.'

Maisie coughs and he turns back to her.

'Look,' he says, 'your mum's stressed. You can understand that, can't you?'

'She never apologises. You always take her side.'

'There are no sides, Maisie, really.'

But he has lost her. She's putting her headphones back on, turning away from him.

He goes downstairs, goes into the dining room, takes out his phone and goes to the window. He keeps a lookout for Kate as he makes the call.

'Yeah, good,' he says, when Luke asks how the job hunt is going.

'Glad to hear it,' Luke says. 'But if you need any help – you know with anything – you will ask, won't you?'

'Actually, funny you should say that because I was calling to ask a favour.'

'Name it,' Luke says. 'Do you want me to put the feelers out again? I can ask—'

'No, it's not that. Would you send Kate a text, tell her Magda's found her dress or something, and you'll get it posted on?'

He has decided he will buy an identical dress and put it back in the wardrobe. She will think she took it to Luke and Sarah's, and everything will be resolved. He cannot ever say how sorry he is to his daughter, but he will put it right.

'Er yeah, sure. That sounds complicated.'

There is an uncomfortable pause before Luke makes a joke about doing anything for an easy life and says of course he can, no problem. 'The things we do,' he says.

'Yeah, the things we do.'

They both laugh.

There was a time when Daniel would have confided in Luke, met up and made a night of it. Like the time they ended up in a jazz bar. They didn't often talk about their wives, not in any kind of revealing way, but after Maisie was born, Kate had been very low. There was no sex for months. He had confessed this to his friend and felt relief. Luke said it was tough when someone you loved held you at a distance – he was sensitive like that, underneath the jokes and bravado. Not many people were privy to that side of Luke.

But not this time. This time is different. Luke would ask too many questions, would want to know why the hell Daniel hadn't confronted her yet. He doesn't know what he would say to that.

16

Kate's boots are caked with mud. The narrow lane is thick with it. It's not yet five o'clock, but she couldn't sleep. She had to get out.

She reaches into her pocket and takes out her mobile. Luke has sent another message. I'll get your **dress posted off today.** He messaged the other day, to tell her Magda found it in the guest room under the bed, which was baffling, because she was sure she hadn't packed it. Even more confusing was the next message. I also **found your tights. They smell of you.** She shoves the phone back in her pocket. Zips her puffa jacket right up.

The sun has not yet appeared above the horizon and there is an early morning chill. Her bare legs are freezing. She is still wearing the stupid flimsy skirt, the one she wore last night.

Three hours ago, the taxi dropped her home. She went into the living room, curled up on the sofa. She couldn't sleep, or rather it was that fitful kind of sleep where she kept jerking herself awake. At quarter to five, she got up. There wasn't a sound in the house, not even the boiler firing up or the faint clicking of radiators. She put on her walking boots and jacket. Shut the front door behind her as quietly as possible.

A low bleat comes from the field.

She balls her hands in her pockets and keeps walking along the track. At the top, further ahead, there is a turning down another smaller track, which eventually leads across the fields. Daniel found this walk when they first moved here. She was pregnant with Maisie. They used to venture out together, exploring. He helped her over the stile as her bump grew. Then later, she would come out on her own. Daniel forced her to get out, said she needed to have some time to herself. He was good like that, just seemed to know, without her having to say anything.

Thinking of Daniel makes her gasp for air. She stops, leans her elbows on her knees as if she might throw up; stays there for a while, bent over in the middle of the lane, until the feeling passes.

She met Alec last night.

The sheep bleats again, behind the hedgerow, triggering more bleating from others. Hollow desperate sounds. She can make out their dark shapes, moving past the gaps in the hedge. She swallows the taste of bile and continues walking, can go at a faster pace now the muddy section is behind her.

At the stile, she jumps onto the step and swings her leg over. There is a ripping sound as the back of her skirt snags on the post. A piece has torn right off. As she goes to step down, she loses her footing and slips. Her leg scrapes along the rough wood. Tears come immediately, spilling onto her cheeks. She gets up and keeps going, leaving her torn piece of skirt stuck to the stile like a marker.

The sun is starting to rise, a shimmer of orange at the

horizon. Her leg stings and she sits down, cannot walk any further. The grass is damp with a raw, violent smell of earth. A thick line of blood is trickling down her shin. She feels in her pocket for a tissue and the blood soaks into it, almost black in the dim light.

She met Alec last night.

Alec. Luke. It's as if something has been unleashed, a dark twin. It wants chaos. It wants everything to come crashing down. It makes her understand, if only for a brief angry second, why her mum wanted to cut herself wide open.

She takes the bloody tissue off her leg. The wound isn't too bad. Blood always makes a cut look worse.

Kate was only ten the first time her mum cut herself. She didn't know what had happened, but she knew enough to go and knock on all the doors, ask someone for help. In films, they always do it in the bathroom. White bathrooms with white baths and glossy tiles that can be cleaned and made to look as if nothing has happened. But her mum did it in bed, the blood dark on the covers. The mattress soaked it up like a sponge, and when Kate went into the bedroom the next day, while her dad was at the hospital, the blood was still there, even though the sheets had gone.

She never understood how her mum could feel so sad that she couldn't even move. When Kate got sad, she felt a rage inside, a voice that told her to make noise. She had to get out, walk, run. Go to the shops and see what she dared take. How could her mum just lie there, static, with so much going on inside?

Then Maisie was born, and Kate understood.

It took longer than they expected for her to fall

pregnant. They had been on the verge of looking into IVF. Just give it another year, they decided, one more year. Neither of them mentioned what had happened when they were students. Neither of them dared say: well, we know it's possible because we got pregnant before. She couldn't ask if he thought they were being punished for what they had done. That was unthinkable. So, she kept saying one more year. And one turned into four. When Maisie finally appeared, there was so much pressure. Those years of waiting. How could she ever live up to such expectations?

When Maisie was a baby, Kate sat on the floor with her, rocking her in the bouncy chair and then later, when Maisie could sit on her own, they built towers together, putting one brick on top of another. It was meant to feel perfect. It was meant to be everything she had waited for, being there with her daughter, teaching her about the world. But Maisie wasn't content, cried every time Kate turned her attention elsewhere. The intensity of it was a joy at first – to feel her daughter's needy pull. But over time, it felt as if she was disappearing from the rest of the world.

'Shut up,' she would shout. 'Just shut up. What do you want from me?'

The day after day of it.

She would run from the room and go to the kitchen, go to any other room, close the door. The screams would pitch higher until she ran back and scooped Maisie up in her arms. She would hold her so tight, afraid that one day she might squeeze her too much, the love and the hate overwhelming. Inseparable.

And then came the dark.

It pulled her down. All she wanted was sleep. To feel nothing. This, she thought. This is what her mum had become.

One day, she strapped Maisie into the pushchair and walked to the shop. It took two hours there and back if she went the long way. It was easy to hide things in the folds of the pushchair's rain hood. She didn't even want the chocolate, the biscuits, the ham, or the tin of soup, but the rush of adrenaline, the feeling of actually being alive. It became an obsession. She had a ritual – walk around the shop a few times, giving the appearance of browsing, picking things up, reading the labels, putting things down. When she was sure nobody could see, she would slip something under the pushchair's hood. Then she would take a pint of milk and a packet of rice cakes to the till. All the other mums bought rice cakes for their babies.

One day, the woman at the till asked if she was going to pay for the other item. She pointed at the small TV screen behind the till, said she wasn't going to report it or anything, but if it happened again, she would have to say something to her manager.

That was the day Kate broke down. That was the day Daniel told her he knew she was struggling. He would do anything to make it right, he said. He suggested she went out, had some time to herself. 'You need to go walking again,' he told her. 'It makes you feel better.' He remembered everything she had ever told him.

Kate looks at her leg. It has stopped bleeding now and she rests her head on her knees. There is a patch of deep orange on the horizon, as if a child has scribbled with a thick crayon.

She met Alec last night.

He was late again and as she waited for him at the bar, it was like being up high and looking down. A swoop in the stomach, a snatch of fear – not about slipping or accidentally falling, but of purposefully stepping over the ledge and jumping.

When he arrived, they found a small table at the back. Alec touched her leg, just above her knee, brushing the hem of her skirt. She was nervous. They talked about the things they had been discussing in their messages: Why do people seek change, even when they crave constancy? Why can't passion last?

'I don't think there's one reason,' she said. 'And not everyone has problems, do they?'

'I'm not sure about that.' He smiled and looked at her with an unbroken intensity. 'People are rarely honest with themselves about how they feel, and even when they are, they don't do anything about it. I bet most husbands and wives are thinking of someone else when they fuck.'

She hated how he presumed she agreed with him yet found herself nodding.

'You're very quiet,' he said. 'You normally have so much to say.'

She can't remember what else they talked about. Just the touch of his fingers on her leg.

After a couple of drinks, he took her to his car. He kept one hand on her the whole time he drove and steered with the other. His rough skin snagged her tights. Then he pulled over. She didn't care where they were.

'I can't get to you.' He ripped a hole in her tights, moved her knickers to one side and pushed his finger into her. So sudden she almost cried out. He kissed her, all the while flicking and pressing with his thumb, reaching further with his fingers. And of course, she felt the wrongness of it, the sense of breaking an invisible bond, but she didn't specifically think of Daniel. Not then. She experienced a kind of fever. A euphoria that drowned out the usual voice in her head. She closed her eyes, disappeared into it until she felt the familiar rush. Then the falling away, the ebb. She opened her eyes and saw her ruined tights, the wet slick on the leather seat.

She became aware of her surroundings – the sound of a lone car going past; the lack of houses; the trees. She noticed that they were parked in a small car park. The air seemed dense and still. There was a Forestry Commission sign further along, down a path, but it was too far away and too dark for Kate to properly read. She was worried then, not knowing where he had taken her.

'Where—' she went to ask, but he felt for her breasts through her top and kissed her hard. His tongue was in her mouth. The taste of him was hot and salt. Then he moved away and looked at her.

'Let's get in the back,' he said, and he opened his door.

The night air was a cold shock. On the back seat he lifted her skirt and pulled down her tights and knickers, slipped them over her feet. She felt stupid and conscious of her awkward body. He pulled down his jeans and underpants and tried to push her head onto his penis. He smelt musty, warm, fleshy. The twist of her body was painful, her legs stretched out, so she couldn't bend. He moved her onto his lap, facing the front. The buckle of his belt stabbed the back of her knee. He fumbled, missing every time, ramming his penis into the wrong place as she squatted over him. Her legs trembled and gave way. But he had made her come already, so she had no choice but to carry on. That was it, wasn't it? She had no choice.

He grabbed her and moved her sideways, squashed her against the back of the driver's seat. She closed her eyes. His fingers went into her bottom, circling and prodding as he kissed the side of her face. 'Not there,' she said, and tried to move away, but he told her to relax. She concentrated on her breathing, hot and humid against the smooth leather. When he finally thrust into her, it was as if he'd punched her throat. He groaned and held onto her hips.

Afterwards, she knelt in the footwell. The smell of shit and something else. Baby wipes. The smell of babies and dimpled, kicking legs. Of Daniel's face as she lay beside their new girl.

Alec offered her the packet of wipes before getting out of the car. He stood by the open door and said nothing as he belted his jeans. A carrier bag had been placed on the floor. She wiped herself quickly and dropped her stained tissues on top of his.

She retches now, a mouthful of lumpy pale sick on the grass, glistening like dew. The rising sun lights up the clouds with fiery pinks, lavender, purple. It is stunning. She wants to fold over until she takes up no space. Stand in the shower, the water so hot it will burn her skin. She thinks of Daniel. Her husband. She loves him. She loves him so much it hurts.

She pushes her hands into her pockets and turns back.

17

The sun breaks from a cloud as Sarah takes in the view through the passenger window. So warm through the glass. One of those deceptive spring days where it could be summer, but as soon as the sun goes in, it feels like winter. She hopes there will be plenty of patio heaters.

'It's along here,' Luke says, steering around a bend.

Sarah holds up the invitation.

'There's the sign. Slow down.'

The trees form an arc over the road. Through the gaps in the branches, Sarah can see Roger and Miranda's house in the distance – a Georgian manor in a film-location setting. Breathtaking views. She remembers how intimidated she had felt the first time Luke brought her here. They had not been married for long, and she was still acclimatising to her new life. Everyone Luke introduced her to seemed so confident, so sure of themselves. It was as if she had become part of an entirely different world.

The car turns down the long driveway. Pleached evergreens sit in a manicured line on either side, like giant square lollipops.

'Oh Zac, Lucy. Look at the garden. Can you see the

house?' she says, turning round. They are both plugged into their music and don't look up.

'It'll be the usual crowd, I expect,' Luke says.

She turns back to face him. 'Yes, I spoke to Miranda yesterday. She was in a flap about the caterers. She's really gone to town with it all.'

'He is fifty.'

'God, I know. You'll be fifty in a few years.'

'Don't remind me,' he says.

'I'll throw you a big party, shall I?'

'Absolutely not. We'll fly somewhere hot so I can look at my gorgeous wife in her bikini.'

He puts his hand on her leg and gives it a squeeze. She checks her reflection in the wing mirror and pulls at the seat belt, smoothing her hand over her stomach. The dress is new, tight-fitting. The girl in the shop persuaded her to buy it, saying nudes were coming back this season. The colour blends seamlessly with her skin. She only bought it because she wants to make sure Luke notices her, not anyone else. But now, she feels slightly ridiculous and imagines how everyone will look at her. She wishes she had put on her safe black dress instead.

In the house, a girl in a catering uniform greets them at the door and hands her and Luke a glass of pale champagne. Zac and Lucy run on ahead. They go into a huge, high-ceilinged room that Sarah imagines was probably the ballroom, where a bouncy castle is slowly being inflated. Rihanna blasts from a big speaker. People are gathered in small groups, not yet freely mingling.

At the other end of the room, young children are gathered around a clown wearing a rainbow wig and brightly coloured clothes. He is making balloon animals and shouts for requests. 'An armadillo,' a clever child shouts; 'a rhinoceros.' The parents laugh. Next to the clown is another man, dressed as a French mime, doing card tricks. Zac and Lucy go over to watch.

In the space between the bouncy castle and the clown, boys skid back and forth on the wooden floor in their socks. A long table is covered with snacks and drinks for the children. Everything has been meticulously organised.

'This is all so very Miranda,' Luke says.

He takes his phone from his blazer pocket. He has been preoccupied with it all morning.

'Take a break from work,' she says. 'Surely Geoff isn't contacting you today?'

She tries to see what is on the screen, but he pockets it quickly and takes her hand, walks her over to the windows. The terrace goes the whole length of the house, with steps down to the lawn. Outside, caterers are unpacking boxes and setting up several trestle tables.

Luke drinks his champagne in one gulp.

'Right, let's find the real party,' he says. He lets go of her hand and looks around.

Sarah sees Roger's brother. She can't remember his name. A bore of a man who drones on about politics. He is talking to a woman.

There is a scuffle of small bodies as one of the skidding boys bangs into a girl with a sequined butterfly on her dress. The girl gets up, crying loudly, clutching her ribbon as one of her plaits slowly unravels.

'I need to get out of here,' Luke says.

He pulls his phone out again and peers at the screen. She leans her head onto his shoulder.

'Was that from Kate?' she says, as he puts the phone back in his pocket.

'Yes.'

'What did she want?'

'Just saying thank you for last weekend.'

'She's already sent me a message.'

'I don't know,' he says, giving a shrug. 'Shall I get us another drink? I'll look for Roger.'

'I'll come with you,' she says.

'You stay. There's Charlotte and Stephen over there.' He presses his hand to the small of her back. She concentrates on her drink, taking rapid sips, doesn't know if she can face making small talk. Luke weaves his way across the room, stopping as he goes. He touches one woman on the shoulder, saying something that makes her tip her head back to laugh; shakes another man's hand. He seems to know everyone. And then he is gone.

Sarah recognises a woman from the gym. She can't remember her name. They often sit together while their children have swimming lessons. The woman comes across and introduces her to the man she is with.

'Martin knows Luke,' the woman says. 'Back in the day, at the bank. Small world, hey? I didn't know Luke was your husband.' She laughs.

The man, who takes a swig from his bottle of beer, proceeds to tell a story about when he worked at the bank, mentions how Luke had such an intuitive knack. 'Never knew anyone else like him,' he says. He goes on to tell a story about how he bumped into Luke only a couple of months ago, and they went to some burlesque bar in Soho.

'Still hasn't changed. I don't know where he finds the energy.'

The woman nods in agreement. 'Oh yes.'

They both talk as if they know Luke so well. It is annoying.

Then Miranda appears, a little out of breath. Sarah cannot help glancing at the low scoop of her neckline, the outline of her breasts, the momentary thought that she will never look that good and perhaps that is why Luke likes to look at other women.

'There you are, darling.' Miranda gives Sarah a quick hug. 'Mwah,' she says in Sarah's ear. 'How long have you been here?'

'Not long. Luke went off to find Roger.'

'He's in the games room. They're pissed already, so God knows what they'll be like later. I've left them to it.' Miranda laughs.

Sarah takes a gulp of champagne. The bubbles scorch the back of her nose.

'Come with me, darling,' Miranda says, linking her arm through Sarah's. 'All this is for the younger children. Bring Zac and Lucy to the barn. I'll show you.' She turns to speak to the other woman saying, 'Oh yours too, tell them to come. There's going to be a disco.'

Zac and Lucy are delighted to be with the older children in the barn, a modern space converted from one of the original farm buildings. There is a large open-plan room, where the disco is already under way. Miranda's nanny is pouring purple-coloured drinks into plastic cups and lining them up. 'Not on the dance floor,' she shouts over the music. 'And leave your cups on the table.'

141

Sarah lingers, trying to get Lucy's attention.

'They'll be fine in here,' Miranda says. 'Hannah's got strict instructions and there's Ellie's nanny and two others as well.'

'Bye,' Sarah calls as she leaves, but nobody can hear her.

In the garden, the caterers are setting up the barbeque and spit roast on the terrace. Miranda stops to speak to them, giving them instructions about where she wants the buffet tables and reminds them to turn the patio heaters on when the sun starts to go down. By the time they are back inside, Sarah's arms are pink from the cold. She tugs at her dress.

More people have arrived. As they walk across the hall, Sarah notices the bouncy castle room is now packed. Miranda leads her on, down the corridor, and they go into another large room, where floor-to-ceiling bookcases run across one wall. It is less busy in here and equipment is being set up for the band. A portable mezzanine stage has been put at one end, and a man in a black leather jacket and ripped jeans sits behind a drum kit, screwing a cymbal onto a stand.

'We thought the acoustics would be perfect in here,' Miranda says, waving at the drummer. He winks at her and takes off his leather jacket. He has black geometric tattoos up both arms. Miranda turns to Sarah, smiling. 'You look fabulous, by the way. Gorgeous dress.'

They go across to the other side of the room, where Mimi and Ellie are sat at a table with a woman Sarah hasn't met before. Mimi stands to give Sarah a hug. She is wearing a floral strappy dress and Ellie, who has recently had her hair cut short, is wearing black. Not a nude among them. They all sit down. Mimi pours them a glass of wine.

'He's offered me a ten per cent share of the business,' says the woman Sarah doesn't know. She talks in a loud voice, but everyone leans in to listen.

'Or a cash settlement plus the house in the Cotswolds. Obviously, the shares are worth more, but I can only get annual dividends. He has a very clever solicitor, so I know either way, even if it sounds like a good deal, I'm definitely being screwed. The only time he's ever put any effort into that.'

Everyone laughs.

'This is Georgie,' Miranda says, 'I don't know if you two have met yet, have you? This is Sarah.'

Georgie smiles. She has dazzling teeth.

'Oh, you're Luke's wife,' Georgie says and reaches over to offer a hand. 'Nice to meet you. How is he? Must be quite beaten up about it, I'm sure.' She makes a face of commiseration.

'I nearly called you,' Mimi said.

'Yes,' says Ellie, briefly touching her arm. 'Is he okay? Must be—'

Sarah hasn't a clue what they are talking about. Georgie interrupts and talks across everyone. 'But what would you *do*, stuck out there, rattling around? Such an upkeep these old properties.' She waves her hand at the room.

Sarah looks to Miranda for help.

'Hasn't Luke said anything?' Miranda whispers. 'His aunt left the house to the National Trust.'

A loud crash from the stage. Before Sarah can gather her thoughts or feel upset about Luke not telling her his news, Georgie is steamrolling on. 'I think the last time I saw Luke was at Glynde,' she says loudly, 'Rufus was there too. I haven't seen him for such an age.' Then she recounts a story about the time Luke dared Rufus to climb up a tree in her garden, and he got so far up that her parents thought they'd have to call the fire brigade. 'Luke was always daring people to do foolish stunts, just like his brother.' She laughs as she says this. Sarah decides Georgie is the most unpleasant person she has ever met.

Sarah finishes her wine and pours herself another. She should be used to it by now. All the anecdotes she has overheard, the names of people she doesn't know. Luke doing this, Luke doing that. She asked him once, why he never told her about his childhood. He shrugged it off, kissed her forehead, said the past was in the past.

Georgie has now moved on to talking about her new flat, and when she will be able to move in. She's going to book the interior designer well in advance because there's such a long waiting list. And while the flat's being gutted, she's going to go down to the cottage in Sussex – at least that's nothing to do with her ex. And he can't touch the trust fund they set up either. She was canny enough to make that iron-clad.

Sarah smiles. These conversations. Sometimes, she steps outside of herself and wonders what her old school friends would say. What would they think if they knew about the sort of people she mingled with? The Georgies with their trust funds, the Mimis with their raft of nannies and endless home help. Her old friend Rachel lives in Sheffield now. They don't see each other any more, but they are Facebook friends. Rachel is a midwife at the Royal Hallamshire hospital. Her Facebook page has political posts about the underfunding of the NHS, about the despicable bankers who were bailed out. When Sarah reads these things, she feels guilty-sick for her privileges. But then she sees photos of Rachel with her husband and children. The ones of them pulling silly faces at family gatherings; standing on the beach, arms outstretched like they are having the time of their lives; Rachel's husband lying on the sofa with the kids piling on top of him; a home-made birthday card with comments underneath about how she's won the lottery, how Phil's such a softie. Sarah feels less guilty then.

She looks across at the stage, where the tattooed man is now moving equipment around and plugging things into a large, square amp. He puts a mic on a stand and taps it. *One two, one two, one two.* He looks at her, an unbroken stare.

'My God,' Miranda whispers, nudging her side.

Ellie says, 'I wouldn't have to fake anything if Simon looked like that.'

A ripple of laughter goes around the table.

Sarah looks down at her lap, wonders why Luke hasn't tried to find her. He said he was going to get them another drink.

'Yes, I know,' Miranda says, in response to something Georgie is talking about. 'What do you think, Sarah?'

And she is pulled back to the table.

By the time she realises she's drunk, the room is heaving, and the band are mid-song. The bass thumps in her chest. Miranda and the others are gone, and she doesn't recognise anybody. It is loud and stuffy. People and faces and arms. Hands clapping. She makes her way through. Someone says sorry as they stagger into her. She has to get out, has to find Luke.

Across the hall and into the other room, the clowns, the bouncy castle, the children have all gone. The long buffet table, previously filled with jam sandwiches and cheese puffs, now has bowls of salads and crudités, a large, cooked salmon with a sunken eye. People queue along the table, helping themselves.

The French doors are open, and the terrace is bathed with the orange glow of patio heaters. The caterers are busy with the barbeque, handing out burgers. A pig is being roasted on a spit. It turns slowly, its skin crackling. Further on from the terrace, more people are gathered around a fire pit with dancing yellow flames. Faces are lit up against the darkness. Sarah stands there for a while, looking out, but she cannot see Luke. Someone taps her on the back, and she turns to see Ellie.

'I lost everyone,' she says. 'Have you seen Luke?'

Ellie is flushed and has wine-stained lips. She shrugs. 'Sorry, no. I've been checking on the kids. Are you coming back in?' She points towards the hall.

Sarah is panicked then, for leaving Zac and Lucy for so long.

'I'll see you in a minute,' she says, and makes a dash across the terrace, past the turning pig, retracing her earlier steps to the barn.

She finds Lucy on a sofa having her nails painted by Miranda's daughter. The disco has finished, and blow-up mattresses cover the floor with girls lying on them in sleeping bags. They are watching a film on a huge TV screen. Tubes of Pringles and bags of sweets are strewn around.

'Just checking you're okay,' Sarah says, tucking in the label that is sticking out of the back of Lucy's top. She is conscious of her words and how they might sound a little slurred. 'Did Daddy bring your things over?'

'Our bags are there,' Lucy says, gesturing with her chin.

Sarah can see the floral rucksack and Zac's bag with the Darth Vader keyring.

'Is your brother okay?'

'They're upstairs,' she says.

'Are you all right?' Sarah asks, but Lucy doesn't look up.

Sarah makes her way to the staircase, concentrates on walking.

Zac is in one of the bedrooms, playing on an Xbox with a boy she doesn't recognise, with other boys crowded round.

'Reload, reload!' one of them shouts.

'I swear to God,' Zac says, his eyes not moving from the screen. 'Stop fucking telling me what to do.'

Sarah resists the urge to go in and snatch the controls away, ask him what he thinks he's doing, gaming for hours, swearing. She stays by the door.

'I think it's probably time to come off that now,' she says. Nobody looks up. 'Zac?' she says, louder. 'Everyone's going to bed soon.'

An older boy gets up and comes over. His eyes dart between her and Zac as if he is checking something. He could almost be university age and is much too old to be here with them. Then she realises he must be Harry, Roger's nephew. He goes to a special school.

'Caitlin said we have twenty more minutes,' he says. He blinks and swallows and stares at her.

'Where's the other nanny? Will she be sleeping up here?'

'Yes,' he says. 'But she's over there.' He points across the landing to the room on the other side.

'Thanks for letting me know,' she says.

Harry remains, still staring. 'You're Zac's mum and Lucy's mum.' He speaks precisely.

147

'Yes, I am.'

'Zac said you aren't a very happy person.'

'Oh, did he? I'm sure he must've just meant . . .' She looks across at Zac. On the screen she sees a soldier slaying a monster with a flaming sword. She has that awful sense of not being properly present, as if she is watching from afar. The room moves in and out.

Harry follows her eyes, looks at the boys and the screen and then looks down at his watch. 'Eighteen and a half minutes left now.' He shakes his head and frowns, then turns away from her and sits back down with the other boys.

Sarah leaves and goes to the top of the stairs. She might be sick. Or cry. Yes, she feels like she might cry. She waits for the sensation to pass and then grips the bannister, takes the stairs one at a time.

Downstairs, Lucy is now on the mattress-covered floor with the others, in her sleeping bag. The film is still on, but a few of the younger girls have fallen asleep. Sarah kneels down and says goodnight.

'Look out for your brother, won't you?'

Lucy smiles but Sarah can tell she wants her to go.

She hates leaving them. Luke tells her she fusses too much but she knows she isn't there for them nearly enough. She walks away quickly and doesn't look back.

Inside, the band have packed up and gone. It is dark in the room now, with flashing disco lights. A small group are dancing, others are sat around the edges, talking and drinking. A man wearing headphones stands behind a table with a record deck, nodding his head to the beat. Sarah looks for Ellie, or any of the others, but can't see them. The whole night searching, that's how it feels. It seems like everyone else is at a different party to her.

'Have you seen Miranda?' she says to a woman who is dancing barefoot.

The woman shakes her head and continues to dance, slowly, like she's in a trance. Sarah goes back out into the hall, decides to go upstairs. Perhaps she will find where Luke has put their bags and she can lie down for a while. She is cold.

At the top of the stairs, there is a landing space with two corridors going off in opposite directions. The door immediately to the left is ajar and she pushes it open. The muted light from a lamp in the corner illuminates enough for Sarah to see two bodies entwined on the bed. The flash of a woman's leg and a man's grabbing hand. She cannot see who it is.

'Just pull them off, Stephen. Pull them off,' the woman says.

Sarah continues down the corridor. So many rooms. She cannot open any more doors, cannot look inside.

And then, she hears Luke's voice – travelling up from a narrow staircase at the end of the corridor. She waits at the top of the stairs, where the light filters up at a diagonal. She remains in the shadows yet can still see all the way down to the bottom. Luke is talking to a woman with dark hair caught up in a messy knot. He reaches to touch her neckline with his fingers. A gentle, intimate gesture. It makes Sarah's insides drag. The woman laughs, tilting her head to the side. Luke holds out a packet of cigarettes and lights one for her with a Zippo lighter. Sarah didn't even know he had one of those.

'Luke,' Sarah says, moving out of the shadows and going down the stairs. She is still drunk and unsteady. The hysterical kind of drunkenness, not the giggly sort, and irrational, like anything might come flying out of her mouth.

He looks up. The woman turns around and Sarah sees she is young, can't be much older than twenty.

'This is Milly,' Luke says. 'Miranda's niece. She was saying she's going to apply to the bank.'

'That's nice.' Sarah stops on the penultimate step, making sure she is a good head and shoulders taller than the girl.

'There's a graduate programme,' Milly says. She flashes her eyes at Luke, smoke coiling from her cigarette.

'If you need any more contacts, just let me know.' Luke sucks on his cigarette, exhaling at the ceiling, where his smoke mingles with Milly's.

'I'm sure she has plenty already.' Sarah wants to slap that look off her face.

'Anyway,' Milly says quickly. 'I'd better find my friends. Get rid of this.' She gestures to the cigarette.

'Yes, you better had,' Sarah says.

Milly turns to Luke. 'Anyway, nice to meet you. Thanks for the advice.'

Sarah notices the way Luke smiles, the way he tips his head and holds Milly's gaze. She watches how he folds his arms in smug satisfaction as Milly gives a little wave and goes off down the corridor. Her shoes clip-clopping across the wooden floor. Her long thin legs with those very silly high heels.

Luke turns back, smoke clouding his face.

'What the hell do you think you're doing?' Sarah says.

'Talking about the bank.'

'You know exactly what I mean.'

He moves closer and strokes her cheek.

'Don't,' she says, going up a step. 'And you shouldn't smoke in here. All the smokers are outside.'

He squashes the half-smoked cigarette between his fingers, puts it in his pocket.

'That's disgusting. You'll have to wash your hands,' she says.

'Why, is my luck in?'

He stands on the step below her. She hates him so much right now, but as he puts his arms around her waist, she lets him. He lifts the hem of her dress a little, touches her leg.

'Let's go to our room,' he says.

He leads her up the stairs, takes her along a different corridor to the one she came down. It bends around on itself until it opens out onto another wide landing. He knows exactly where he is going. She feels a crushing sense of sadness.

Luke pushes on a door, and it opens into a small room with a queen-sized bed.

'I thought we'd be cosy in here,' he says.

She fumbles for a switch on the bedside lamp. Luke falls onto the bed, his arms outstretched. There are dark red velvet curtains at the window, and she draws them closed.

'Come here,' he says.

She sits on the edge of the bed and slips off her shoes. She notices an oily stain on her dress and wonders how long it has been there, scratches at it with her nail. Luke grabs her arm, pulls her down towards him.

'No,' she says, pushing herself up. 'I don't want to lie down. And you stink.'

'Come on,' he says. 'Take your dress off. I never see you these days.'

'What are you talking about?' She looks at him, his puffy eyelids, his pupils wide and black. 'You're drunk.'

'So are you,' he says, grabbing her dress. 'Take this off.'

She pushes his hand away. 'What were you doing with that girl?'

He sits up, leans against the padded headboard, fumbling in his pocket. He takes out a small silver vial, unscrews the lid and hunches over, sniffing into his hand.

She watches him screw the lid back on.

'I don't know you,' she says.

'You don't know me?' He laughs, a nasty sound. 'Fucking empty,' he says, throwing the vial across the room.

'Has that started up again? You promised you wouldn't do that any more.'

'For fuck's sake, calm down. Of course it hasn't. Just a treat. It's a party, Sarah. Chill out.'

'You said you wanted to make everything right. After last time, you said—' She can feel the tears, the weight on her chest.

'I don't need this shit,' he says.

He pushes past her to get off the bed. She can smell his sour sweat.

'And you wonder why I work so late.' He bends over her, pokes his forefinger into her chest. 'My frigid wife.'

'Get off me.' She remembers Pete used to call her that. How dare he say that to her.

She stands and pushes him as hard as she can. He staggers back into a chest of drawers. A china vase with painted yellow and blue flowers wobbles. They stand watching it, even after it is still.

'And tell me, why does everyone know about your aunt?' she says.

'What are you talking about now? Who?'

'Everyone seemed to know. About your parents' house. Why does everyone else know things I don't?'

He sighs and pinches the end of his nose, gives a hard sniff, like a child who refuses to use a tissue.

'Well?'

'It's old news.'

'Is it? I'm sick and tired of this, of how you treat me.'

'You're overreacting.'

'Am I?'

He looks away and fumbles in his pocket again, says 'fuck' under his breath. His skin is greasy, and his face looks bloated.

'It's been a horrible night,' she says, covering her face.

'You need to lie down. Don't worry, I won't do anything.' He holds his hands up. 'I wouldn't want to anyway. It's like fucking a statue.'

A loud slap across his cheek. She feels the sting in her palm.

'Get out,' she says. 'Just fucking well get out.'

He raises one hand high in the air, although she is too angry to flinch.

'Go on,' she says. 'Hit me. What would your precious brother think if he could see you now? And your parents? You're a waste of space. No wonder they didn't love you.'

He clenches his hand into a fist and punches the wall. The wallpaper splits across the dent. And then he is gone. She can hear him banging down the corridor like a pinball.

18

Two weeks have passed, and Kate is having a Friday night out with some of the mums from Flo's new school. A social gathering for Naomi's birthday. The pub is busy, a continuous hum of voices. Kate is sitting at the end of the banquette next to a woman she recognises but hasn't spoken to at length before. Oona, she thinks the woman is called, or maybe Tina.

'Florence settled in okay?' the woman asks.

Kate nods. 'I was worried about her joining mid-term and leaving her friends, but she's really happy.'

'That's good. They adapt so much quicker than we do. Where did you move her from?'

'Oh, just a school the other side of Guildford.'

The woman waits for more information, but Kate smiles in a way that ends the conversation. She doesn't like talking about Flo's previous school, the private one. It used to be something she wanted more than anything, a better education for her children. What she and Daniel had both wanted. That's why he had applied for the job at the bank all those years ago, to give them a better life. Only it was never meant to cause him so much stress.

She overheard him on the phone to Luke the other day, saying something about changing ideals, being forced into things for the money. Something about the cost of sending the girls to private school.

Why hadn't he ever told her? Was he insinuating it was her fault?

The woman is talking, something about the local schools.

'It was easier when there was less choice. You never know now if you've made the right decision, do you?'

'No,' Kate says. 'You don't.'

Her phone is pinging in her bag. She ignores it, puts her bag on the floor at the side of her feet.

'The new Head has done wonders,' the woman is now saying. 'You're lucky you haven't had to put up with the drama of the last few years. The problems they've had . . .'

Kate smiles and nods, drinks her wine, tries to ignore her phone.

Luke is still sending her texts. A casual Hey how are you? And then they tell each other about their days. He told her yesterday he liked messaging her, that he never has to explain himself to her. You get me, he wrote. It isn't too strange, she decided. They are, after all, old friends. She has forced herself not to dwell on the other weekend. It makes things feel too complicated and she wants to keep the recollection hazy.

Another message from yesterday: I read this and thought of you. He attached a quote by Nietzsche: 'Ultimately, it is the desire not the desired that we love'.

She guessed he was drunk and didn't reply. This morning, he sent a follow-up message explaining he had sent it to generate ideas for her book. She replied then, thanking him, told him it was really thoughtful.

What do you think about the quote? he asked.

Not sure. Do you think desire is more about generating a feeling than the actuality of a person?

I think it's both, he wrote.

She didn't reply. Before she left the house tonight, he messaged again.

How's the book coming along?

Great. It's really coming together

She hasn't actually done any more work on her book. Not since the incident with Alec. She cannot face it.

There is a chorus of laughs. Kate doesn't catch what they are talking about, but laughs along, pretending she can hear. They are sitting at such a long table. Although she doesn't mind. At least they don't know her well enough to notice that the smile she is putting on isn't real. If any of them knew her better, they might reach out and whisper *Are you okay?* with a sympathetic voice. If someone did that, it would all come pouring out.

Naomi is at the far end of the table. Kate can only hear a few broken sentences: 'Trust him to say . . . would you believe . . . going there next half-term . . .'

She talks to Naomi whenever she does the morning school run. They stand together in the playground, waving their daughters off, and then they carry on talking as they walk back to where they've parked their cars.

'It's like I'm the one starting a new school,' she said to Naomi that first morning. 'I think I'm more nervous than she is.'

They sought each other out after that. She likes Naomi. A happy kind of person, someone who always finds a break

156

in the clouds on a rainy day. So, when Naomi invited her to come along tonight, Kate said yes. They haven't shared any kind of real honesty yet, but she likes how they laugh at the same things, and she can tell by the way Naomi's face is relaxed when they talk, the way her eyes crease up when she smiles, that Naomi isn't being fake.

Earlier, when she was getting ready, Kate had looked at herself in the mirror. She thought about her friends and the messages from Luke and how she couldn't be truly honest with any of them. Daniel is the only person she has ever properly talked to. Other people have best friends, they have mothers, fathers, siblings. Some people even open up to their hairdresser. But she's condensed all of herself into one person. It used to give her a feeling of security, knowing Daniel was the only person who really knew who she was, but now she isn't even sure if that is true. She feels stranded. How can she explain anything to Daniel when what she most wants to talk about is the fact that she can't talk to him any more?

The hours go by. Kate has more wine. She laughs along to more stories, joins in with their jokes about how hot the new PE teacher is.

Then everyone is standing, and Naomi is thanking them for coming, asking if anyone needs a lift home.

'I'll give Daniel a call,' Kate says, steadying herself on the table as she stands.

'Why don't you come with me?' Naomi says. 'If you're okay to wait a bit. I booked a taxi, but it won't be here yet. We can have another drink.'

Kate nods.

'I've hardly talked to you all night,' Naomi says, linking her arm through Kate's, guiding her to a table.

Kate is glad of the attention, but it also makes her insides feel sickened and weak. She has an urge to tell Naomi how bad things have become at home. If they had a spare room, Daniel would have moved into it by now, for sure. When they are lying in bed, she can sense that he can't bear to be next to her. Perhaps if she tells Naomi this, confesses what she has done, Naomi will say it is perfectly understandable. She can find some peace then, because right now she's afraid she will do another terrible thing, because that's what happens, isn't it? One thing to leads to another. *Help me*, Kate wants to cry. She wants someone to hold her and say: *You're not a terrible person. I understand*.

Naomi goes to the bar and when she comes back with their drinks, she shuffles onto the banquette next to Kate.

'Cheers,' Naomi says.

'Happy birthday!'

'I can't believe I've got twenty quid left,' Naomi says. 'Neil gave me sixty and he won't believe it. Not quite the mad celebration I thought it'd be.' She laughs.

Kate can feel herself slipping, the smile not so easy to find. Naomi seems oblivious to the way she's struggling to fight the tears.

'I was shocked when he gave me the cash, to be honest,' Naomi continues, taking a sip of her rum and Coke. The ice cubes sing in her glass. 'He's been going on about us having to be careful until his next big job comes in. And he got me so many presents. He's taking me out tomorrow night, even organised a babysitter. I think he felt guilty because he forgot our anniversary last month . . .'

Kate can't hold it in any longer. Her eyes are stinging.

'I've just got to—' she says. The room becomes a blur

through the tears. She gets up and hurries towards the toilets.

What happens next is unclear, a bang of bodies, an icy splash down her front, her hand reaching for a table, then crashing onto the floor. A face with long black eyelashes, shimmery eyeshadow. 'Are you all right?' the face says. 'I'm so sorry. Let me help you.'

And Kate finds she can't get up because she is holding onto the leg of a chair, crying.

Naomi is there and she is talking to the girl with the long eyelashes and then the girl walks away. Kate is helped off the floor and sat on a chair. Paper towels are being pressed to her chest.

'I'm sorry.' She is helpless to do anything, allows Naomi to blot the wet patch on her top. 'Sorry,' is all she can say.

'It wasn't your fault,' Naomi says. 'She wasn't looking where she was going. Are you okay? Nothing hurt?'

The sympathy is too much, the concern, the recognition. Kate can't stop the tears.

'Come on, you need some air.' Naomi helps her off the chair. 'You're shaking.'

People stare as they walk past tables to the door that leads into the beer garden. The night is cool but not too cold. Naomi ushers her to a wooden bench and sits next to her, legs straddled like she's riding a horse.

'I got your bag,' she says, putting it on the table. 'Are you okay?'

Kate tries to smile, tries to say *Yes, I'm fine*, but instead what comes out is: 'I don't know. I don't know what's happening to me.'

Naomi puts an arm around her briefly, an awkward half-hug.

'Shall I get you some water?' she says. 'Did you bang your head? Do you want me to call Daniel?'

So many questions. And the tears keep coming, like a stopper's been pulled out.

Naomi says she didn't think Kate was looking herself all night. 'I didn't get the chance to come over and I thought you'd be fine with Tina. Tina's lovely.'

Kate nods through her tears.

'What's wrong?' Naomi says, giving her arm a squeeze.

It seems to Kate that she is really saying: *Tell me everything*, so Kate doesn't pause for breath, tells Naomi how Daniel doesn't see who she is any more; how she's writing a book and started chatting to men on a website to do some research; even though she didn't want to, she met Alec, and when she met him, she had this weird feeling inside that was like being sick but also being alive; she isn't sure what happened with Luke but something definitely happened and now he's sending her messages and it's like she's two people – the person she used to think she was and this new person and when Daniel looks at her now, it's as if he's expecting to see the person she used to be and he can't connect with this new person at all. But isn't she still the same person? What if this is who she's always been, and the reason Daniel can't see her is because he never really saw her in the first place? And if that's true, how can we ever know anyone and isn't love just a series of expectations and if she isn't what Daniel expects does that mean he's stopped loving her?

Naomi listens. Doesn't say a word.

And then they are in a car, hurtling down the dual carriageway. Naomi is resting her head back, looking out of the window. The night feels as if it has passed quickly and yet it is also never-ending. Kate cannot place the events in any order – falling onto the floor, the shock of the ice, drinking wine as the others laughed, Naomi's face as her words gushed out. Kate holds onto her bag and stares at the flashing lights of the oncoming cars.

19

It is almost midday, and the park is busy. Luke usually comes earlier on Saturdays, but it turned messy last night. He slows to a walk and checks his watch. Forty minutes is a terrible time, nowhere near his personal best. He hasn't been bothering with these weekend runs recently and needs to get back into his usual routine.

He coughs as he walks onto the grass, hawking up some phlegm and spitting it out, before continuing towards a large horse chestnut. He leans against the trunk and stretches out his quads, one side and then the other. The bark is hard and dry against his palm. A pack of runners go by, disappearing into the distance. They are fast. He once considered joining an organised group, years ago, but those days of serious running are long gone. Anyway, he prefers to choose his own routes, come out whenever he feels like it.

He slips off his rucksack and rests it on the damp grass. His bottle has an inch of water left and he drinks it in one gulp. Across the lake, a couple of Canada geese launch themselves into the water. One pecks at the other before swimming away.

The feeling is intense today. A physical pain, almost like a burn. And even though he knows the rush will be fleeting, he has to have it. In fact, he will die without it. There is a voice telling him this time is going to be different. *This time you can stay in that place for ever and be invincible.*

Recently, things have been getting completely out of control. Last weekend at Roger's party was particularly bad. He vaguely remembers Miranda's niece and then some other woman he knew from years ago. Anyway, that was Sarah's fault for being so spiteful. He was genuinely trying, and she threw him off course. The other week, he could have really crossed a line with Kate, couldn't he? Doesn't that show he can do it, that he's making a change? He scuffs his foot over an exposed tree root, kicks at it with his trainer. Who's he kidding? He knows he's only biding his time, finding out how much he can make her want him, despite herself. It's part of the thrill. He wants to fuck her, knowing that she can't make herself stop. That's the real reason he did it – wanking over her stomach, all the while knowing Daniel was there, down in the basement, in the guest room, that he might wake any minute and find them. The look on her face as she lay there and let him do it.

He is disgusting. Vile. Unforgivable.

In the summer holidays, when he was about fourteen or fifteen, he used to take girls he knew back to the barn. They'd listen to music on the radio, drink a few swigs of whisky, smoke a couple of cigarettes. He never did much with them – kissing, a bit of fingering, blow jobs – because the excitement was in being there with them, having them want him. His brother could have walked in at any time.

Seb discovered him only once. It was the summer his

163

brother had come back from his first year at Oxford. Luke was just sixteen. The girl had long dark hair. He held it off her face as she went down on him. She knelt on the hay-strewn floor, and he knew he couldn't stop, not even when she started gagging. That gave him such a thrill, knowing she was doing it to make him happy. Or maybe it was because he knew Seb would find them. He had wanted to see the look on his brother's face.

Seb hadn't said anything, just stood in the doorway, watching. The girl didn't know he was there, continued until Luke came in her mouth. Afterwards, when the girl had gone home, Luke walked back to the house. Seb was lying on a lounger on the terrace, and he glanced up from his drink, looking at Luke over the top of his sunglasses. Neither of them moved until Seb broke their gaze. Later that night, Seb came into his room. Luke understood then what it was to hate and love, to want and not want. Nobody could make him feel like Seb.

The Canada geese squawk and time resumes. Luke swings his rucksack over his shoulder, and he walks towards the path. The feeling today is so intense. Raging. He can't even stand the breeze against his face – the air makes him real, tells him he is present, that his body is solid. He just wants to disappear.

He continues to walk, consciously trying to avoid the usual triggers – the café and the benches where runners pause to take a breath. It's all too easy to strike up a conversation.

A lone jogger approaches, her ponytail swishing like a pendulum. She holds eye contact, smiles at him. But he keeps walking. It has to stop, he tells himself. He wants it to stop. But the more he focuses on stopping, the worse it gets. Take last night – he told himself he would go home. He didn't need anything else, just his wife, his children. And when he went for a drink with the team after work, he purposefully sat with a sobering pint of Guinness. Sipped it slowly. He even walked away from a woman who came onto him, went to the gents, congratulated himself on having such resolve. See, there wasn't a problem, was there? Everything was under control. He'd go home soon, home to his beautiful wife. He checked himself in the mirror, splashed water on his face, straightened his tie.

Then Stu came in. 'All right,' he said. 'Fancy some good stuff? Best I've had for a while, man. Pure as fuck. Blow your head off good.'

Everything conspires to make him carry on.

So he did a few lines. Took the woman who came onto him outside, fucked her against the wall at the back of the club. He went and got himself a few whisky chasers, did a few more lines. Before he realised, he wasn't going home. He was outside Eloise's door.

Luke stands at the edge of the lake. A gaggle of geese swim towards a child, who throws some bread into the water. The birds fight and peck their way to the front.

'More bread,' the child shouts, turning to his mother. 'More bread, more bread.'

Luke has an image then, of sitting on the floor of the barn, hidden behind the bales of hay. The sweet, sour smell. He must have been eleven or twelve. Seb was home on a weekend exeat from school. That was the year Seb really changed, when he was sent away to school. It seemed to extinguish his kindness.

Seb is grinning, making him take long swigs from a bottle of whisky.

'Have more,' Seb is saying. 'More.'

'I don't want to. Please.' Luke puts the bottle down, his throat burning, pleads with his brother *no more*. He only wants to play the games they used to play, ride their bikes, take turns on the river swing. But Seb is different.

'You don't get to say when you stop.' Seb picks the bottle up and forces it into Luke's hand, pushes it to his mouth.

The more Luke asks him to stop, the more his brother makes him drink. Standing over him with an unfamiliar threatening look in his eyes. Until Luke is sick in the corner.

When it was over, and they were walking back to the house, Seb told him it was a lesson. 'People use your weaknesses, you know,' he said. 'Turn them back on you.'

Seb pulled him into a hug and kept him close for the rest of the day, was especially attentive, as if the extra love balanced everything out. That night, he came into Luke's room, as he always did, got into his bed, curled around him. They lay like that for a while, like sleeping animals, until Seb kissed his back, his neck, felt all over his body with his hands. He said Luke needed to stay still. And Luke kept still.

Luke is almost out of the park now and walks quickly, avoiding the tourists taking photos of the Albert Memorial. The golden prince glinting in the sunlight. What adoration, what glorification. How could any man be loved like that? It is nauseating. He makes his way onto Exhibition Road and flags down a taxi.

At home, after a shower, he goes down to his study. The house is empty and quiet. Sarah and the children are out shopping and won't be back for a while. His phone buzzes. A reply from Kate: **Perhaps desire is only about the things that are forbidden**

That makes him feel angry. Why is she saying that? Stupid woman, he thinks. She knows nothing. He puts his phone away in his drawer. Logs on to his computer.

Online, he finds his usual site. Michelle isn't available. There's a tempting redhead, but she looks too young. He doesn't like them too young. The older ones give him more of a challenge.

Anika sits on her bed. The room could be anywhere in the world, but he likes to imagine she is nearby. She is wearing a white shirt and a black skirt that clings to her thighs. She isn't wearing any stockings. Just bare legs. Olive skin.

She types: **Hello**

There aren't many others logged on and she's ignoring the guests, only bothering with the members. She leans forward to type again.

Are you shy? We can take things private if you prefer

She looks across to the right, off camera, twirls a strand of hair around her finger, puts it in her mouth before looking right at him again. She loosens one button, so her cleavage is more visible.

He types: **Don't do that. Stop**

She stares at him, unsure, suggests they go to private mode, but he ignores her. He finds it irresistible how agitated she is becoming.

He types: **I just want to watch you for a minute**

She moves towards the screen, her eyes looking down while she types.

I'd like to get to know you better. Would you like to get to know me?

He clicks off and goes back to the home page, looks through the long list of other girls, knowing all the while how furious she will be that she has lost out. After ten minutes, he goes back.

He types: You'd need to do everything I ask

She thinks.

Let's get to know one another privately

He types: First I need you to agree to do anything I ask

She pauses, then nods.

OK

He pays with his card – one hundred and twenty pounds for thirty minutes. She clicks the screen to private mode. He accepts the use of the microphone but turns off his camera.

Afterwards, everything slows. It always does. He remains in the chair until the last of it fades and then goes across to the guest room. It is an impersonal space, like being in a hotel and he pulls back the bedcover, climbs under the duvet, balls himself up. The sinking feeling drags him down and he allows himself to fall. Perhaps he sleeps, but it isn't for long, as the house is still silent when he opens his eyes. He gets out of bed and shakes the duvet back into place, smooths the bedcover.

It is as if he had never been there.

20

Sarah's dad has had a fall. She got the call just before nine o'clock. Sunday morning, the phone ringing – it could only be bad news. Her mum was distraught, a jumble of information, stating facts that were difficult to decipher, with confusing details about Celia who lives over the road and Errol who lives around the corner. It was Errol who found him – that much Sarah managed to understand.

Sarah sits on the sofa in the living room of her parents' bungalow. Her dad is in the armchair, propped up with cushions and a blanket over his knees. He refuses to rest in bed.

'I'm fine,' he keeps saying. 'I'm fine.'

'It was lucky Errol was in,' her mum says from the other armchair. 'Otherwise, he'd have been lying there for hours, bleeding to death.' Her mum doesn't look at her dad, directs her comments at the carpet. In a voice with sharp edges, she explains to Sarah what happened.

At eight o'clock that morning, he had decided to go and get the papers. Normally they are delivered, but he just upped and left, without saying a word – he's never done anything like that before. And, of course, he didn't bother to take his stick. Outside Errol's house, he'd tripped on a raised section of paving stone and fell. He must have put his hands out, to try and break his fall, because his palms were badly grazed. Thankfully, Errol was in his kitchen, looking out for his son, who was coming over for the day. He'd thought the noise was kids from the neighbouring road – they often mess around as they cut through the cul-de-sac to the park – but he spotted the body, face down at the end of the drive. Errol rang Celia, the only number he had, who dashed across to raise the alarm.

Her mum finishes the tale and crosses her arms.

'But they said no broken bones, right?' Sarah says this to her dad. She just wants him to look at her, so she knows he's all right.

'I'm fine,' he snaps. He touches his head lightly, where the steri-strip runs parallel to his eyebrow. 'Ju-just gra-gr-grazes.' He still doesn't look at her, doesn't even seem pleased that she is there. She's never seen him like this before.

'A bit more than a graze,' her mum says, scowling. 'They said he'll have to see the doctor again next week. Have some more tests to check it wasn't a stroke.'

There is a stilted pause. Her dad looks down at the folded newspaper in his lap, at the crossword. Sarah isn't sure he is actually doing it. She can't help feeling angry with him too, the way he's ignoring her, after she dropped everything to be here.

Earlier this morning, after her mum's call, she made sure the children were dressed and gave Luke instructions for the day. Take them to one of the museums, she suggested, have lunch at the pizza place they like. As she drove along the motorway, trying to keep her speed under ninety,

170

she told herself it would be good for them to spend some proper time with Luke. And it would be good for him as well. She can't remember the last time she left him solely in charge. Usually, she is able to organise for Magda to come over, but she didn't like to call her so early on a Sunday morning. But now the thought of Luke being with the children is making her uneasy. She often has to smooth any misunderstandings over Zac's behaviour. Luke can be harsh with him sometimes. And he won't know how to talk to Lucy, to make sure she doesn't retreat entirely. Luke has never had to manage any of these things.

Her mum rustles a piece of paper, checking through the leaflets they were given at the hospital. Her dad continues to gaze at the crossword. Sarah feels useless, sitting there doing nothing. All she can think about is sending a message to Luke.

'I'll make us all a cup of tea,' she says, and gets up before either of her parents can reply.

In the kitchen, she composes a text, telling Luke that her dad seems stable, and she'll probably leave in a couple of hours. Is everything OK? She pauses before pressing send, wonders if it would be better to call. Then she imagines the irritation in his voice as she tries not to sound like she's checking up on him. He will know she is nervous about him being in charge of the children. But really, she is still worried about their argument at the party last weekend. Has it caused some kind of permanent damage? He went out again Friday night, stayed late when he said he wasn't going to, came in stinking of cigarettes. Punishing her. It's as if an invisible line has been crossed. They have never been so cruel to each other before.

She presses send, then remembers she can't get reception

inside the bungalow. It is probably a good thing, anyway. She puts her phone back in her bag and fills the kettle. As it comes to the boil, her mum appears.

'I think he'll need some sugar in his tea,' she says. 'For the shock. Will you put a teaspoon in?'

'He seems really angry,' Sarah says. This makes her mum look up and they exchange a momentary acknowledgement.

'Yes, well, he doesn't like being told what to do, does he?'

'I don't understand why he went out, not if you have the papers delivered.'

'He said he needed some air.' Her mum moves the carton of milk closer to the mugs and then opens the cupboard at the side of her head, reaches for the sugar bowl. Sarah can see she is struggling to remain composed, does that thing where she presses her lips together, pulls her chin into her neck.

'Are you all right?' She goes to touch her mum's arm, but her mum dives back into the cupboard.

'Mum? Are you okay?'

Her mum puts a packet of biscuits down on the counter, keeps her hand wrapped around it. She seems to visibly wrangle with herself, and then pulls up straight. 'Oh, I'm fine. Don't you worry about me. I bought these.' She holds the biscuits in the air. 'They were on offer, two for one, so I got one of each sort. Your brothers used to like these when they were little. Although I'm sure you're used to fancy biscuits now.'

Sarah pours boiling water into the mugs. She really shouldn't let it get to her, the way her mum rejects any attempt to create closeness between them. She once brought

172

a boyfriend home from university, the sort of normal boy she thought her mum would like. He wanted to work in a museum. But all her mum could say afterwards was that she was surprised Sarah would want to be with someone like that. Did she really want to spend her life with someone who lacked ambition, who had no financial security? She can never win.

Sarah stirs a teaspoon of sugar into her dad's mug. She says, 'I better be getting home after we've had our tea. Dad seems to be settled now.'

Her mum pauses and sniffs, then slides some of the biscuits onto a plate. 'I did think you might stay for lunch,' she says. 'I was going to get some ham from the shop. And then I thought you could be with your dad while I go to the service. I missed the one I usually go to and—'

'Service?'

'Yes, at St Mary's.'

'You're going to church?'

Her parents have never been to church and not once, not in the whole of her childhood, has she ever heard her mum mention God.

'It helps me find peace.' She looks at the floor. When she looks up, Sarah feels the unpleasant sting of her gaze.

'Your dad pushes me too far and I just need to get out, sometimes. I've met some nice people.' She doesn't wait for Sarah to respond and goes back into the living room holding the plate of biscuits.

When her mum leaves for church, Sarah doesn't bother to ask how long she will be. The familiar wall is there, and Sarah knows it is pointless even trying. Her dad is awake now. He slept through most of *A Man for All*

Seasons, although she is glad to see he is brighter. As her mum shouts 'Cheerio' and the front door clicks shut, he even smiles. His eyes look kindly upon her, the way they usually do.

'Dad, you will be careful, won't you?' she says, edging forward on the sofa to touch his hand.

He frowns, but she can tell he is doing it to try and make her laugh.

'I mean it. You have to use your stick.'

'Hate that th-thing,' he says.

'I know, but you need to use it. And what were you doing going out at that time anyway? The papers get delivered.'

'Was-wasn't papers,' he says, frowning again. He winces and touches the steri-strip. 'Your mum . . .' He shakes his head. 'It's ju-just . . . she can't stop . . . noyn noyn. Shit.' He tries to form the right words, his lips nibbling the air. She knows exactly what he means.

On her way home, she calls the landline and then Luke's mobile, but there isn't an answer from either. She wonders whether she ought to say something about their argument at the party last weekend – pictures them sitting together on the sofa, Luke's arm around her as they both tell each other they are sorry. *I didn't mean what I said.* They will both smile and say it is all forgotten. Imagining this makes her feel lighter, as if something has been lifted away.

She thinks about her parents. When her mum came back from church, she went and sat in the living room. Her dad was there, but neither of them offered a single word to the other. It struck Sarah, as she watched how they were with each other, that they have always been that way, for as long as she can remember. No memories of them kissing, no tender holding of a hand. They stayed together when they probably should have parted years ago. Her dad should have chosen Elaine.

Her marriage is nothing like her parents'. It feels re-assuring to think this. And she is so relieved that instead of taking the shorter route home, she stops at the twenty-four-hour supermarket and buys a tub of vanilla ice cream and a treacle tart. Treacle tart is Luke's favourite. And a bottle of wine. Yes, they will sit on the sofa together and he will tell her he is sorry.

When she gets home, the house is quiet. She puts the ice cream in the freezer and is about to try Luke's mobile again when she hears faint voices. She goes into the hall, strains to listen. The voices are coming from the basement.

Downstairs, she sees Luke's study door is ajar and she pushes it further open. It takes a moment for her to take in what she is seeing. Luke is sitting in his chair, staring at the computer screen. His jeans are around his ankles.

'That's it. Slowly. I want to see how wet you are,' he says.

His hand is on his hard penis. But it is the image on the screen that is horrifying. The face of the woman is con-torted. She is naked apart from her shoes, her legs splayed apart. Shiny black shoes with long spiky heels. Her fingers viciously jamming into herself.

'Like this, Luke?' the woman is saying. 'Is this what you want to do to me?'

Sarah cannot move.

Luke senses her then, turns around wide-eyed. Fumbles for his trousers.

'Oh God, Sarah. I . . .'

She runs. Up the stairs, into the hall, then up and up. All the while the image of those heels, the fingers. *Like this, Luke.*

In the bedroom, she slams the door. She could pack his things, or better still, throw them out of the window, let him collect them from the garden. She could change the locks. Tell him he isn't allowed to ever see the children again. How stupid she is. Just stupid.

The door opens and Luke comes towards her, his hands outstretched. She climbs onto the bed, away from him.

'Sarah. Look . . .'

'Get out. Pack your bags and get out.'

'Sarah, come on. You're overreacting.'

'You're disgusting. Do you know that? You need help.'

She wants to throw something, claw at his face. He stands at the foot of the bed. Neither of them moves or speaks.

'Where are my children?' she says, finally.

'They're with Miranda. I'm picking them up at six thirty.'

'So you could stay at home and wank over a whore?'

He glares at her. His face is full of fury.

'Miranda called the house after you left, offered to take the kids to Thorpe Park. She said she couldn't get you on your mobile.'

'How very convenient. You didn't think of calling my parents . . . or going with them, to actually spend time with them? Or would that have spoilt your day?'

'I'm not going to say anything while you're being like this.'

He heads for the door, pauses, comes rushing back in, as if he's thought better of it. His finger points aggressively.

'All high and fucking mighty, aren't you? When you're the one needing help.'

'Is that what you think? You're sick.'

'And you're not?'

He keeps pointing his finger. Everything she planned to say is a jumble. What could she say to him, anyway? How on earth is this ever going to be fixed? How has she let it go on for so long?

'You need to leave now. Pack a bag.' Her heart thumps.

'I'm not going anywhere,' he says. 'You pack a fucking bag.'

He picks up one of his trainers and throws it across the room. It hits the wall and falls to the floor. A grey streak is left on the pristine white. They both stare at the wall as if he's knocked it down.

'I can't do this. I can't . . .' she says.

Neither of them moves.

'I heard you once. Stood outside the door, could hear what you were doing. Do you know how that makes me feel?'

He lets out a long breath.

'Do you still love me?' she whispers.

He looks at her and frowns, shakes his head, as if he is having some kind of internal dispute. 'Of course I do.' He comes over to the bed, sits next to her.

She cannot stop the tears.

'Sarah don't cry. I'm so sorry,' he says.

He holds her, which makes her cry more, and she buries her face into his chest. It will be okay, she tells herself. It needed to come out into the open and this will be good for them. She doesn't really want him to go. She will get him to talk, get him some help.

'We could find someone for you to talk to,' she says, slowly.

His arms soften, and for a moment she thinks he is going to confess. Then he lets go of her and turns away.

'I'm no good for you,' he says. His voice is hard and her heart drops.

'We can figure it out,' she says. 'We'll get help. We'll find the best person there is, and we can—'

'Don't,' he says.

She reaches for his hand; realises what she needs to do. He mustn't leave her.

21

It is Thursday evening. Daniel doesn't move his eyes from the rear-view mirror. He is parked on the road by the leisure centre, close to the cinema. Far enough away not to be seen. He has already driven around the car park and found Kate's car, but he needs to see her, needs to know that she is with her friends like she said.

'We should all go out together sometime,' he said, before she left. 'Naomi seems nice, whenever I've spoken to her at the school.'

Kate's cheeks had flushed. 'They aren't really your sort of people,' she said, which made him flinch. They've always socialised with each other's friends.

Movement in the mirror, a couple of men walking past. Kate said she was meeting her friends in the pub, that they were having a drink before the film, and he wonders how long he should wait. Perhaps they have already gone in. An older woman walks past the car and stares back at him. He must look ridiculous, squashed up against the side of the car, spying in his mirror like some kind of stalker.

In years to come, he wonders if he will look back on this evening and think of it as the catalyst, the trigger point, the peak – he plots things in his mind like a graph, with definite points on an axis. Everything that happens is going to be determined by the action he takes tonight. He won't regret his decision, but he wonders if he will ever wish he had been brave enough to do something sooner.

And there she is. He sees her walking towards the doors, the back of her head, her jacket – the one she calls dark red that looks more like purple – and then she is gone. There were some other women with her, the short one he recognised from the school and also Naomi.

Now he can go home.

When he gets back, he goes upstairs to check on Flo first. He left in such a hurry, on impulse, and now he feels guilty. Flo is asleep, her head turned to one side. He clicks off her bedside lamp and pulls the door to. Maisie is in her room, on her bed, mobile phone in hand.

'You've been ages,' she says, letting the phone fall into her lap. 'I texted you and then called, but your phone was ringing in the kitchen. We've already got milk.'

He stands in the doorway.

'Do we?' he says. 'I must've missed it. Anyway, I needed to get petrol.' He raises his eyes to the ceiling, pulls a goofy face. A pathetic attempt to get her on side, but it seems to work. She smiles at him.

'Come on. Bed,' he says. 'Put your phone away. Your mum'll go mad if she knows I've let you go on it.'

'She gave it back, didn't she? The closest thing to an apology I've ever heard.' She looks at him, as if to test his loyalty and then laughs.

He hates how she can play him off against Kate, but he doesn't say anything. It's just a relief to be home.

As he leaves, he keeps the door open an inch. She will shut it as soon as he is gone, but he likes to keep the illusion that he can check on her later, like he used to. He lingers at the top of the stairs and when he can hear the sound of her getting ready for bed – the shuffle of clothing, her duvet being pulled back – he goes downstairs.

Kate's laptop is on the coffee table. He sits on the sofa with it. After weeks of procrastination, of going back and forth – telling himself everything is fine, all the while knowing it isn't – he is actually going to do it.

The spy software should be quick to download. While it installs, he will have a proper look at her emails, see what her internet history reveals. He has the absurd notion that he is in charge of what he will find. As if he can choose whether it will be good or bad. A part of him actually wants to find something, just to know how it will feel, just to see what will happen. Would he tell her it's over? If he found an email from another man, what would he do? Perhaps a confirmation of a hotel, a date. A reply. Kate telling this man how much she enjoyed being with him. It is so real, this imaginary thread, and he feels such a swell of hatred, his mind gets into such a fog that when he enters the password, he gets it wrong. He tries again but it is still wrong.

There is a bright glare of headlights through the adjoining door to the dining room. She can't be back yet, but there she is, parking on the drive. He closes the laptop and sprints to the kitchen, where he takes a dirty plate from the side, starts rinsing it under the tap. When she comes in, he is a little out of breath, his heart hammering.

'Oh, you're still clearing up,' she says.

He clears his throat, tries to calm his breath. 'You're

back early,' he says. He puts the plate down on the draining board, turns around.

'We caught an early showing,' she says. 'But I think I'll go up. I don't feel well.' Her voice is far away, as if she's been crying.

'The early showing?' he says. 'Are you sure?'

'Of course I'm sure. What's the matter with you?'

He gives her a mouth shrug, but she still doesn't relent.

'I'm doing a proper backup of our laptops,' he says. 'It's long overdue. You don't need yours, do you?'

She stands there, not saying anything. She looks sad. Tired. For a split second, he remembers who they really are. *Let's stop all of this.* Then she narrows her eyes and turns away from him, and the feeling is gone.

The password comes to him suddenly, the letters, the numbers, all in the right order.

'So, is that okay?' he says.

'Yes, whatever,' she says, over her shoulder. 'I need to go to bed.'

'I'll get on with it then.'

He waits until she is gone and the sounds of her moving about have stopped. As he goes into the living room, his mind analyses what just happened. It is confusing. If she was messaging men, having an affair, he is sure she wouldn't let him have her laptop.

He sits back on the sofa. Regardless, he will continue. In a few clicks it is done. The file is invisible, just like the marketing blurb said. The software is installed, and she will be none the wiser.

He scrolls through her emails, her internet history. There is nothing. The adrenaline fades and his body feels heavy. What should he do now?

On her desktop, there is a folder labelled *Daniel & Kate*. He clicks it open. It is a file containing their photos. A few years ago, they spent ages going through their boxes of old albums, getting them digitised, even the ones of him as a boy standing next to distant relatives. They are all here – pictures of him when he was young, holidays with his parents. The photos of Kate only go back to university. He asked her once, why she didn't want to keep any from when she was young, none of her mum. He could understand why she didn't want any of her dad, but at least she should have some of her mum. The ones of her smiling. But she said she didn't want any of them. They lit a fire – one of those galvanised incinerators they had bought for the garden waste – and sat around it, like they were having a campfire. She threw the old photos in, watched as the flames licked higher.

'You're the only family I want,' she said, blinking at the wall of heat. 'Did I tell you what my dad said when he found out I was pregnant?'

He didn't say anything, put his arm around her, instinctively knew that she needed to talk. She had done the same thing the day she found out her mum had gone. He had been at his student house, about to leave for a lecture when she knocked at his door. She had always been wary whenever he asked about her parents, but that day, the stories had spilled out, the pain she had kept hidden. All she needed was for him to listen.

In the garden all those years later, when she burned the photos, he held her and said nothing, let her say the things she needed to say, let her repeat the stories he had already heard. She was fearless, but she was also fragile. He knew that. She made him promise that he would never let her go.

He flicks through the photos until he can no longer stand it, closes the laptop and goes back into the dining room.

22

Kate sits on the end of the bed. Her jacket is buttoned up, her boots still on. Daniel is downstairs, although she can't hear him. She thought he might come and ask if she is okay.

When she got back from the cinema, she parked behind Daniel's car and sat for a while, staring at their house, shaken by what had happened. Only, as she looked, she hadn't seen the house she had left earlier. Instead, she saw the old windows that needed painting, the bottle-green front door, the tarnished brass letter plate. It was daytime and a young couple were going up the path. The man carefully guided the woman past the row of woody rose bushes. He stopped and looked around, said, 'I think we could make a driveway here. It would fit two cars, just about. Get rid of these old roses.' The woman looped her arm through his and said, 'It's perfect.' The man told her she needed to be nonchalant in front of the estate agent. 'Talk about the other house we saw. Say in a loud voice you prefer that one.' The woman nodded and absently stroked her stomach. She was pregnant, just eight weeks, not showing at all, but she wore elasticated trousers. She

185

was so excited to be pregnant and couldn't wait to start wearing maternity clothes.

In the house, the estate agent showed them around. They asked to have a look on their own and went up to the front bedroom. It had a view of the fields, beyond the row of houses opposite. 'Imagine waking up to that every day,' she said. And they did imagine it and the man said, 'Think of the walks we can do at the weekend, right here on our doorstep.' The woman smiled and said, 'Look who's being nonchalant now?' They laughed and turned away from the window, but before they went back downstairs, the man grabbed the woman in a passionate embrace. 'I love you,' he said and kissed her, as if they were having a clandestine meeting, snatching a final moment together.

Kate sat in the car, watching the ghosts of that couple until they disappeared. The rose bushes faded into the driveway, the old green door was replaced by the new blue one, and she once again saw the house she had left a few hours before. The tears came then, dripping off her chin and running down her neck. But she wasn't only crying about what had happened that evening. It was the whole mess of what she had done. She cried until her eyes were swollen and sore. When she went into the house, she told Daniel she was going to bed. She thought he would notice how upset she was, but he said nothing. He didn't even come over to hold her. He seemed almost disgusted by her presence.

Kate remains perched on the end of the bed. She knows she cannot continue to sit there, so she eases her left boot off with the right, pushing against her heel, wriggling her foot, until the boot finally gives way. She throws both boots to the side, aiming in front of the wardrobe, but they fall short.

Her phone buzzes in her bag and she takes it out, almost expecting to see a message from Naomi, but it is from Luke.

Go for it. Tell her about your book

She told him yesterday about her email to Joanna Shultze, the head of department at the university. There is a rumour about a full-time senior lecturer position, and she wants to meet up with Joanna to find out as much as she can.

She types: I don't think so

Luke responds immediately: Why not?

Kate doesn't want to explain. She can't bear to think about her book, has been considering giving up the whole idea. There is a blank space where the words should be. Love, sex, unfulfilled desires. She can't bear to think about it.

Luke sends another message: Tell her how much of a money-spinner it will be

And another: It's always about the money

And another: Show them what an asset you'll be

He is getting annoying now. Luke doesn't understand the way it works. It isn't about money. It's the unique ideas, the profound thoughts. But she doesn't have any of those and she just doesn't have what it takes.

She writes: I don't know. It's not good enough

That's an excuse. What are you afraid of?

She wants him to stop and leave her alone. She's had enough judgement for one night.

Nothing. I just don't want to do it any more

She throws the phone onto the bed. It doesn't matter what he thinks.

From the road, a car's headlights strobe across the room, catching the framed photo on her bedside table. For over sixteen years the photo has sat there, along with the lamp and the silver box, where she keeps the baby curls from the girls' first haircuts.

She leans over and picks the frame up. The photo is of her and Daniel, both of them wearing T-shirts and jeans. Still the best wedding photo, better than all the others, even the ones of her in her wedding dress and Daniel in his fancy suit. A man at the airport took it, said he used to be a professional photographer. *What luck*, they had said. The man told them the secret knack of a good portrait was to keep people talking. 'Cos if you get it just right, they show you things they never meant for you to see.'

Kate stares at the photo. What can she see? She sees a naive girl, a boy who loves her.

Her phone buzzes.

Are you OK?

She doesn't want Luke's messages to stop. Not really. They are her only comfort.

I've been better

She shuffles up the bed.

What's wrong?

For a second, she imagines telling him. The release of having someone understand. She went to him once, when she and Daniel had their first row. He made her promise not to worry. 'He's got the wrong idea and it can all be fixed.'

But she knows Luke cannot fix this.

I'll be OK. I'll let you know how the meeting goes. It's next week

She turns off her phone and lies down, curls up as small

as she can. She hates how pathetic she is being, but she has never felt so alone, or so humiliated. Those women she thought were her friends, those things they said about her – she can't stop the scene from replaying in her mind.

At the cinema, she had waited in the foyer while Naomi and the others went to the toilets. Before, in the pub, there had been a strange atmosphere. The conversation had been stilted, awkward even, and she had caught Naomi and Debbie giving each other a look, as if there was something going on. She told herself she was imagining it.

In the foyer, she picked up a leaflet about up-and-coming films, then decided she probably ought to go to the toilet after all. The others were still in the cubicles, and she went into a free one at the far end. As she sat with her jeans and knickers around her knees, she heard flushing. She listened as they went and stood by the mirrors and washed their hands. Naomi said she couldn't believe what Kate had been doing. Why had Debbie even invited her? One of the others said they couldn't believe it either. Kate had seemed so nice, not like *that* at all. Naomi said it had made her feel ill hearing about the website, about the man in the car, and the other man she'd done *God knows what* with. Naomi had been through enough with Neil. She couldn't be friends with someone like that. *What a slut.*

Kate tries to curl herself into an even tighter ball. It is cold. Another car goes past, a loud exhaust puncturing the quiet. She grabs the edge of the duvet and folds it over herself. She finds herself slipping in and out of sleep.

A cough from below makes her stir. Daniel. She goes downstairs and sees he is in the dining room. She peers round the door, watches him until he notices her.

'I was just finishing,' he says, closing the lid of his laptop. 'I thought you were asleep.'

'I was getting changed.'

'But you've still got your jacket on.'

She looks down.

'Oh, yes,' she says. 'I mean, I fell asleep but then I woke up and I'm getting changed now.'

Daniel stands. The space between them – her in the doorway, him at the head of the table – is disproportionately stretched.

'So, was it any good?'

'What?'

'The film. Was it good? I can't remember what you said you were going to see.'

'I told you I left early. I wasn't feeling well.'

Her eyes cannot settle on his face.

'I thought you said you went to the early showing.'

'No, I didn't say that. I meant I left early, you misunderstood me.'

It's like needles when he looks at her that way.

'I said I wasn't feeling well. Why are you so angry?'

He shakes his head and looks at the table. 'I'm going to bed.' He rubs his eyes. His glasses fall down his nose. 'It's been a long day,' he says, pushing them back up.

That usually melts her, his funny tired face.

He looks at her blankly. She wants to go to him; tell him she doesn't know what is happening to them, but she wants it to stop. They used to be bound together so tight.

He walks past her.

'Are you coming?' he asks.

'I'll be up in a minute.'

She waits until she can hear the creak of floorboards

on the landing, then goes into the living room and picks up her laptop. She hasn't been on the site since Alec, but there is an urgency to erase what she has done. With one click her profile is gone. She puts Naomi and the others, all of their words and glaring judgements into a big black hole.

23

The sun appears briefly, casting shadows over the field. It is almost one o'clock. Luke sits on the damp grass at the edge of the treeline, taking a swig of whisky. The bottle was full when he arrived and now it is nicely broken in. He looks down towards the barn and then across to the house. It has been a long time since he has been here.

He had a sudden impulse to come. His appointment at the clinic is meant to be at one thirty. An initial meeting to ascertain his therapeutic route and a group session with other people who have similar problems. The literature the clinic sent in an email said he would find the group sessions especially helpful. He doesn't need a fucking therapist, doesn't need to be in a fucking *group*. He'd only agreed to it to get Sarah off his back, so everything could go back to normal.

Now he is here, he realises what he must do – he has his lighter, his whisky. It is something he should have done before.

If he squints, he can see the window of his old bedroom. The third one along from the right. If he looks hard enough, he can see a boy at night, in his bedroom. A speck at the window, listening to a screaming fox.

The last time he slept in his room, it was the Christmas before his parents' car accident. He was in his second year at university, home for the holidays. Eighteen months after Seb's funeral.

There were so many people at the house that year, people he hadn't met before. They all seemed to know who he was. 'Hello, you're looking well,' they said, as if he should be anything but. He had brought a girlfriend with him. An American girl with long legs.

Christmas dinner was an elaborate affair and Luke couldn't help wondering if so many people had been invited to help water down his presence. He was sat away from his parents, in between his aunt and uncle. The American was seated further up, on the opposite side of the table. He watched as she tried to make conversation with his mother.

'It's not you,' he said later, when they were in bed. 'It's me she hates.'

His old bed had been replaced by a double and the room had been redecorated. Striped wallpaper and co-ordinating curtains. His old toys and comics, even his mirror and clock, everything had been boxed up and put in the storeroom. Every scrap of him erased. For a moment, he pretended nothing had changed at all and he was back in his old single bed with the heavy blankets. He half expected to hear soft footsteps, cold hands reaching around his chest and a breath of a voice in his ear saying, 'Move up, it's freezing.' At breakfast his father would read the paper and groan about politicians, and he and Seb would groan as well, even though they didn't really understand. Their mother would roll her eyes in a jokey way and say that politicians stank more than the kippers.

When the American was finally asleep, Luke put on his coat to go down to the barn. The draw of the place was too strong. He had never believed in ghosts, but the barn hung onto a strange energy after Seb had gone, something that couldn't be explained. A charge that made the hairs on his arms prickle. He stood in the middle of the empty floor, right on the spot where it had happened, where Seb had fallen. Being there made him feel like he wanted to stay for ever and yet run far away. That's what being with Seb was like.

Staring across the field now, he takes another swig of whisky. A bank of cloud covers the sun and the trees' long shadow disappears. His phone pings in his jacket pocket. It is Sarah.

Shall we have takeaway tonight?

She hasn't left him alone since the upset the other day. He knows she wants reassurance, and he will give it to her soon. Maybe he wants to punish her a little longer for threatening to leave him. *Ping*. Another message.

And good luck! Let me know when you've finished

Does she really imagine he would go? A cosy chat with a man who will be just as screwed up as he is – he knows what those *therapists* are like. A gathering of pathetic losers. Sitting around, listening to everyone's sob stories: *Hello, my name's Luke and I'm a mess.* Not a fucking chance. Later, he will tell her it went well, that there is no need for concern. That's all she needs to hear.

He types a reply: **Ordering in sounds perfect. Let's do Thai**

He had a fantasy on his way over here that he would climb up and sit on the beam, swing his legs for a while, then let himself fall. He would crack onto the hard floor, maybe remain conscious for a few minutes until the blood soaked into his brain. Look up at the beam before the lights went out. It would be the same view Seb would have seen.

His phone pings again.

I love you

He puts his phone away.

If he were gone, would she mourn for him? Probably she would be happy. Love is just a word that people say to get the feeling they need. When they first met, she used to say it all the time, as if it was an involuntary tic. Why do people do that? *I love you* really means *I want you to love me.*

Earlier in the week, he had to fill in an online form in preparation for the therapy session. He already knew he wasn't going to go, but he had to play along. Sarah hovered outside his study, poking her head in, asking if he wanted a coffee.

'Is it straightforward?' she said. He could feel her eyes straining to see what was on the screen.

'It's fine. Please don't fuss.'

'Sorry,' she said. 'I love you.'

The form was typical. Describe his childhood in five words; what was his relationship with his mother like, his schooling; how many times per week does he watch porn, masturbate; how long are his sessions; has he had any extra-marital affairs or one night stands; has he used prostitutes; on a scale of one to ten, with one being mild and ten severe and debilitating, how would he rate his recent need for sex.

He had to fill in a form like that, years ago, when his parents thought he needed help. When they thought he was to blame for what happened to Seb. The therapist was a dumpy woman who wore shapeless jumpers.

What is your first thought when you wake? Do you plan your day around having a drink or taking drugs? Do you find it difficult to cope in life without drink or drugs? Would people say you have difficulty controlling your anger?

'I'm not angry,' he told her. 'And the drugs weren't mine.'

They were Seb's. The trouble is, when you've spent your whole life covering up for someone else, nobody believes a word you say.

He gets up and walks slowly down the field, holding the whisky bottle by its neck. The field is overrun with nettles and thistles, not even remnants of the wildflower meadow his father had planted all those years ago. As he gets nearer, the barn seems smaller than he remembers. Twitch grass crawls over the cracked concrete platform in front of the doors. Crumbling brickwork and rotting wood. When he was a boy, he used to squeeze through a gap where the loose boards were easily prised apart. He goes around to see if the gap is still there. He could pour some whisky in and light a bit of old wood to get it going.

'What do you think you're doing here?'

Luke sees the boots before he hears the voice. He continues to crouch, the whisky sloshing in the bottle.

'Just having a look at the old place,' Luke says, standing slowly. He doesn't recognise this man. He has deep furrows across his forehead and his skin is brown and leathery. Just like Mr Jebbs, the manager who ran the farm when he was a boy, but it isn't him. Jebbs would be dead by now.

'This isn't part of the estate,' the man says. 'You shouldn't be here. It's private property. The entrance to the house is down that way, but they're not opening it up yet.'

'I'm not here for the house.' Luke stands and offers a hand.

The man steps back and ignores the gesture, looks at the bottle.

'You don't know who I am, do you?' Luke says. 'How long have you worked here?'

'This is private land. You need to leave.' The man remains, unsmiling and stern.

'Who runs the farm now?'

'You can go to the office if you need to speak to someone.' He widens his stance and crosses his arms. 'This is private land.'

Luke holds up a hand in mock surrender, and as he walks away, he shouts back, 'You know, there's a footpath running right around the edge of this field. Not many people know, but it is a public byway.'

The man watches him walk back up the field.

Luke cuts across to the other corner, towards the river. He finds the two big birch trees and makes his way along the scrubby bit of land that leads down to the ditch, which he and Seb used to jump over on their bikes. The route is overgrown, but he finds his way easily, brushing past brambles that try to hook onto his jacket sleeve, moving closer to the burbling sounds of the river. He spent a lot of time here as a boy, and as he goes down into the clearing, he feels a pain in his chest. He didn't know what it would feel like to come back.

The alder is still there, where the narrow part of the river curves around, its trunk still leaning out at an impossible angle from the bank. And the rope still hangs from the white willow, although the seat they made from an old

197

Frisbee is gone and the rope is short and frayed. Luke takes a breath and steps onto the shingle, takes off his jacket and lays it down next to the bottle of whisky.

The water is low and clear, and it gurgles over the stones. He knows that in bad weather the silt gets stirred up, making the water murky and brown. And he knows how the shingle would feel under bare feet, sharp at first, at the start of summer, until the tender skin remembers.

Further along, there is a stepping-stone platform. His father let him have some flagstones from the garden, after the new patio had been laid. Seb helped load the wheelbarrow and they pushed it all the way across the field, through the trees and down the bank to the edge of the river.

Luke takes a swig from the bottle and sets it back down on the shingle. He rolls up the sleeves of his shirt and picks up a flat grey stone. Then he flicks his wrist and lets it fly across the water. It bounces once, skims the surface, and disappears. His record was five times.

He remembers the girl then. She smelt of summer holidays. Seb had already gone back to school weeks before and Luke had just turned thirteen. He was in his final year at the local prep and before long he too would be sent away.

'What you looking at?' she said.

It was a shock to find her standing there, in his and Seb's place. She was older than him and spoke like the men who worked on the farm. He hadn't seen her around before.

She watched him balance on the tree trunk, placing his feet like a trapeze artist, hovering over the deepest bit. He said he would teach her how to do it, if she liked. She laughed when she almost slipped in. They talked and skimmed stones, both taking turns to practise. By the end of the afternoon, she was as good as him. They shared the bacon sandwiches he'd brought with him. It was nearly dark when she said she had to go.

'See you,' she said.

He liked the way she made him feel and there was a tug of disappointment as she said goodbye. It was an instinctive thing, when he reached across and pulled her head towards him, put his lips on hers. She lay on the shingle, and he lay next to her. The smell of her was sickly sweet, like bubblegum and suntan lotion. She took off her knickers and showed him what to do. It was over quickly.

'I like you,' she said, afterwards.

They sat and flicked more stones into the water, and it was peaceful. Yes, he remembers that, how peaceful it had felt. He didn't see her again and he didn't tell Seb.

And then Luke thinks of the summer it happened, the summer he turned eighteen. His parents gave him a signet ring – a gold ring with the family crest, just like Seb's, just like his father's. There was a big party at the weekend, and on the actual day of his birthday, Seb took him to the pub. Both of them were drunk by the time they walked through the woods. They messed about on the rope swing. Seb was relaxed and happy. That was the thing with Seb – he was two people and Luke never knew which one he was going to be.

It was a few days later when Luke was starting to pack for university. Seb came into his room. He said they should go down to the barn.

'Come on,' he said. 'Let's see you off in style.'

He held up a bottle of whisky. He wasn't different, no

different to any other day. People talk about signs, about knowing when something terrible is about to happen, but there was nothing. Signs only ever appear in hindsight.

In the barn, Seb dragged a couple of hay bales across for them to sit on. He lit a cigarette.

'I don't think I like the idea of you being at university,' Seb said, clicking his jaw to make smoke rings. 'All those girls.' He passed the cigarette to Luke and opened the bottle.

They sat drinking the odd swig, not saying much, watching the sun sink low through the open door. Seb never usually left the door open, but he didn't seem to care that day. Jebbs would've gone mad if he'd seen them smoking by the bales.

'You'll be all right,' Seb said. 'I know you're going to be brilliant.' Then he said he wanted to climb up and sit at the top. 'Like we used to, when we were younger, do you remember?'

Luke did remember but they were skinny things back then and could clamber up the hay bales to the mezzanine ledge and shin along the beam, no problem. But Seb wouldn't listen, insisted they went up there.

Sitting on the beam, Seb took two packets of white powder from his pocket, opened them out.

'What's that?' Luke said, even though he knew. There were boys at school who did it all the time.

'We're going to have a good time,' Seb said, and then he took out another bag with coloured pills that looked like sweets.

Sometimes, when Luke thinks back to that day, he wonders if he did push him. A hand on his back, a quick shove. That's all it would have taken and perhaps that is what happened. Perhaps Seb started on at him, started kissing his neck, his mouth. Perhaps he made him lie down on that mezzanine ledge and unbuckle his jeans. Perhaps he held onto his shoulder as he shoved himself inside. But Luke doesn't remember any of that. All he sees is being on the ground, next to the hay bales, and rolling Seb onto his side. He tries to clear his airways, presses on his chest – he learned first aid in the Scouts – then stuffing things into his pockets – the coke, the pills, the cigarettes – and running. Running as hard as he could to the river. And then seeing the vomit on his hands, his shoes. He is standing barefoot in the river, washing it away, hoping the water will make everything disappear. There was an empty feeling, like a void had opened up inside him. But there was also a kind of a release, like he'd been set free.

It was dark when his father found him.

'So, this is where you are,' his father said. He snatched the bag of pills that was poking out of his pocket, made him turn everything else out onto the ground. His father wouldn't believe him when he said they were all Seb's. 'What have you done?' he said. 'Your mother will never forgive you for this. Never. You will never be forgiven.' He grabbed Luke's hand and yanked the ring off his little finger, threw it hard. It bounced off the stepping-stone pile and disappeared into the water.

Luke stands on the shingle now, looking in, remembering. He feels the grip of his father's hand, the sharp tug on his finger.

Before he realises what he is doing, he is wading in. Water fills his shoes, soaks through his jeans. He is on his knees, digging at the riverbed, water slicing into his arms, his chest. Where would it have gone? Is it buried here, under the stones? He pulls out a flat piece of flint and throws it across the water with all his strength. It bounces one, twice, three, four times. Disappears.

24

The cushions sit across the sofa in a perfect line. The house is silent, the children at their after-school clubs. Luke is at work. Sarah took the day off today, planned on doing some research, calling a few colleges. She is thinking about a new direction, perhaps studying interior design. She has also decided to call Elaine.

She stands away from the sofa and puts her hands on her hips, sniffs under her arms. It's not the unpleasant acrid smell that she sometimes gets a whiff of when she is about to come on her period, but not nice either. She decides that she will choose some new cushions. Perhaps she will redo the whole room. It just isn't working.

When Zac was born, and she was at home on maternity leave, she planned a complete refurbishment. Room by room, she went through the house, spent hours choosing colour schemes, finding the right curtains, accessories. Her friends told her she was mad to decorate so soon after having a baby, but they didn't understand. It helped when she was having those off days, especially when Zac struggled to settle. There is something comforting about getting a room just right, the satisfaction it brings.

The cushions are completely wrong. She throws them on the floor and starts again, stacks them in pairs at either end.

Luke had his appointment with the therapist on Saturday. She is trying not to think about it. Luke says she has a tendency for over-analysing. At first, when she made the appointment, it felt like a safety net had been placed beneath them. Okay, she thought, the doctor can take over now, he will make everything right. But as the day grew nearer, she worried whether Luke would even go. Would he do what he always did – be repentant and then let things slide back to the way they were? He was gone for hours. She had to stop herself from sending too many messages. When he came home, he dashed upstairs and leaped in the shower before she even had a chance to say hello. Afterwards, he explained that he was late because he had needed to go for a walk. That he needed to think. Then he told her he wouldn't be continuing with the sessions. 'There's nothing wrong,' he said. He didn't blink or flinch as he said this, looked straight at her. She couldn't say she didn't believe him.

'All men do it,' he said in his explaining voice. 'And the doctor said you might well be projecting your inhibitions onto me. You know, the problems you have with sex.'

'I don't have problems,' she said.

'It's okay. I know.' He smiled at her in a way that was confusing.

He changed the subject, talked about going out for dinner. Called for the children and said they should go out to the cinema. He made it impossible for her to say anything else.

So now she is in this strange place where she doesn't know what to do next. Their week has resumed, everything back to how it was. Although his late-night visits to the study have stopped. At least she can be thankful for that.

Turning away from the sofa she pauses at the mantelpiece, repositions the bronze dish Luke bought her for their eighth anniversary. A dish designed as a feather. She runs her finger down the smooth central midrib. It came with a card, explaining how no two feathers are the same, like fingerprints, and how the artist was inspired by their contradictory nature – fragile, yet powerful.

In the kitchen, she puts the oven on low to preheat, lays the plates out ready for the children's dinner. The pie Magda made is in the fridge. They will be home in an hour. Her eyes scan the room, checking for things to do. She knows she is procrastinating.

With the phone in her hand, she goes over to the sofa and sits down, tapping in the number before she can change her mind. She wrote it on a piece of paper, and it sits on the coffee table, symmetrically placed in the middle. The receptionist answers and she is put through.

'Passenger transport, how can I help you?'

It is Elaine. Her voice is unmistakable, cheerful. A glass-half-full kind of person. Sarah remembers the times she used to go to her dad's office for a lift home after netball. 'Wish I could have my time again,' Elaine used to say. 'So many possibilities, so many different kinds of jobs.' It gave Sarah such a boost to hear that, instead of the constant gloom from her mum, who always spoke of limitation and how hard it was going to be to start a career.

'Is that Elaine?'

'Yes, how can I help you?'

'Hello, Elaine, I don't know if you remember me, but it's Sarah, Colin Talbot's daughter.'

There is a pause.

'Oh yes, Sarah. How are you, dear? How's your dad doing?'

'He's about the same. I understand you went to see him a couple of months ago. So nice of you to visit.'

'I hope it helped. It's tricky when the speech is affected like that.'

'Oh no, he loved you visiting. I hope you can go again. In fact, I was hoping you—'

'It takes time, doesn't it? My friend's husband had a mild one a few years ago, and even he had to see a physio. Not a physio … what are they called? Those people who help with exercises for buttoning up clothes, holding cutlery. What are they called?'

'I was thinking maybe you'd like to come for another visit. Dad would love to—'

'Occupational therapist. That's it. He had occupational therapy. For several weeks. He was marvellous after that. His speech was always okay, though. Maybe it takes longer with speech. It's not like doing up a button, is it?'

'So, I was thinking it might be nice for him to see you again.'

Sarah's hand feels clammy, her arm stiff from where she has been holding the phone so tight. She loosens her grip as she waits for Elaine to respond. The pause feels infinite. Perhaps this was a terrible idea, after all.

'Well, I'm sure Derek said he'd go for another visit. And all his golfing friends. Your dad had a lot of golfing buddies, didn't he?'

Elaine sounds breathless now, like she's moving about.

Sarah imagines her tidying up, putting staplers and pads of paper straight, getting ready to go home.

'I didn't mean to disturb you, but I just thought it would be nice. Dad misses seeing people. I think he'd like to see you again.'

'Everyone in the office says it isn't the same without him. I'm in a different department now, but I see the others all the time. Been here sixteen years, can you believe it? And I was in highways for nine before that. I'll be retiring next year.'

'Maybe we can put something in the diary.'

'I'll certainly pass the message on to Derek, dear.'

Sarah gets up and walks over to the French doors, traces her finger around one of the rectangular panes.

'I'm sure he'd be happy if you were to visit by yourself. You know where the bungalow is now. I could let you know when . . .' She is about to say when her mother won't be there but realises how that would sound. She feels flustered and isn't exactly sure what she is trying to achieve.

'Oh,' Elaine says. 'I'm not sure that would be—'

'I know. I'm sorry. I didn't mean—'

'I'll let Derek know you called. I better be going. I've got a few things to finish.'

'Of course. I'm sorry.'

'Lovely to hear from you.'

'Yes, it's—'

'Give your dad my regards, won't you?'

Sarah puts the phone down next to the piece of paper on the coffee table. *Highways and Transport*, she wrote in her neatest handwriting. She feels the crawl of embarrassment, the creeping self-conscious pang of having done something foolish.

25

Kate commutes to the university every Friday. She loves the sensation as the train picks up speed. Even when it's crowded, she doesn't mind. The anonymity of sitting there, not needing to speak. She managed to get a window seat today, and she lets herself sink back as the concrete platform recedes.

She is going in earlier than usual, for her meeting with Joanna, the head of department. One of the associate professors will be leaving in four months' time. The position will be advertised soon, she has discovered through the grapevine. Her colleagues are being supportive about her applying and, like Luke, they also said Kate should just *go for it*. She is hoping Joanna tells her the same.

Her phone buzzes in her bag. A message from Luke: **Good luck**. It makes her smile then frown. She doesn't know why she hasn't told Daniel about the meeting. Last night, when he seemed more relaxed than usual, she went to say something, then stopped herself. She isn't sure why.

She looks down at the folder on her lap. It contains her outline plan and a jumble of notes for her book. Taking off the elastic string at each corner, she opens it and reads the heading on the first page: *Marriage and an altered sense of belonging.* Her idea is to bridge the gap between academia and the commercial markets, which she thinks the department might find interesting. But they will probably be looking for academic rigour, something to be published in the journals. She shouldn't mention it, only brought it because she wants to prove to herself that she isn't a coward. What Luke said to her in his texts about her being afraid has struck a nerve.

She closes the folder and reattaches the elastic, tucks it out of sight against the cold wall. The train is speeding along now, and she watches the landscape go by.

Waterloo station is busy, people pouring on and off platforms. She shows her ticket at the gate and joins the surging crowd. Someone knocks into her, going the opposite way, almost spinning her around. 'Watch it,' she says, but the boy in the hoodie keeps going, his hands shoved deep into the pockets of his jeans.

Down on the platform, the forewind signals the tube and she is reminded of the film about a life splitting into two possible versions. Kate wonders what her other self might be doing now. Is she also standing on a platform on her way to a meeting, or is she already at the university, already a professor in the department? What decisions did that other self make? Did she open the curtains this morning and find the courage to say to her husband: I'm so worried that if I don't get this job I'll never get to where I want to be, and how is it that I'm managing to hold down two jobs and pay the bills, yet I still feel like I'm a failure?

The tube arrives and she finds a spot holding onto a yellow pole, between a tall man with a briefcase and a girl of about eighteen. The train continues, extra people cramming on at each stop. Kate is forced closer to the girl. She notices her fingers, the dark nail varnish on bitten-down nails, the bruised tiredness in her face. She seems sad. As Kate takes her in, their eyes meet, and Kate instinctively turns away. Then she wonders if the girl has anyone looking out for her. Perhaps their silent connection was what the girl needed. Kate should have smiled, and the girl would have been uplifted. When Kate was that age, it was overwhelming sometimes, coping with the fierceness of the world. She had only wanted someone to see her and be kind. Kate looks across, but the girl is readying herself to get off. The train slows to a stop and as the doors beep open, Kate follows the girl onto the platform. She almost catches up with her, but the girl is engulfed by the crowd.

Kate continues up the stairs and along the corridor. A busker is singing. She finds some coins at the bottom of her purse and drops them into his guitar case. He winks at her.

I'd like to discuss my idea for a research project. I'm also writing a book I think would benefit the department.

She imagines saying the words, can see herself sitting in Joanna's office, sees the smiles, the encouraging nods. She can hear Joanna saying that her book sounds very interesting and that she would be a perfect candidate for the position. Over and over until she is sure this is exactly what will happen. She steps onto the escalator, clutching her bag with two hands.

Six hours later, after her last tutorial, Kate finds herself standing over the road from Hyde Park. She meant to go home, but instead walked past the tube station and kept walking until she found herself here. There is a break in the traffic, and she crosses the road. She wants to be hidden, lost in the trees and veers off the path. The grass is damp, but she doesn't care about getting her feet wet.

Her phone buzzes in her bag. A message from Luke.

How did it go?

She shouldn't reply. She should be telling Daniel about the meeting, not Luke. Daniel should be the one messaging her, asking how it went. Daniel should be soothing her worries. Daniel is the one she wants. But Luke appears to be the only friend she has right now.

She composes a reply.

Terrible. Joanna hates the book idea

I'm sure that's not true

Absolutely true. I'm in Hyde Park. Think I might throw myself in the lake

Don't do that. You'll scare the ducks

She laughs aloud.

I didn't take you for a duck lover

There's a lot about me you don't know

I think I know enough

Like the lake, I have hidden depths

Hidden shallows, you mean?

Very funny. Go to the café by the lake. I'll see you there in thirty minutes

I should be getting home

That's an order. You officially need cheering up

At the café, she finds a table. It isn't particularly warm, but she wants to sit outside. She pulls up the collar of her coat. The water is dark and corrugated, reflecting the grey sky.

They used to come here a lot when they were students,

in the warmer months. Just up there on the grass by the trees. They would stay until late, drinking and messing about. Kate sees an image of them. Daniel is kissing her.

'Don't look so glum,' a voice behind her says. Luke stands with two wine glasses and a bottle of white.

'You made me jump,' she says.

'At least the ducks are safe.' He gives her a grin and puts the wine on the table. 'I thought you'd be inside.'

'I wanted to be by the water.' She notices his well-cut suit, the shirt that has already been unbuttoned, the loosened tie.

'So, how are you?' he says, sitting down and pouring them a glass.

'Thanks,' she says. 'I've been better.'

'Let's drink to days that are better, then.' He gives her a nudge with his elbow. 'Come on, cheer up.'

'I'm okay,' she says. 'I shouldn't have mentioned my book. It's not properly sorted out in my mind, and now I've blown it. Such an idiot. I sounded like a pathetic schoolgirl.'

'Hardly. You always beat yourself up too much.'

She wants to know what he means, but he continues talking, says her book sounds like it's just the sort of thing publishers would want. 'People can't get enough of reading about it, can they?' he says. 'Because nobody has the answer.'

'What, about love? Or sex?' she says. 'Isn't one just a biological disguise for the other?' She takes a gulp of wine.

'That's probably true.' He laughs, but in a way that suggests he is feeling uncomfortable.

A young mother with a buggy goes past the table. Luke looks, then turns to the other side, as if he is trying to find a distraction. Perhaps he is wishing he hadn't come after all.

'Don't listen to me,' she says. 'I'm just pissed off.'

She smiles at him and clinks her glass against his. They talk about how it would be good to have a holiday, like the one they had in the Lake District. Luke says if Daniel wasn't so sensitive about being out of work, he'd have booked something for Christmas.

They drink and talk, Luke drinking the most, and the bottle is soon empty. He goes to get another.

'What?' he says, as he sits back down. 'You think I'm an old soak, don't you?'

'I wasn't thinking about you at all,' she says, looking away.

They sit watching the water, drinking more wine. She notices the way he turns the stem of the glass between his fingers. How he closes his eyes briefly when he swallows. How his Adam's apple bobs up and down. His arm resting on the table. She notices all of this because it is something that she is aware of these days, not the person inside, not the individual who is performing the action, but the body itself.

By the time the second bottle is almost gone, she cannot recall the thread of their conversation. They are playing a game – the one they used to play as students, imagining the lives of the people walking past. Kate has chosen a young woman with an athletic figure. Luke decides that for her day job, she does admin for an office of accountants, but in her spare time she is pursuing her childhood dream of winning a medal at the Olympics for synchronised swimming. She meets her fellow teammates at five am every day, where they practise their brilliantly choreographed routine to the sounds of Katrina and the Waves.

Kate laughs.

'Okay, how about him?' Luke says, pointing to a stylish man wearing a roll-neck and Crombie coat.

'Oh God,' she says. 'I don't know. My mind's a blank. You're too good at this.'

'I remain victorious,' he says, flexing an arm. 'You guys were always rubbish.' He gives her a wide smile.

She says, 'What would you think about me, if you didn't know me, and I walked by?'

He leans back in his chair and stretches, puts his hands behind his head, his elbows jutting out to each side.

'Hmm,' he says. 'That's not really a fair question because I do know you, don't I?'

'Go on, just pretend,' she says.

'All right then. I'd say that you were someone who always wants to do the right thing, always wants to do well and make people happy, and you've got a respectable job and a happy marriage and happy children but there's this other side of you that's wild and dangerous and you're afraid that one day you won't be able to contain it and it'll make you ruin everything.' He stares out across the water as he says this, and then brings his arms down, holds his hands in his lap.

Something catches in her throat. He must realise the change of mood because he then says with a laugh, 'God, I don't know. I'd probably say that you were a corporate solicitor who'd just had a big meeting and the rest of your team are scared of you because you have such a ferocious reputation.'

He blinks as a piece of hair flops into his eyes, and he rakes it back with his fingers.

'Really? You think I look like a solicitor?' she says.

'No,' he says. 'Not at all. It's impossible to say, isn't it? We've known each other for too long and I just see who I know, rather than what other people see.'

She wants to hear more, wants to know what he thought of her the first time they met, but he says it in a way that ends the matter.

They finish the dregs of the bottle. She feels drunk, but in a quiet way, like she is watching from outside of herself.

She sees the rippling water, dark and cold, but she also sees the sun, the white sparks and the blue – both days, now and then – superimposed upon each other as if no time has passed. She sees herself in Daniel's arms, hears them talking about the house they will buy, the places they will go, the books she will write, the life they will have. She sees them as if they are right there, and she wants to know how she had such certainty then? How did she know what Daniel felt? How was she able to surrender herself to him so entirely?

'There's this photo in my bedroom,' she says, not looking at Luke but out across the lake, almost hypnotised by the way the water seems to move back and forth yet remain in the same place. 'It's been there for years but it was like I'd only just seen it. We look so young. It was taken by a man at the airport, after the wedding. Daniel had surprised me with tickets to Mauritius. Do you remember that? Anyway, this man, he said he used to be a photographer. He said he liked taking pictures of people because you always see something in a photo that you can't normally see when someone's there in front of you.'

She turns to Luke and is about to say more, but Luke's hand is reaching out, as if he is going to touch her face.

'Oh,' she says.

'A leaf in your hair.' He shows her the flat of his palm, but whatever he plucked out blows away before she can see. 'What were you saying?' He leans closer and the way he looks at her makes her cheeks grow hot.

'It doesn't matter,' she says. 'I'm just rambling.' She moves away and sits back, even though she wants to move closer so she can feel his hand brush against her cheek again.

The wind picks up and rolls against the water, lifting it into tiny peaks. She pulls at the collar of her coat and before she can say anything else, Luke has got hold of her arm, and they are standing.

He steers her down the steps and onto the path. She tells him they shouldn't have drunk so much. They are on the grass, heading towards a cluster of trees. She is under the branches, leaning up against the scratchy trunk. His hand is up her skirt, touching her leg. The words are in her head, telling him stop. Telling him no. No. She can't make the words come out. She can't speak or move at all.

'You and me,' he says. 'I've always known we were the same.'

His hand is in her knickers, and he rubs his thumb over the nub of her, kisses her on the mouth. She feels his tongue.

'I'd love to see you properly,' he says. He squeezes her breast through her top. 'Will you send me a picture?'

He kisses her again, and then he is gone.

It is only much later, gone midnight, when she is stirring from the sofa and it is pitch dark, that she realises what she has done. She turns on the reading lamp and looks down at her hands. Speckles of dried blood on the heel of her palms, the mild sting of a bruise; a vague memory of someone helping her up from the path.

On the coffee table there is an empty Big Mac box, a half-drunk glass of wine and a chocolate wrapper. There is a text message from Luke on her phone.

I want to taste you

She scrolls back, sees the messages she sent hours ago, ones that she has no recollection of sending, including a photo – her unbuttoned blouse, her bare breasts. She deletes the message thread, blocks his number, then deletes his contact details in her address book. It isn't enough. She wants to turn back the clock and scrub it clean. How can she make it all go away?

She opens up her laptop and types a new email.

I don't know what's been happening. We shouldn't have met or done any of those things. Delete the texts, the photos. I don't know what I've been doing. Just forget it ever happened.

26

The music thumps through the wall of the gents' toilets. Luke stands in front of the mirror and pinches his nose between his thumb and forefinger. He leans in. The dim light makes his eyes appear as if they are hollow voids.

'Happy birthday Seb,' he says to his dark reflection. His brother would have been fifty today.

After the funeral, Luke was given a leaflet. Something about how to cope with loss. The stages of grief. Anger was one of the stages. He'd folded the leaflet and put it in his pocket, kept it in his bedside drawer, and when he had left to go to university, he dropped it in his suitcase. He couldn't have said why he kept it. Seb would have laughed at such pathetic drivel, but perhaps it was something to do with how death had made him see things more clearly. It was unforgivable the things Seb had done to him, but he had allowed it to happen, hadn't he? He had remained silent, remained still. He had done nothing but concede. What did that make him?

He stares at the mirror until his phone buzzes in his pocket. Sarah has sent him another message, won't let up. He told her before he left the house that he didn't know how long he would be, and he tells her again that he won't be late.

She replies immediately: It's Saturday Luke and I'm fed up with this. What time will you be back?

I don't know, he starts to type, and then changes his mind. Instead, to shut her up, he types: In an hour. He has no intention of being back by then.

Seb used to do that, make insinuations, make him feel so bad he would have to do something to take the feeling away. And even though Luke knew Seb was telling a pack of lies – hinting that their parents thought he was stupid, that they were disappointed – he had to find a way to inflict some kind of punishment. It made no sense afterwards, but in the moment, he would blame his parents for what Seb was saying, and when nobody was looking, he would go into their bedroom. Perhaps he would take a china ornament, or the special crystal frame, the one with the photo of them on their wedding day. He would take it to his room, where he would get the pair of compasses from his pencil case and work away at a corner until he had chipped a piece off. A tiny diamond. Later, he would feel sick with guilt and when his mother came to say goodnight, he would hold onto her for the longest time, pressing his face into her dress, breathing in her scent, wanting to say sorry but not able to let it out. 'What is it?' she would say. 'Oh Luke, it's all right.'

He already knows the guilt he will feel later, when he comes in so late Sarah will have moved from anger to sadness, but he can't help himself. He couldn't help himself with Kate last night, either.

A man comes in to take a piss. He stands at a urinal and then turns to the sinks, stands next to Luke and gives his hands a quick flick under the tap. He looks young, about the same age Luke was when he first joined this club. Luke notices he has a signet ring on his little finger, a plain gold one.

'It's my brother's birthday today,' Luke says. The euphoria of the hit is already levelling out and he could do with another.

The man gives a nod in the direction of the mirror.

'Do you have any?' Luke says, waving the empty packet at him.

The man laughs, shakes his head and leaves, the door swinging slowly shut. Luke dabs the remnants with a wet finger and rubs it into his gums, screws the paper into a bullet and aims it at a urinal.

Back in the bar, Luke orders a double and has a look around. The woman he saw before is still at one of the tables. He picks up his glass and walks over.

'Looks like we're both on our own,' he says. 'Shall we be alone together?'

She smiles. 'I'm waiting for a friend but she's always late.' She squints at her watch. 'I'm giving her half an hour.'

'Can I get you another drink?' he says. 'A dry white, is it?'

'My friend should be here any minute.'

'I'll get one for her too, that's not a problem.' He smiles, but she doesn't seem happy, although he caught her looking at him in a way that tells him she is definitely interested. Sometimes they just need an extra push.

'Thanks, but it's okay,' she says. 'We have some business to discuss.'

'At least let me get you a drink. I'll keep you company until she gets here.'

220

She gives her watch another cursory glance and he can see she is thinking about it. As he goes to walk away, she says, 'Okay, why not. Thank you.'

With a fresh round of drinks, Luke pulls out the chair next to her. She is wearing a dress with three-quarter length sleeves and as she reaches for her drink, he can see the delicate network of veins inside her wrist. She looks at him, is about to say something but stops herself. He can tell she wants him to take the lead.

He says, 'So what business are you in? They're lucky to have someone so dedicated to be working this late at the weekend.'

Her face brightens and she gives a little self-conscious laugh. 'I wish I *was* working for someone. We're trying to set up our own business – an online shop selling beach towels. It's impossible to find anyone willing to invest.'

He frowns, making an effort to appear that he is thinking.

'I know people,' he says.

She stares at him. 'Do you?'

'I run a hedge fund. I know a lot of people.'

Her phone vibrates on the table.

'Hold on,' she says, picking it up. She looks at him as she talks. 'Oh,' she says, 'really? I'm here waiting.' Her forehead creases into a frown. 'Well . . . Okay. Yes, Okay.'

She finishes the call and drops her phone into her bag. 'My friend can't come now,' she huffs. 'But she's been speaking to someone who wants to meet us next week. That's a good sign, isn't it?'

Luke nods. 'If you don't have any luck, I can put some people your way. In fact, I might be interested myself. If you have a business plan, I can take a look.'

She smiles, although he can tell she is sceptical.

'I'm Luke, by the way,' he says, and offers his hand.

She is soft and warm. 'Gemma,' she says, looking pleased all of a sudden. Sometimes, all it needs is a moment of skin-to-skin connection.

After more drinks and another trip to the gents, where he manages to acquire some coke and a couple of pills, he has that buzzing out-of-body feeling.

'Another one?' he says. She doesn't drink very quickly.

Gemma shakes her head. 'Thanks, but I really need to go.'

'Back to yours?'

'You are funny.'

Both his jaw and his leg feel as if they are hammering in opposite directions, and he isn't sure whether to hold his leg or his face. He runs the back of his hand across his mouth, almost expects to see blood dripping from his nose, but it is clear.

'Are you okay?' she asks.

'What?'

'I said are you okay?'

'Where are we going, then? The night is still young.'

She laughs. 'I'm going home, but thanks for the advice. I might take you up on your offer if we don't have any luck with this other guy.'

The bar is quite busy now and he shoulders his way through the crowd to follow her. The ground feels slanted. And then, he isn't sure how, he's on the floor. He's at the bottom of the stairs in a crumpled heap and Gemma is standing over him, as if he's had a heart attack.

'Oh shit!' she is saying. 'Are you all right?'

He tries to tell her he is fine, but his words don't seem to be coming out properly. The floor is gritty, like someone's spilt something and the edge of the first step of the stairs has one of those metal strips running across it, like a train track. He pushes himself up to stand and she's next to him, grabbing his arm. 'Let me help you,' she says. 'Are you okay?'

She's like a fucking parrot. He wants to tell her to get off, to leave him alone, but he also wants to be with her. He feels himself sway and grips the bannister rail. If he could just have another little bump, he'll be fine. Or a drink. Yes, that's what he needs, another drink. He struggles to place his foot on the step – bloody filthy stairs – and slips, falls again, hitting the ground.

'I'll get someone, stay there,' she says. 'Just stay there.' And she goes.

He lies there for a while until he feels able to push himself up. Gemma is there, already has his arm. She is surprisingly strong. He reaches into his pocket, is sure he had something left. Just a quick one and he'll be sorted. A quick sniff and he'll be as sober as a—

Another hand is holding his other arm, and Luke looks up to see the man he'd met in the gents earlier.

'Hey. Where did you come from?'

The man doesn't reply.

'It's my brother's birthday today,' Luke says. 'Happy birthday,' he shouts and his voice echoes in the stairwell.

'Let's get him in a taxi, quick,' Gemma says. 'Thanks so much for helping. I couldn't just leave him, and he doesn't seem to be with anyone.'

'I can hear you,' Luke says. 'And I'm okay, I can walk myself. I'm absolutely fine.'

They are outside, and the man is flagging a black cab.

'Make sure you take him straight home,' Gemma says to the driver.

Luke is inside the cab now, sitting down. Gemma holds the door open and leans in. 'What's your address? The driver needs your address.'

'Britten Street,' he says.

'What number?'

'Britten Street. Just take me there.'

The door slams and Gemma and the man are gone.

A bright pink china flamingo sits on the table next to an art deco lamp. Gilt frames with black-and-white photos on the wall. There is one of a man on a bench, arms folded, his legs stretched out, wearing muddy wellington boots. There is another one with a girl staring up at a lost balloon. The balloon is red. He has been here so many times before but never noticed these pictures on the wall. This is a home, where there are pictures on the wall, a lamp on the table.

Eloise appears at the doorway of her bedroom.

'You're late,' she says. 'I was expecting you a while ago. You're lucky I'm still free.'

He goes into the bedroom and takes off his jacket. The room is moving in and out. His shoulder hurts. He isn't sure what those pills were, but Eloise's head is alive, covered in a mass of coloured fireflies. They turn her head into geometric pixels, like she's been sucked into a computer game.

His clothes are off, and he is crawling on the bed. The covers smell clean, like the sheets when he was a boy. Eloise is lying next to him and touches his penis. He wants to curl up in these sheets, have her curl up behind him.

'You're too wasted tonight,' she says. 'If you're going to stay for a while, you'll still have to pay.'

'Take whatever you want. I don't care,' he says.

Her mouth is on his and he kisses her.

'Sshh,' she says. 'You relax.'

'It's Seb's birthday today,' he says. 'His birthday . . .'

She kisses him and he feels tears on her wet lips, can taste salt. Then he realises they are his tears. She reaches down to touch him again, but he pulls his knees in, makes his body into a ball. He is cold. He sobs into the pillow, can't stop these racking sobs. I'm disgusting, he thinks, or is he saying it aloud? I will never be forgiven.

The shivering won't stop, as if his whole body is in ice. She pulls him to her, and he puts his head on her chest.

'It's okay,' she says. 'Everything's going to be okay.'

27

At least Daniel started the day with good news. The client he has been priming for weeks has finally made an investment and he now has his very first commission. The fund director phoned and said he liked his approach, hinted at the possibility of something permanent. After the call ended, Daniel actually punched the air, like a schoolboy. Nobody thought he had it in him, not even Kate. He decided he would buy a bottle of champagne, properly celebrate later, once she was home. Yes! The relief was overwhelming. They were saved. He would take her out, surprise her with dinner. She would kiss him and say how sorry she was for being so distant, for their arguments, for the way she has been blaming him. He would say none of it mattered. She wouldn't ever need know how stupid he had been to think they were broken.

But that was an hour ago.

That was before.

Now, he's trying to process the email he has just found.

He looks out of the dining room window. A shuffling figure goes past, the woman from a few doors down – not Mrs Thompson with her dog, but Mrs Davies from number twenty-seven, pulling one of those old-lady bags on wheels. Her husband died last year, and people said she'd never be able to manage, that she would sell up and move near her daughter in Wales. Kate told him once that the woman's husband had been domineering. An old-fashioned marriage, where he controlled their finances, controlled everything. Kate said she even had to ask his permission to visit her own mother. 'How on earth do you know that?' he said. 'People talk,' she said. Who are these people, he wonders? And what do they say about him and Kate?

The irony is, he was going to delete the software, stop the spying nonsense. It was neurotic, unhelpful, and he hadn't found anything, anyway. He logged on to have one last check, to give himself a kind of final assurance. The window came up with a list of activity alerts as usual. There it was. An email addressed to Luke.

He gets up from the table and goes to the understairs cupboard. It's as if he's planned this day, already knows exactly what he needs to do. The suitcase is beneath black sacks of musty clothes, boxes of junk. He pulls it out and takes it upstairs, lays it on the bed, yanks his drawers open. He cannot think what he might need, cannot think at all. He empties a couple of drawers into the case, takes a few shirts off their hangers, chucks them in and presses down on the lid, zips it shut.

And then he is front of his parents' house. He doesn't want them to know he is there just yet, and parks up alongside the kerb, a little way down the road, in front of the green hedge-wall of their neighbour's house.

He looks in the rear-view mirror. His suitcase sits like a child on the back seat. He looks at his hands on the steering wheel. They don't feel like his hands. The sun is warm through the glass. A van drives past and makes the car shudder. He knows he needs to take the next step, but he can't. It's as if he has been punctured.

When another vehicle goes by, he forces himself to move. He leaves the suitcase and goes up to the house, presses the doorbell.

'What a surprise,' his dad says as he opens the door.

Daniel remains on the path. Surely his dad can see what has happened. He won't need to say the words aloud, will he?

'Where are the girls? Is Kate with you?'

'They're at school, Dad. It's Monday. I just needed to come over. I just—'

'Of course, it's Monday! Days tend to merge when you're retired,' he laughs.

Daniel steps over the threshold and follows his dad into the kitchen. His body feels lumbering, clumsy, like he isn't in control of his movements. He sits at the table, opposite his dad, who pushes a pile of catalogues to one side, and moves a box filled with different bags of seeds. His dad laughs, says he never thought he'd be the sort of man to get excited about a delivery of seeds.

'Mum not here?' Daniel says.

'She's at her friend's. Sorting out some charity thing later in the month. She's busier now than ever.' He flaps his hand in the air and laughs again.

Daniel has never noticed before how much he laughs.

'I'll make us a tea . . . or would you like a coffee?' His dad gets up and goes across to the kitchen.

'Tea's fine,' Daniel says, and he wonders if he should get up too. Sitting is difficult, like he might come apart if he remains still for too long.

'Biscuits?' his dad shouts above the noise of the kettle.

'No, I'm fine. Thanks.'

The kettle boils and two mugs of tea appear on the table. His dad sits down and sighs with contentment. 'Not working today, then?' he says. 'I guess doing this commission thingy you can pick and choose your hours. How's it going?' He winces as he sips his too-hot tea.

Daniel tells him the good news, and how there might be the promise of something more permanent. He finds himself explaining his decision to take up the offer, that he never thought he would enjoy it in sales but thinks he can make a real go of it.

'The money's so much better,' he says. 'I might even be able to afford Maisie's fees next year.'

It really is the best news, but his insides don't match what he is saying and his dad eyes him suspiciously.

'That's great,' his dad says. 'I knew everything would work out.' Then he goes on to tell Daniel about the treatment he gave the lawn last week, how he's determined to get it looking good this year.

Daniel nods, all the while battling a strange out-of-body sensation. He looks at his keys on the table. Such a bad idea, coming here, when all he needs is to be somewhere quiet, where nobody knows him, where he won't have to talk or answer any questions. Where he can sleep. That's all he needs, sleep. He feels so tired, yet his thoughts are racing ten-to-the-dozen, and he keeps conjuring the image of Kate, her back turned from him, someone's fingers tracing down her back. Only this time, it's Luke's fingers – how had he not known that before? – moving down her back and making her moan.

'I've got to . . . I'll be back in a minute.' He gets up

from the chair. 'No – I must go. I need to . . .' He sits back down. What the hell is he doing?

'Daniel, what is it?' his dad says, and then says something else. All Daniel can hear is a jumble of sounds.

'Daniel?'

He studies the edge of the table where he can see a splotch of furniture wax which his mum must have missed. He tries to squash it in, but it is hard and dry.

'I've left,' he says.

'Left? What do you mean?'

'I need to stay with you and Mum for a while. My suitcase is in the car.'

He stands and grabs his keys, goes to leave. His dad stands too, follows him.

Daniel has a strange choke in his throat, like the time their dog died, and he found him in his basket one morning, floppy, as if his bones had dissolved. There was the immediate need to cry, but it wouldn't come out right. It was more like laughter.

His dad is next to him now. 'What's going on, son?'

'Kate's having an affair.'

'An affair. What do you mean? Who with?'

Questions, questions. He can't cope with the questions. The questions make the images come back, the finger tracing down her back . . . Luke. He shakes his head.

'I don't want to go into it. Just someone we know.'

'Are you sure?'

'Yes.'

'Well, you can't just up and leave. Come and sit back down. Let's talk it through. What about the girls, the house? I've heard stories about men who just leave – they lose everything. Have you spoken to Kate? How serious is this?'

230

His dad stands there in his neatly ironed shirt, his chinos with the crease down the front. His seed catalogues. His nice lawn. Everything is in a simple neat box for his dad, and that's exactly how Daniel used to think his life would be. And he wants to explain that he's tried so hard for everything to be right. He never expected to have a single regret – no point in regretting something that's already happened, right? But how can he move on from this? How can he have no regrets when the two people he trusted most in the world – 'I just need to think,' he says.

'You can't drop everything like that. All marriages go through bad patches.'

'She's been seeing someone else, for God's sake!'

He should have checked himself into a hotel. He leaves his dad standing there and goes into the hall. Sunlight streams through the fanlights and throws a lattice cage across the floor. Who is he? Even his parents' house is a strange place.

'Daniel?' His dad comes and puts a hand on his shoulder. 'It'll be okay, we can talk it through, son.'

'I don't want to talk about it,' he shouts. He is too embarrassed to turn around.

'Come on,' his dad says.

He steers Daniel back to the table, where he collapses onto a chair. He is depleted, the adrenaline replaced now by a saturating heaviness.

His dad makes more tea. He always makes tea when there is anything wrong. Like the time Daniel had been rejected for a summer internship he had wanted, and then that same summer, he lost his deposit on his student house. It wasn't what his dad had said in those moments, it was the fact that he was there, like being bolstered by an invisible army.

But it doesn't feel like that now.

The kitchen is filled with the burble of the kettle, the clatter of a spoon on the worktop, the pfft of the cork lid from the jar with TEA written across the front. Usually a comfort, these sounds.

'Your mum and me went through a bad patch once,' his dad says, setting the mugs down. He sits and has a momentary faraway look before snapping himself back. 'Well, more like a whole ruddy field!' He gives one of his laughs.

Daniel sighs.

'It's hard, I know,' his dad says with more of a sombre tone. 'You have to keep reminding yourself why. This is just a reminder, that's all.'

'I don't need reminding of anything. She's the one who's done this. They both have.'

His dad frowns. 'It's not that simple. You can't run away—'

'I'm not running away.' It's like they're on opposing sides. 'I shouldn't have come,' he says.

'I do understand what you're going through, you know.' His dad leans over the table. 'So, here's what you're going to do. You're going to come out into the garden and help me with the rest of the seedlings. Then you'll go home and unpack that suitcase before Kate finds out. And you'll wake up tomorrow and keep going. And you'll keep on going until it's okay. I can tell you a few things about how to keep a marriage . . .'

Daniel cannot listen any longer. He swallows his tea. Stares at the keys on the table. His girls bought him that keyring for Father's Day one year – a silver letter D: Daniel and Daddy. As he looks at it, he doesn't think of the girls, or even Kate. He thinks of Luke. How could he? It is the worst kind of betrayal.

When Luke's parents died, they were in their second year at university. Luke was a mess for several months, missing lectures, drinking, doing too much coke. Daniel had been the one to prop him up. He had given Luke his lecture notes, had even written essays for him. He had stayed up late, listening to Luke ramble on about things that never made sense. But Daniel had listened anyway and said supportive things. Luke once said he thought of him like a brother. On Daniel's stag night, when Daniel had admitted how nervous he was about getting married, Luke had grabbed him by the shoulders. 'What you and Kate have,' he had said, giving him a shake, 'you two are fucking sorted. You've got it all.'

His mug is empty, and his dad is still talking.

'. . . and that'll be the end of it, and one day, it'll be like nothing has changed and then you'll realise what it's really been about.'

His dad claps his hands together. 'Right,' he says, with finality. 'You ready?' He stands, brushing his trousers, smiling as if he's just completed a satisfying task.

Back at home, he does what his dad told him to do. His clothes are back in his wardrobe and drawers as if nothing had happened. In half an hour, he will leave to collect the girls from school as usual. Then Kate will be home. They will have dinner.

He needs to decide what he is going to say when she is there in front of him. He has two options – he could confront her, let it all come crashing down, or he could say nothing. His dad's voice is in his head. But there is another voice telling him to stop being such a weak fool, to tell Kate it is over. But what if he walks away and ruins them for good; what if, in years to come, he will look back and realise how it could have been saved? What if his dad is right?

He hadn't wanted to tell his dad about the email, but in the end, it just came out. They had gone into the garden. As they walked towards the greenhouse, his dad told him about the different fertiliser he was using on the lawn, how it was already making a big difference to the quality of growth. The air warmed and cooled each time the sun moved between the banks of clouds. In the greenhouse, his dad took a tray of seedlings and handed them to Daniel.

'We need to plant these in that space next to the courgettes.'

And for some reason this made Daniel angry. His dad, obsessing over his lawn, handing him pots like nothing out of the ordinary had just happened. He couldn't stand it. So, he put the tray of pots on the side and came out with it, told him about the email he had found.

His dad nodded, patted him on the shoulder. Daniel nodded in reciprocation. *Now you understand. Now you see.* And he expected he would go and get his case, unpack his things in his old room. Discuss the best solicitor. But his dad said he was making something out of nothing. 'Was that all you found? Just that?' he said. He waffled on about women and hormones and menopause and the last rush before the slow. How all marriages go through it. He told him to put it out of his mind, focus on his job, not make any hasty decisions.

In the bedroom, Daniel closes the lid on the empty suitcase and zips it closed, takes it downstairs and puts it away in the cupboard. He cannot account for the way his dad thinks, cannot understand why he gave such thoughtless advice. Who would tell a man to go back to a woman who's done what Kate has done? How can his dad think he can carry on after that?

From the kitchen, the sound of his mobile rings out. He closes the cupboard and reaches his phone before it rings off.

'Hello?' he says, although he knows who it is. He rang Sarah half an hour ago.

'Hello, Daniel? I saw your missed calls. Is everything all right?'

Sarah sounds impatient, almost annoyed that she is having to speak to him.

'Yes, sorry. I needed to talk to you about something. Have you got a minute? Something private.'

'Oh,' she says. 'Yes okay.'

He can hear the sound of muffled voices in the background, getting louder and then fading away. A door closing.

'I've got two minutes.' Her voice echoes as if she is standing in a stairwell. He imagines her there, in her office building, leaning against a cold concrete wall.

'I'm not sure where to start,' he says.

'What's happened?'

'I found an email.'

'An email? I don't understand.'

'She said they—'

He pauses and realises he can't say it like this, not over the phone.

'Look, can we meet? I can come tomorrow, meet you for lunch, for a coffee.'

'Of course. But I don't understand? You've got me worried now.'

'I'll explain everything tomorrow. One o'clock? You're just down from Holborn tube, aren't you?'

'Yes, there's a pub opposite my office that's good for lunch. I'll meet you there.'

'Okay,' he says. 'See you tomorrow.'

He hangs up and puts the phone back on charge before taking a breath. He will tell Sarah first, before he speaks to Kate. It will be dealt with carefully and calmly, he decides, without any need for hysterics. He presses his hand firmly against his chest and then goes upstairs to put the rest of his things away.

28

Sarah has decided to quit her job. Last night she barely slept, listening to Luke's huffing snores, like he was responding to her every thought. It suddenly seemed so obvious. She has been so very unhappy. Luke will be better when she is happy.

She swallows the rest of her tea and puts the empty mug in the sink. The taxi should be here any minute and she checks for it out of the window. The faint drone of Magda's hoovering resumes.

When she spoke to her mum on the phone the other day, she almost changed her mind. She shouldn't have called, because her mum is the last person she should talk to about her career. But at the time, she just needed to hear her voice. She wanted reassurance.

'So, I thought I could do some courses. Maybe train to be an interior designer.'

'I never wanted to say anything,' her mum said after a short pause. 'But it always surprised me when you announced what you were going to do. You were always so good at history. You'd have made a good teacher. It's worried me, seeing you so stressed about your work. I said to myself that one day you'd end up snapping under the pressure of it all.'

What rubbish. Her mum hasn't got a clue what her job entails, how good she is at it. Always trying to make her feel incapable. Always going on about her inability to cope, as if she actually wants her to crumble. Was that it? Did she want Sarah to fail, to make her feel better about her own life?

Her mum continued, saying how much better Sarah would feel once she didn't have to cope with all the stress and pressure of it, and London – she said London like it was an unobtainable prize – was all so very cut-throat. Her brothers were so much better at all of that. They were the businessmen of the family. It wasn't a failure to admit that you weren't very good at something. Sarah should be glad she's in a position to stop working – she should have done it years ago.

Sarah came away from the call feeling furious. She would damn well get a creative director job, keep going. She would be so much more successful than her brothers. That would show them.

Then she took a breath.

She realised that it wouldn't matter if she became prime minister – her mum would still find a way to make her feel that she was useless. The real problem was her mum was dissatisfied with her own life. It was such a simple thought, yet it brought such a revelation. She knew then what she had to do.

Her mobile rings in her bag.

'Hello?'

'Is that Mrs Linton?' a man's voice says.

'Yes.'

'I should be with you in about thirty minutes,' he says. 'There's a hold-up on Vauxhall Bridge but the office says I'm still the nearest one to you.'

'I need to be there for one,' she says and looks at her watch.

'Nothing I can do, love,' he says. 'The roads are solid.'

She tells the man okay and ends the call, dials Daniel's number.

'Hello, Daniel?'

'Yes.'

'My taxi's been delayed. I'm sorry, can we make it half-past one?'

'You're getting a taxi?'

'Yes, I've got the day off.'

'Oh,' and then, 'we could meet somewhere else if that's easier. Or I could come to you. I'm at Waterloo, about to get the tube.'

'No, we'll meet where we said. I'll see you soon.'

She puts her phone down on the side. It feels good to make firm decisions. Everything is clearing, like coming out of a fog. Even lunch with Daniel feels like she is finding clarity. He called her out of the blue yesterday, clearly in a state. The poor man is obviously too embarrassed to ask Luke for the money he needs. She has already decided to help. *Will five thousand cover it?* Hell, she might even give it as a gift instead of a loan.

While she waits for the taxi, she calls Luke.

'I'm off out in a minute. Just wanted to check you were okay.'

'Everything's fine,' he says.

She tells him she's having lunch with Daniel, although there is no need for him to know about Daniel's predicament. Luke needs to focus on his recovery. She reminds him to come straight home.

'I'll get some Epsom salts,' she says. 'I read they're good for detoxing, and you can put them in a bath later.'

'Okay,' he says.

He is monosyllabic but she doesn't care. She is stronger now she's the one leading. They say goodbye.

Saturday night was the turning point. He came home in the early hours, drunk and rambling, his eyes like saucers. At first, it brought the usual panic, the anger she was too afraid to show, that always turned to a hollowed-out feeling. But something happened. It was like seeing the hidden images in an illusion. She saw him differently. He needed her and she needed to be different.

When he woke the next morning, she told him to stay in bed. She made him soup. When his mobile rang, she took it away. It felt good to be unafraid.

She sees Daniel at a table on the far side of the pub and waves. He waves back and she makes her way over to him, weaving through the tables. It is busy today.

They hug. He looks flushed and nervous. He keeps rubbing at his cheek with his hand. She takes off her jacket and shuffles along the velveteen banquette. He sits opposite. There's a jug of water on the table and he pours some into her glass. For a few seconds they sit in silence and then both talk at the same time.

'They do good burgers,' she begins, at the same time he says, 'Thanks for agreeing to meet.'

'Sorry. You first,' he says.

'I was just saying about the burgers,' she says. 'People from the office come here and say how good they are. And the steak sandwich.'

'Yeah, I've decided on that. Shall I go and order?'

'Let me get this. I'll go.'

She starts to shuffle out, moving her bag and jacket out of the way, but he is already standing. There is further awkwardness as they both insist upon paying, until she gives in and tells him she'll have the feta cheese salad and a glass of white wine, thank you.

When he returns with their drinks, he seems more relaxed. But as they talk, Sarah notices that she is the one who keeps asking questions. The conversation is stilted, like they are marking time. It is irritating how he is dragging it out, but she can't be the one to bring it up.

'How're Kate and the girls?' she says.

He seems to flinch. 'Yes, okay. How's your dad?'

'Much better, yes.'

Daniel's mouth moves as if to approximate a smile. She looks away and notices the couple at the table to her left, who are laughing and talking in a way that suggests they haven't seen each other for a while. She turns back to the table.

'I spoke to Elaine. Did I tell you? No, maybe that was after you visited. So, I called her again this morning and she's going to meet Dad for lunch. I'll be there as well, of course.'

'Elaine? You'll have to remind me . . .'

'You know, Dad's old secretary.'

'Oh yes. I don't understand, why would you—'

'Well, my dad said he stayed for me, and my mum probably thinks she has to stick it out. I can't bear to see them

241

like that any more. They don't love each other one bit.'

Daniel forces his mouth into a strange upside-down smile. She isn't sure why she is saying any of this to him, is annoyed with herself for even bringing it up. She sits back and folds her arms, looks out of the window, although there is nothing to see except the side wall of a building across the road.

'So, what's this all about?' she says. 'I'm all ears.' She unfolds her arms. It will be hard for him to ask for help.

He clears his throat, looks in his lap. 'I'm not sure where to start.'

He puts his hand on the table. His finger traces an imaginary square, across and down, across and up.

'You see, I should have done something when I knew things weren't right. It's like you were just saying, about your mum and dad, about them not admitting anything was wrong. I haven't been able to admit what's been going on.'

He sighs and seems annoyed by his fingers sketching of their own accord, snatches his hand off the table and drinks his beer in several frantic gulps. Foam remains on his lip, and he wipes it away with the back of his hand.

'I'm not sure I understand,' she says.

He reaches into his pocket and pulls out a folded piece of paper.

'I think it's best you read this.' He holds it out, watches intently as she unfolds it.

She sees Luke's email address, Kate's. She reads it twice over and puts the piece of paper down on the table. The creases mean that it won't lie flat, so she folds it back up and puts her hand over it. She feels surprisingly calm.

'When did you find out?'

242

'Yesterday. I packed a suitcase, went to my parents, but my dad told me I was overreacting, that everyone goes through this. It's what happens. We're at that age.'

'At that age,' she echoes.

'I've thought for a while . . . but I didn't imagine.'

'Are there other emails, other messages?'

'I don't know,' he says. 'I really don't know.'

Outside, it is raining. Large drops stick to the window, blurring the view across the street. She keeps her hand pressed over the paper.

A man in a white shirt and black jeans brings their meals. She looks down at the bowl in front of her. Sharp spikes of rocket, large chunks of sweating cheese.

'I can't eat this,' she says to Daniel, once the man has gone.

All she can think about is the last time she saw Kate and how they'd sat opposite one another, smiling. Kate had stuffed a profiterole in her mouth. And then she remembers how she and Luke had curled up together on the sofa, after Kate and Dan had gone home. She had felt so guilty about how she had been avoiding sex, was so worried about losing him, that she forced herself to give him a blow job.

She feels sick.

Daniel passes her a wrapped knife and fork. 'Sorry,' he says, as if he is the one who has been found out.

'I really can't,' she says, putting the cutlery down. Tears appear and she blots them with the heel of her hand. Daniel stares into his lap. Why is he just sitting there? She pushes her bowl into the middle of the table.

'What has Kate said about this?' She flicks her hand at the folded piece of paper.

243

'I haven't spoken to her yet.'

'What? Why not? You found it yesterday and you still haven't spoken to her. What's the matter with you?'

'I wanted to speak to you first. I wanted—' He pulls at his collar, rubs his neck. 'Look, I just want to make sure I handle this the right way.'

'The right way!'

She snatches up the folded paper, puts it in her bag, starts shuffling out, dragging her jacket and bag behind her.

'I have to go,' she says.

'Oh.' He looks genuinely shocked. 'I thought . . .' He looks like a lost boy.

She could tell him what she has been going through – the drinking, the drugs, the porn. The nights Luke goes out, the nights when she is left wondering if he'll ever come back. She can feel her anger splintering into despair.

'I can't,' she says.

He blinks at her.

She balances her bag on her lap while she fumbles with her jacket, constricted between the stupid seat and the stupid table. Everything blurs as the tears come and she rushes out of the pub, banging her hip as she slaloms between the tables.

29

The rain hits the window like hail, making Luke look up from his desk. He's been staring at the same figures for the past forty-five minutes. Time is purposefully slow. It's day three of being sober and it's like wading through treacle. A whole hour before he can leave and he's only got a couple of Happy Cherry sweets left. He puts them both in his mouth, licks his finger and wipes it around the inside of the packet. The sugar gives minor relief. He needs more. The feeling is excruciating. More more more. And orange juice. Lots of orange juice.

His mobile buzzes against the desk. He had put it on silent, but he picks it up.

'Yes,' he says.

'I'm off out in a minute but I just wanted to check you were okay.' It's Sarah. Her voice is so happy, so bright. Like the ting of crystal.

'I'm fine.'

She goes on about Epsom salts and that she's going to have lunch with Daniel. Why is she meeting his friend? He doesn't care, tries to end the call as quickly as possible. Doesn't she know how he is feeling?

He puts his mobile back down and rests his head on the desk. Of course, her understanding, her generosity, it is appreciated. And it was quite the surprise. At the weekend, when she confronted him about the drinking and the drugs, he thought it was the end. But she put him back to bed, made him soup. The comedown was bad, and she nursed him like he had the flu. She wasn't upset in the way he expected. She has been different these past few days. He just can't decide if it is a good or bad thing.

The desk phone rings, loud as a fire alarm. Geoff says he wants to see him in his office, please. Please! The old bastard never says please, although he delivers his request in a way that means *now*. Luke says, 'Of course,' and puts the phone down. He knows Geoff's game. He could go and see him now, but he's not so out of it that he'll be spoken to that way. The first sign of weakness – letting people push you down. It's a constant battle.

After twenty minutes or so, he gets up and drags himself across the main office. Tom is quiet as he passes. Nobody looks up. Keyboards click. In Geoff's office, Luke leaves the door open, but Geoff gestures for it to be closed.

'Have a seat,' he says. All very formal.

Geoff is behind his desk, glasses perched halfway down his nose. He looks over them as Luke sits in the chair facing him.

'What's up?' Luke says.

'I'll get straight to the point.' Geoff removes his glasses, folds them slowly and puts them down, as if he's stalling for time, or more likely, creating dramatic effect. He does like to feel important.

'If this is about the bio-tech. Yeah, it was a gamble, but—'

'It's not about that.'

Luke's head is hammering.

'I think you need to take some extended leave.' Geoff looks away and inhales before turning back. 'You need to sort yourself out.'

Luke notices the perfect alignment of Geoff's pen on the desk. Papers in a pile at the side, everything in a precise line.

'I've already spoken to Tom. He knows your client list, already deals with some of them.'

Luke springs from the chair. His palms are sticky as he presses them flat onto the desk.

'Sit down, Luke.' Geoff sighs and gets up from his chair, goes to the window and stands looking out with his arms folded. 'I've had Stephen draw up the paperwork. Spend some time with that lovely wife of yours. Take the kids on holiday. Talk to a professional, someone who can help.'

'I don't know what the fuck you're talking about.'

Geoff turns back around and sighs again. 'Let me be clear. You have no other option.'

Luke makes a lunge for the desk. He could take the old bastard by the neck, choke that look off his face. Instead, he pushes the pile of paperwork onto the floor and grabs Geoff's pen. Once it is in his hand, he isn't entirely sure what to do. There's a screaming pain in his head. Little flashes of light he has to keep blinking away. He throws the pen with force, aiming at the window, just missing Geoff's head. It taps against the thick glass and falls to the carpet.

'Security?' Geoff is on the phone. 'Yes, floor seven. Can you—'

247

Luke holds up his hands. 'Okay, okay. I'll go,' he says. 'There's no need for that.'

Geoff pauses, the phone still held against his ear. 'No. It's fine. Just a misunderstanding. Thank you.' He hangs up.

Luke goes back into the main office. Talking into phones, typing, the printer churning out paper, everything so loud and obtrusive. In his own office, he grabs his jacket and shoves his laptop and mobile into his bag. He leaves the empty packet of Happy Cherries on the desk.

Outside, he walks without thought of where he is going. It strikes him that Geoff has always wanted to get rid of him. He only used him to get the fund up and running. Geoff's a dictator, not a collaborator, cannot cope with even the slightest deviation from what he thinks is right, no vision whatsoever. The fund will collapse without him, but by then he will have already sold his stock and Geoff will be left with nothing. Yes, that's what he's going to do. He's going to sell his stock to someone who will bring them ruin, then they'll all be sorry.

He sticks his hand out for a taxi.

'Britten Street, SW3.' The driver nods, and Luke gets in.

As the taxi heads towards Hyde Park Corner, he decides that if Eloise isn't in, he'll go to the club and find someone else. He sends Eloise a message and lets his phone fall into his lap, rests his head back, although he can't relax. His leg jiggles up and down.

When he gets to Britten Street, Eloise buzzes him up. 'You caught me just in time,' she says. 'I was on my way out.'

He follows her into the bedroom. A pair of jeans, inside

248

out, are on the floor, a T-shirt on the bed. She hurriedly picks them up and throws them into the wardrobe. She takes a small bottle from a drawer and holds it up.

He nods. 'Yeah, perfect.'

'I've got a bit of coke as well. Probably half a gram. You can have them both for an extra hundred.'

He takes the twenties from his wallet.

She shuffles them between her hands, counting them out like a child, the notes scraping against each other.

'I said a hundred.'

'That's all I have with me. I'll give it to you next time.' He doesn't smile, doesn't feel like smiling.

'You're in a funny mood today.' She hands him the bottle and the packet.

'I need you to work your magic,' he says, sitting down on the bed. He considers having the line first but puts the packet in his pocket and opens the bottle. The first sniff gives an instant hit, a euphoric rush to his head.

'Fucking perfect,' he says.

She has already unbuckled his trousers, her mouth already on him, her tongue. She continues while he lies back, enjoying the contrasting sensations in his cock, in his head. Back and forth, taking a sniff then letting the rush settle, trying to keep himself at a continual high.

He grows bored and gets her to lie down. He takes off the rest of his clothes and tells her to take off her kimono. She looks perfect, expectant, willing to please. He grabs one of her breasts, squeezes until she winces, but she doesn't tell him to stop. She would never do that. She wants him to be happy.

Still feeling her breast, he uses his other hand to slide his fingers inside. He jabs and presses until she gets really wet. Such a powerful release, this feeling. So powerful, he could crush her in his hands.

'Careful,' she says. 'You're eager today.'

He takes his fingers out and makes her lick them clean, then kneels over her.

'Hold on,' she says, and she moves away, slithers up the bed and reaches into the jar on her bedside table. The condom is the same as usual, the thin ones that she always uses, but it makes him recoil. He throws it on the floor.

'I don't want this,' he says.

She frowns and goes to speak.

'I said, I don't fucking want it.'

He's fucking sick of following other people's rules. Fucking Geoff and his smug grin. Sarah and her expectations. He needs to clear his mind of it all.

When he is done, he collapses on the bed, breathless. She lies next to him, stroking the side of his face.

'Sorry,' he says. 'I'm so sorry.' He is back inside his body now, doesn't know where he went, doesn't know what he is apologising for.

'I've really got to go,' she says. 'You can have longer next time.'

She gets off the bed and puts on her kimono, wraps it tightly around her. He dresses quickly and makes his way down to the street. The light is searing as he heads towards the Kings Road. The cars whoosh past.

At home, there is television noise coming from the sitting room and he can hear Lucy's and Sarah's voices. He carries on upstairs, gets into bed, doesn't even bother to take off his shoes. He wants the roaring in his head to stop.

When he opens his eyes, Sarah is there at the side of the

bed. 'Luke,' she says. Her voice is far away and strange, like he's in a dream. 'What are you doing?'

He pulls his knees up to his chest. He cannot explain anything.

'Are you ill? What are you doing?'

I'm not well, he thinks he says, but he no longer has control over the words coming out of his mouth.

'I need to talk to you,' she says. 'You need to sit up.'

She pulls the duvet away.

'You're dressed. And your shoes. What are you doing?'

He sits up and lets his feet fall.

'Have you been taking something? You're a mess. Have you been drinking?'

He rubs his hands over his face. The pain in his head is crucifying.

'I've got the worst headache.'

She remains, staring, emotionless. He can see she is holding a piece of paper.

'How long has it been going on?' she says. She shakes the piece of paper in his face.

He slides off the bed onto the floor, tries to reach for her to sit with him. If he can hold her, she will calm down. Everything will be resolved if he can hold her. He has let things get out of hand, just needs to explain.

'Don't touch me,' she says.

An image of Seb's funeral. How they had all looked at him. Everyone already decided that he was the black sheep, that he was to blame. His mother had told him to sit at the end of the pew and he had reached out to her. She couldn't blame him for ever, surely? She must have known what Seb was like, what he did for all those years? But she had flicked her hand at him, like she was shooing a fly.

Sarah is waving the paper in front of his face again. 'How long has it been going on?' she says. 'That's all I need to know. Then you can pack your things and go.' The edge of the paper touches his nose. He turns his head, pushes it away. She isn't letting him explain anything.

'We can go away, somewhere new,' he says. 'Everything will be different.'

'You make me sick.' Her face is hardened. 'You need to leave now. I don't care where you go. Just leave.'

She throws the paper at him, and it glides like a paper aeroplane to the floor. He looks at it but can't register what he's seeing. He reaches into his pocket, sure that he has something. A Happy Cherry, that's what he needs. There is nothing in his pockets.

Sarah is still there.

'I'm sorry,' he says.

'I can't even look at you.' Her voice is cold, not even a quiver. She moves towards the door. 'I just want you to leave.'

And she is gone.

30

One Sunday afternoon, when Daniel was nine or ten, he watched *The Great Escape* with his dad. The curtains had been drawn, the volume on the telly turned up loud. Just like the cinema. They sat next to each other on the sofa and ate chocolate Hobnobs from a plate with red and gold flowers. Daniel loved Sunday films with his dad.

The Great Escape was the best – that's what his dad had said. But Daniel was fidgety and couldn't properly understand what was happening. There was a lot of talking, with men discussing things in serious voices. Before the film started, his dad had explained it was about the war, about some Allied soldiers who had been captured by Nazis and taken to a prisoner-of-war camp. *Shhh* his dad said, whenever he asked a question. *Just watch it now*. Daniel grabbed a few Hobnobs and slid onto the floor. He sat cross-legged and made mouse-sized bites, nibbling them slowly, one by one, spilling crumbs down his front. Every so often, he would check to see if his dad was still staring at the telly, then he'd lick the chocolate off his fingers and brush the crumbs from his jumper onto the carpet.

Then the music changed. One of the captured soldiers,

the one who wore a navy triangular hat, turned away from the main gathering. He walked in between the wooden huts, towards the fence. Trudging steps. He looked like he was in a trance, eyes fixed forward. At his side, he held the handle of a metal can. He stopped when he reached the low tripwire. The music quivered; everything was tense. He dropped his metal can with a clank. Daniel pulled his knees up to his chest.

The next few seconds was a rush of men. Nazis pointing their guns, a scuffle. The man in the triangle hat broke free and stepped over the wire, made it to the fence and started to climb. Before he reached the top, machine guns were fired from the tower. His back arched; his hat fell. The camera lingered on him. His limp body hung from one elbow. Then the picture cut to the rest of the men, who were being held back by the Nazis pointing guns. An American, the one who stood out from the others in a red top, bent down to pick up the fallen triangle hat and folded it in his hand. That man was called Virgil Hilts, the Cooler King. Daniel hugged his knees tight. His eyes didn't move from the screen until the credits rolled. He didn't even have another biscuit.

Afterwards, his dad got up and turned off the telly, said *What a corker of a film* and went into the kitchen. Daniel remained. He felt strange, a surge of something he hadn't felt before. It wasn't sadness – even though most of them got killed and Hilts got captured – it was something different, something more complicated.

'Can we watch it next week?' he asked, when he finally got up from the floor.

'Won't come on again for a while. Maybe next year,' his dad said.

Daniel lay in bed that night and replayed as much as he could remember, running through, scene by scene. All the way to the end, where he felt the weight of sadness that wasn't quite sadness. It squirmed around, those feelings he couldn't name.

He saved his pocket money, and for Christmas he bought the DVD for his dad from the section in HMV called Old Classics. Daniel watched it every weekend until he was told he may as well have it for himself. When his dad asked why he liked it so much, Daniel said he didn't know. But he did. Even though he could recite almost all of it, and knew exactly what would happen, he still put his hands to his face when it got to the bit where Hilts jumped his motorbike over the final fence. He watched that part through his fingers every time. Just one day, he believed that motorbike would make it over.

Daniel is in the front room, at the dining table. He isn't doing much, just sitting there. The girls are upstairs getting changed and he's already prepared dinner, bought a pasta sauce, cooked some mince, put the spaghetti in a saucepan ready for the water. It feels important to keep things simple, make everything run like clockwork, so he is able to get through the next few hours. His mind keeps racing, snatching at moments in time: when he was a boy, when he was at university, when he first met Luke, when he met Kate. The times when Kate had said how much fun Luke was, or how she knew how Luke felt after his parents died – *he had a complicated relationship with his parents, and I understand what that's like.*

It's as if he is searching for answers, trawling through the years, trying to pin an explanation onto something tangible – an actual event that will give him the answer. *Yes, that's it*, he wants to be able to say. *That's the exact moment.* It occurs to him that he has always tried to deny terrible things, as if his will alone could make things turn out differently. Perhaps he does stick his head in the sand. Sarah intimated as much, earlier, when he met her for lunch.

What a fool he has been.

The telephone rings and breaks his thoughts. The answerphone cuts in and he can hear Kate's voice telling the caller to please leave a message. Whoever it is, they hang up. He cannot face talking to anyone. All he can focus on now is what is about to happen. He reminds himself that there will be no need for drama. It will be important to remain calm. The facts will be stated, like he's in a courtroom. She won't be given the opportunity to talk, not until he has said what he needs to say.

He has imagined the scene in detail. He's going to wait until the girls are in bed and then go into the living room where she will be sitting in her chair, her hands folded in her lap. He will tell her that he knows everything. He will need to take charge once he's told her, tell her he's already spoken to a solicitor because he knows she will cause a scene. He will tell her that he also saw those messages she sent to another man on that website. He will tell her he knows about the email to Luke, the mention of a photo. His friend, for fuck's sake. His best friend.

Once Kate is home from work, Daniel keeps to his plan and says nothing. She looks tired and sad. *Good*, he thinks.

Over dinner, Flo chatters on, oblivious. Kate pokes her spaghetti with her fork. Maisie asks if Kate is okay.

256

'I had a big lunch,' Kate says and continues to prod. He cannot help staring, hates the way Kate is holding her fork, hunched over the table like she's trying to engender sympathy. He forces his eyes back to his plate. His pile of spaghetti doesn't seem to be getting any smaller and he struggles to force it down.

Flo finishes her last mouthful and Kate smiles at her.

'You've got sauce all round your mouth, monkey.'

Maisie gets up, says she's going to have a bath and Flo says it's her turn first. They go into the hall, bickering with each other, and he watches, keeps staring at the door even after they have gone. Their feet bang up the stairs and there are shrieks and squeals. Usually, Kate would be shouting after them, telling them to stop arguing, but today she is quiet. It's as if she knows what is coming. And he thinks of the girls' faces when he tells them – what will they say? Maisie will hate him, will blame him for sure.

He gets up and takes his plate over to the bin, scrapes the rest of his dinner away.

'Not hungry?' Kate says.

'Not really.'

Kate stands and brings her plate over.

'Do you mind clearing up,' she says. 'I'm going to bed. I don't feel well, and I've got a hellish day at the school tomorrow.'

'But it's not even seven,' he says.

She looks at him.

'I know about Luke,' he says quickly.

Kate half turns. Her eyes dart over the worktops, the cupboards, the bowl of fruit in the corner. Looking at everything but him.

'What do you mean?' she says.

257

'I know everything. The email, the photo.'
She looks down at the floor.
'I want a divorce,' he says.

31

Kate is on her way to give her usual Friday class at the university. She walks along Taviton Street, past the familiar Georgian terraces. Nothing is right, yet it looks the same – the neat railings, the windows, the glossy panelled front doors.

These past few days have been unbearable. She isn't sure how she is managing to continue as normal. In the mornings, she gets out of bed – the bed where Daniel has agreed to sleep until they can talk to the girls – and goes across the landing to the bathroom. Once she is dressed, she goes downstairs and takes the box of cornflakes from the cupboard, pours it into four bowls. She gives the box a shake to check how much is left – she can always ask Daniel to pick up another box. Only, she can't. She can't even look at him without a heavy stone in her stomach.

These past few days everything might have appeared the same, but the outside and the inside are two completely different places.

She runs her hand along the pointed arrow ends of the railing. She rarely allows herself to think about her mother but wonders now if this is how she felt when she was having a bad week, being fractured from the world. For the first time it comes to her: maybe her dad didn't do his disappearing act because her mum was having a bad week; maybe her mum was ill because her dad kept going off.

Kate pauses before she reaches the steps, stops alongside the raised flower bed. The brick is cool against her palm, slightly damp, although it hasn't rained. She takes her hand away and brushes it lightly against the side of her cardigan. She knows she is stalling but she needs just a few more minutes before she is ready to face her class; their eyes, their silent words. People are making her feel too much. Even the strangers on the train this morning made her catch her breath – the old lady asking if the seat was taken, the man checking tickets at the gate.

Daniel left an envelope in the kitchen this morning. He got up early, dressed in a suit, muttered something about a meeting. She wanted to ask if it was an interview, but by the time she went downstairs, he had gone. He sent her a text message:

Please read and sign the letter I left next to the kettle. It's in everyone's best interests.

Cold and formal. So, that was how it was going to be.

The letter was a printed-out separation agreement, with a space at the end for her signature. Daniel had already signed it. She ripped it up and put it in the bin.

In front of the university building, she leans on the edge of the wall. She has that same heavy, desolate feeling as the day she found out her mum had cut herself for the last time.

'Have a good Easter break,' a cheery voice says beside her.

'Oh yes,' she says, jumping to her feet.

She follows her colleague into the building.

When the class has finished, and she is gathering her papers together, Kate decides she will go to the nearby gardens and have a break before her final tutorials. Some air will do her good. The trees – she needs to be under the trees.

'What are the secondary texts?' Three students are standing in front of the small desk.

'I put them up at the end, on the final slide,' she says, pointing to the screen behind her. It isn't the slide with the essay questions and the list of books, but an image of the Maasai. The students exchange glances.

'I'll email it,' she says.

After the students have gone, she keeps staring at the image of the jumping Maasai men. Daniel is leaving her and there is nothing she can do. She imagines what he would do if she reached out to him. Would he put his arms around her? If she begged him to, would he stay?

She picks up her things and heads out. When she opens the door, she finds Sarah in front of her, waiting on the pavement.

'I called reception, they told me where to find you,' Sarah says. She looks pale and tired.

They face each other – Kate at the top of the steps, Sarah at the bottom.

'I was about to go to the garden,' Kate says. 'It's just along there . . .'

Sarah doesn't move. She shoves her hands into her pockets. Her raincoat is creased and unbuttoned, with the tie belt dangling at her sides. Her hair is flatter than usual, greasy-looking. She seems different, less polished. Less perfect. Kate doesn't move either and remains at the top of the steps.

'Can we talk?' Sarah says. Her face is hard, unreadable.

'I've got about an hour.'

Sarah nods and they walk in silence, with Sarah half a step behind. Kate feels the air against her face, hears the sound of a distant pneumatic drill. The silence and noise of it all.

'Virginia Woolf lived here,' Kate says as they go past a row of tall white houses, one with a blue circular plaque. She has a need to talk, to fill the silent gap. 'I've never read any of her books, have you? Always meant to, and I had a friend . . .'

Kate has to step back to allow a group of girls to pass. The girls talk quickly with animated hand gestures, smiles. They are Spanish perhaps, or Italian. It is comforting not understanding the words, just hearing the sounds.

Sarah is still silent as they go into the gardens. Kate finds an empty bench and they sit down, an arm's length between them. Kate puts her bag on her lap. It helps to keep hold of the strap. She looks ahead, as if they are strangers, and focuses on the wide rectangle of green. A group of students are on the grass, engrossed in conversation.

A man coughs on the bench along to the right. There is a carrier bag bunched up in his hand and he is restless, keeps craning his neck to look around, as if he's waiting for someone. He sees Kate looking at him and she turns her head back to the front, looks at the trees, the bulging knots at the top of the branches where they must have been repeatedly lopped. She counts the knots: one, two, three, four. Sarah's silence is too much.

'Daniel used to meet me here after my lectures when we

262

were students,' Kate says. 'He'd bring sandwiches. Always chicken salad for me, cheese and pickle for him. Even if it was raining and—'

'I know about you and Luke. Daniel showed me the email.' Sarah's tone is flat. 'Well? Aren't you going to say anything?'

'It's not what you think.'

Kate can't stop counting in her head. One, two, three, four. Onetwothreefour.

'I just need to know how long it's been going on.'

'Nothing's been going on.'

'I'm not stupid. And you had the nerve to come to my house, to behave like that in front of me.'

Kate hates the way her cheeks are blazing. 'Nothing happened,' she says.

'I've seen the email. There's no point denying it.'

Kate keeps staring straight ahead.

'How long has it been going on?' Sarah spits the words. 'How long, Kate? At least look at me.'

'You want to know?' She turns around. 'Really? How long he's been sending me messages? Or how long my life's been falling apart?'

A tear escapes. She brushes it away and returns her hand to her bag. The strap presses into the middle of her palm and she imagines how it would feel if it was sharp.

The man at the neighbouring bench gets up and walks past. One of his trainers has a broken lace, too short to be properly tied and his shoe slips on his foot as he walks. The outline of a bottle is visible through the thin plastic of the carrier bag. Kate thinks of the night they did shots, rubbing herself clean in the shower. She still cannot face the thought of what she might have done.

'Please. Just tell me,' Sarah says. 'I don't care any more. I need to know or else I'll go mad.'

Kate feels surprisingly calm.

'He sent me a text and said you'd found my dress. He said you'd be posting it. Then he asked about my book, said he was fascinated about—'

'Your dress?'

'Yes, the one I left in the guest room, the one you post-ed back.'

'I didn't post anything.' Sarah's face becomes taut again.

'I'm not lying, you can ask Daniel. He was there when it was delivered. It's hanging in my wardrobe. He said you'd written a note and—'

'I didn't write anything. What are you talking about?'

'I didn't see the note. Maybe it was Magda—'

'I don't know what the hell's going on.'

A mottled dent forms on Sarah's chin and she slaps her hand over her mouth as if to contain a scream.

'I'm sorry,' Kate says. The words feel like ice. 'He kissed me in the park. I was upset . . . it's no excuse but I'm having a really hard time right now.'

Sarah's eyes are full of pain. 'And the photo?' she says, her body slumped, as if she is resigned now to hearing the worst. 'What did you mean in the email?'

'I don't even remember taking it. I don't know what to say.'

She cannot admit that she doesn't want to remember, that she is afraid.

Sarah sighs, rubs her eye. She isn't wearing any make-up.

'We messaged each other,' Kate says. 'He asked about my book. Daniel doesn't ask me anything. He's so stressed

264

about finding a job. I should've talked to him, but . . .'

'Okay,' Sarah says. She shakes her head but seems to accept the explanation.

They both look ahead at the grass. The group of students have dispersed now, leaving only a boy and girl. The boy is teasing the girl and she pushes him playfully until he falls backwards. They mess around, him laughing, her squealing, until he pins her down and kisses her. They kiss the way young people kiss, like it could be the end of the world.

Kate doesn't think of Daniel, not directly. Or force herself to examine why she did what she did. She recalls something her mum once said a long time ago, on a weekend when her dad had shouted and stormed off. Her mum had shut the door on him with a slam, and instead of crawling into bed, like she usually did, she told Kate they would go out as well. They went into town, to the museum with insects in tanks and displays with buttons to press. They went to the Oxfam shop where her mum bought them each a new outfit. They went to Wimpy and had beefburgers and strawberry milkshakes, knickerbocker glories. Kate was too young to understand that her mum was being reckless. Her mum pulled Kate into a hug, said that sometimes it was difficult to carry on, especially when you felt things too much. That she loved Kate's dad but sometimes loving him felt like drowning and flying, all at the same time.

Sarah clears her throat and goes to speak, but Kate says, 'Nobody really knows what's going on inside you, do they?'

Sarah says, 'Look, I just want to say—' But Kate already knows what Sarah wants to say. She can't hear it. Not yet.

'I was only eight when I found my mum, when she cut herself the first time,' Kate says, swallowing. 'I thought it was my fault because I'd taken some money from her purse. Dad had been angry all week because he didn't have enough money to pay the gas bill. He'd gone off, like he usually did when things got too much. And when he came back, Mum was in the hospital. He said I needed to be good. Looked at me like I'd done it to her. And when we went to the hospital, I remember seeing her in bed, her arms all bandaged up. I sat in the chair, trying to look happy, trying to think of what to say to make it better. I thought, when I'm older I'll know. When I'm older . . .'

Sarah tries to interrupt.

'But the thing is, we don't ever know, do we?'

'Just tell me what happened,' Sarah says, touching her arm. 'Please.'

Kate tells her then. Not about scrubbing herself in the shower or Alec or the men on the website, but about the messages Luke sent, how it was nice to have someone who cared. She tells Sarah that Luke touched her, but she didn't want him to. She tells her she feels so ashamed. There is more, she knows there is more, but she will not make herself remember.

'I felt so alone,' Kate says. 'I'm sorry.'

The tears are warm on her cheeks.

Sarah looks away. When she speaks, her voice is changed, softer. 'I wanted to hate you so much today,' she says. 'I told myself that if you were the reason for everything that's happened, then I wouldn't have to . . . But really, I know it's nothing to do with you.' Her voice

266

trembles. 'I found him in his study. A naked woman on the screen, talking to him.' She pauses.

Kate remains quiet.

'He goes down to his computer most nights. And he comes home late all the time, stinking. I think he's been . . .' Sarah loses composure then, dissolves into tears. 'It's been so terrible,' she sobs.

Kate gives her a hug, lets her cry. Finds a tissue in her bag.

On the grass in front of them, the boy and girl brush themselves off to stand. The boy says something, and the girl laughs. He kisses her and they walk away, his arm around her.

'I used to think love was a magical thing,' Sarah says, sniffing and wiping her nose on the tissue. 'They don't have a clue, do they?'

'No.' Kate gives a weary smile.

They sit in silence again, but now it is different. There is a sense that things have been settled, that they are on the other side of it. Although Kate knows it can't be how it was before. Everything has changed now.

'You know, I was always petrified of you,' Sarah says suddenly. 'I couldn't stand it when the three of you were together, like I wasn't part of your club.'

'I thought you hated me.'

'Really?' Sarah says. She seems surprised. 'But I tried so hard to be your friend.'

The roar of a distant bus on the main road. A pigeon flying down to peck at crumbs on the path. Kate is newly aware of the world outside. She checks her watch, has ten minutes before her tutorials start.

'I'm sorry, I have to get back,' she says.

Sarah pulls herself up, buttons her raincoat, ties her belt with a kind of finality. 'I'm sorry, I shouldn't have come here. Only Daniel contacted me and—'

'Daniel wants a divorce.'

'Oh.'

Kate looks at her watch again. 'I really have to go . . . my students.' She shuffles to the edge of the bench.

'Yes, of course, you go. I'm sorry.'

There is an awkward moment, neither of them knowing what to say, then Sarah gives her a hug. 'Maybe we can meet up again?' she says.

'Yes,' Kate says, and she means it.

They leave in opposite directions. Kate goes back along the pavement to the university building. She attempts to focus her thoughts for the tutorials. She feels giddy and leans against the railing along the side of the pavement. The houses loom over her. The pavement comes up.

Virginia Woolf lived here, she tells herself, trying to anchor her mind. Isla's face comes to her – the girl she was friends with in her first year at university. Isla was the one who introduced her to Daniel. She had piles of books on the floor of her tiny student room and kept trying to get Kate to read some of them.

Kate can see Daniel then – at the party where they met. He is standing in front of her, pushing his glasses up his nose. Afterwards, they went for a walk around the park. It must have been sub-zero that night, but she hadn't felt cold at all. She hadn't thought it was possible to feel that way with anyone.

Sarah is wrong. It is like magic.

Kate looks at the red painted doors, the line of windows. She takes out her phone.

'Jean?' she says. 'I'll have to cancel my tutorials . . . Yes . . . I think I'm coming down with something. Can you put a note on my door? Thanks.'

She puts her phone back in her bag and turns the other way, towards the main road. She has no thoughts now, just the physical sensations of moving her legs, her bag brushing against her skirt. Overhead, the distant roar of a plane merges with the noise of the traffic, the pneumatic drilling that has started up again.

32

Daniel closes the front door and takes off his shoes. The house is quiet. His immediate thought is to check in the kitchen for the envelope. He propped it against the kettle before he left for his meeting. *KATE* written across the front in capitals. The solicitor had said a separation agreement made the divorce process so much easier. Kate won't make it easy.

He lets out a sigh. The envelope has gone.

In the garden, he sees the cat from next door on the fence. It stares at him then jumps down. The evening is still light, the birds singing. The house is so quiet.

He has been gone all day. Earlier, he met his new bosses for lunch and signed the contract for his new job. They had been so impressed by the deal he made the other week, they offered him a permanent position. They welcomed him to the team. If things were different, he would be arriving home to celebrations, to eager faces asking how it went, keen to hear his news. 'Well done,' Kate would be saying. She would kiss him, and he would have that invincible feeling in his chest.

He runs the tap and fills a glass, stands over the sink

while he drinks it quickly. A plate has been left there, the toast crumbs floating around like skating insects. He puts the empty glass down on the draining board and goes into the hall. Kate must be back from university because her car is in the driveway. He cannot hear the girls, then he remembers they both have sleepovers. That was why he decided today would be the best day to give Kate the documents. Any discussions could happen without the worry of upsetting the girls.

He makes his way upstairs.

In the bathroom, there is a soaking towel slung over the side of the bath, a small puddle underneath. The contents of the wall cabinet have been turned out, strewn across the floor in a mess. Cough medicine, the old bottle of Calpol, dental floss, plasters, painkillers. An old rolled-up tube of athlete's foot cream.

'Kate?' he says, in a quiet voice at first, then louder. 'Kate.'

He leaves the mess of the bathroom and goes into the bedroom. Kate is there, on the far side of the bed, sat on the floor. He can see the top of her head, but she doesn't turn round.

'What are you doing?' he says.

She is hunched over her lap. There is a towel wrapped around her arm.

'Kate? What are you doing?'

He crouches next to her, and she lets him peel away the towel. Red lines score the underside of her arm. A deep puncture wound dribbles dark blood. He presses the towel back in place.

'What have you done?' He immediately thinks of the envelope he left for her, the text he sent. He recalls how it had felt when he told her he wanted a divorce.

She whimpers.

He gets her up onto the bed, has to lift her like she's a child. Another towel falls from her lap, soaked with blood, along with a knife from the kitchen – the bread knife of all things, its two-pronged end like a serpent's tongue. He pushes it to the side. She leans into him, sobbing.

'Let's get you cleaned up,' he says.

'Don't go,' she says. She continues to sob, but quietly, with thick jagged breaths, as if she has been crying for some time.

'It's going to be all right,' he says. She is shaking.

She presses her face into his ribs. *Just the smell of you*, she used to say. *Just the smell of you.*

'Kate. We need to get you cleaned up. Can you sit?'

He manages to move her onto the bed, where she sits against the headboard. He waits for her to settle before going to the bathroom. The first aid kit is in the corner – he remembers seeing it there – and he brings the tube of antiseptic cream as well.

She opens her eyes when he stands next to her.

'You need to take the towel off,' he says.

He swabs the sterile wipe across the scratches. 'Ow,' she says. He did this once before, when she decided to cut down an overgrown bush in the garden. It was only later in the evening she noticed her arms were criss-crossed with angry lines.

'What have you done?' he says again.

'Ow. Be careful.'

'I am.'

He avoids the stab wound, which is still bleeding, and holds her wrist while he cleans around it.

'What happened?' He says this more to himself than to her. How could she do this?

'I don't know.'

'You've made a real mess.'

She pulls her arm away.

'Don't,' he says. 'Let me finish.'

She gives him back her arm and he dabs on some antiseptic cream. He isn't sure whether to bandage the wound but decides to use a large square plaster instead.

'There,' he says. 'You need to be careful with it.'

He rests her arm back on her lap.

Downstairs, he waits for the kettle to boil. No thoughts but of how strong he needs to make the tea and whether he should add one or two teaspoons of sugar. He squashes the teabag with the back of the teaspoon until the water is dark. When he opens the bin, he sees the white envelope and the ripped-up pieces of the agreement. He drops the teabag on top. The wet soaks across, making the paper translucent, the typed words blurring.

In the bedroom she has propped herself up with pillows. She cradles her wounded arm. He sets the tea down on her bedside table and sits on the edge of the bed.

'It's got sugar,' he says. 'For the shock.'

She looks at him. Her eyes are puffy, her face blotchy with grey streaks down her cheeks.

'We should get you to a doctor.' He tries to see if blood has seeped through the plaster. 'It'll need checking. You might need stitches.'

'No!' She edges away.

He holds up his hands, as if she is pointing a gun, and then slowly lowers them. 'Okay, I won't call anyone. I just want to know you're all right.'

273

She curls her feet underneath her, as if she can't allow herself to take up too much space.

'Kate? What happened?'

'I don't know,' she whispers. Tears fall, tracking silently down her cheeks, making dark splotches on her pale top.

'But why did you—'

'I don't know, Daniel. I don't know.'

'Did you want him?' he says. 'Did you enjoy it?'

She pulls her knees up and buries her face.

'No! You don't understand.'

'How can I understand? You've told me nothing,' he shouts.

He gets up and crosses to the window. None of it feels real, as if they are on a stage. Soon the curtain will be lifted, and he can step across to where everything makes sense.

'I took your stupid form,' she says. 'I ripped it up and put it in the bin.' A distorted laugh escapes. She wipes her nose across the back of her hand. 'I'm not signing anything. I'll make it impossible.'

'I know,' he says.

He remains motionless at the window. Out there, life continues, and it seems to him that no matter what he decides to do, he will suffer regret. He has never felt that before, regret for a path not taken, regret for things not said. He has always known exactly what to do. Perhaps he always did what others expected. It is time, he realises, to find his own way. Decide who he wants to be.

He turns abruptly from the window and looks at her.

'Tell me everything,' he says. 'I need you to be honest.'

She looks up at him. He goes back to the bed and sinks

274

down on the edge. He cannot get too close because he doesn't trust himself. One touch, one look. He's a car spinning on an endless stretch of ice.

She takes a breath. 'He started sending me messages. I couldn't talk to you, and it was nice to have someone interested in what I was doing. He kissed me at the park. I didn't want him to kiss me, Daniel. He left and I told him he needed to stop messaging me. It was all a mistake. You know what Luke's like.'

He does know, which makes it feel worse, not better.

'And what about that website?' he says.

'The website?'

He shakes his head. 'Come on,' he says. 'Just tell me.'

'I met someone for a coffee.'

And there it is. Finally. He shakes his head again and looks away. 'Who is he?'

'No one. He just answered my questions. It was research for my book.'

'Research. Is that what you call it? And this was the night you came home so late it was actually morning?' She is shocked by that, stalled. 'Yes, I'm not stupid. I know what time you came in.'

'You don't need to shout. I'm sat right here.'

He grips the edge of the bed. 'Did you sleep with him?'

She is the one to look away now.

'Tell me,' he says.

'I met him for a coffee. It was quick and then—'

'Oh, it was quick, was it? A quickie in a hotel with—'

'No!' She sobs. 'It was horrible . . . I can't . . . just horrible . . .'

He looks at the carpet. A blur of colour.

'So awful you kept doing it? Is that right?'

'No,' she repeats, 'no – what do you take me for?'

'What do I take you for?' He looks at her, although all he can see now is a hotel, a bed, a hand undoing the zip of her dress. And then him. Luke's hand.

He gets up, presses his finger to his head, taps it hard. He wants to drill it into his brain, how fucking stupid he's been. 'Well, let me think,' he says, as sarcastically as he can. 'Someone who fucks around, someone who'd send a dirty photo to her husband's best friend.'

'I didn't mean—'

He waves his hand at her, can't listen to it for a second longer.

He finds himself back at the window, staring out at the darkening sky. Exactly where he was on the night he discovered what she was doing. He has been such a fucking coward. So weak. Why didn't he shake her awake? *Look what's happening to us*. Most of all, he should have said, I'm afraid that everything we are isn't good enough.

'Why couldn't you believe in me?' he says, turning away from the window. 'I needed you to see how hard it was, watching you go out every day. I knew you didn't want to be teaching again. And then you'd come home and question me about what I'd done all day, as if I was doing nothing. Couldn't you see how it made me feel like a failure?'

She swallows, as if her throat is sore. 'I didn't know,' she says quietly. 'I'm sorry . . . Daniel, I'm so sorry.' Tears are running down her face.

He goes over to the bed and sits down, touches her – can't help himself. For a moment he is able to pretend that nothing else exists. Just this here: his hand, her knee. She is warm. And he knows, a split-second realisation, that what

276

he has been grappling with is the irrefutable reality that he loves her. He hates her, yet he loves her. There it is.

'Don't leave me,' she says.

'I'm not going to leave you.' The words come out instinctively and he knows them to be true.

Her eyes search his face, and he is aware that it is now dark. He clicks on the lamp and brings the room back. The colours. She blinks against the light.

'We should get something to eat,' he says, seeing the untouched mug on the bedside table. Her tea will be cold.

The lamplight throws their blurred reflections onto the dark window, and he is aware of how visible they must be to the houses opposite. He goes across to draw the curtains, looks down at his car parked behind hers, pausing to let the wash of emotion pass over him. The same feeling of emerging from the grips of a terrible headache. The relief of a receding pain.

'Will we be okay?' she says.

'I'm not sure.'

'Don't say that. It sounds like you're saying no.'

'I'm not saying no. What do you want me to say?'

'I want you to say everything is going to be all right, like you said before. You said that didn't you? And you meant it?'

'Yes,' he says. 'Everything is going to be all right.'

He goes to her then, pulls her close, crushing her to him, her hot breath on his neck.

33

In town, Sarah parks outside the restaurant. There are plenty of free spaces, which is unusual for the last Saturday of the Easter holidays. She supposes a lot of people have gone away and wonders if she ought to take the children for a day trip down to the coast tomorrow, before the schools go back. It would help to get away, to put some distance there. She needs to figure out what she is going to do. It has been two weeks since Luke left. He sent her a text from his hotel room this morning. I miss my wife

She waits in front of an estate agent's window. Her dad is slow to get out of the car. He won't be helped. They didn't speak much during the car journey, just the comments she always makes about work, the children's schools, how Zac scored a goal at his recent football game. Everything still in its usual groove. She cannot bring herself to say anything about Luke yet. She doesn't know where to start.

A few days ago, Lucy asked where he was. She told her that he had to go away for a while.

'Daddy hasn't been feeling well and he needs some time on his own,' she said.

Lucy had nodded, giving the impression that she understood the hidden subtext.

'You're always happier when Daddy isn't here,' she had said, later.

In the estate agent's window, she sees a bungalow for sale that looks similar to her mum and dad's. And a cottage with fields all around. She could move away from London, live somewhere with a beautiful view, somewhere secluded. But then she imagines what it would be like and decides that it would be too disruptive for the children. Anyway, she hasn't come to a final decision yet.

The wind gusts, whipping up her hair, blowing it over her face. Her dad is out of the car and stepping onto the pavement.

'God, it's windy today, isn't it?' she says, locking the car. Her eyes smart and she has to keep blinking.

Her dad doesn't say anything, his gaze fixed to the pavement. His left leg drags, causes him embarrassment, although he refuses to use his stick.

'I booked the table for twelve thirty,' she says. 'And it's only quarter-past, so plenty of time.'

She holds out her arm but knows he won't take it. It would be for her benefit, anyway. She isn't sure what she is doing. The logic of arranging this lunch is suddenly difficult to grasp.

They go into the restaurant. A girl of university age greets them. She has a tiny nose stud, and it twinkles in the overhead lights as she shows them to a table in the corner. Sarah's dad walks slowly and when they reach the table, the girl says she will give them a minute.

Sarah takes her dad's jacket and hangs it over his chair. She sits opposite him and looks around. It has changed so much. There used to be an old-fashioned coat stand near the door, a small desk where Mr De Luca stood to greet his guests and photographs on the walls of different places in Italy. Mr De Luca always wore smart trousers that her dad called slacks. She used to feel so grown up coming here. Her dad would let her have a sip of his wine.

'This is nice,' she says. 'It's been so long since I've been here.'

A jumble of words that she can't understand and then, '. . . al-always had m-m-m-melon and ham. Ravioli.'

He's talking about her mum and how she was never adventurous, always ordered the same things. He looks off to the side and smiles, like he's remembering. She pictures her mum back at the bungalow, helping Zac measure flour, telling him not to add too many raisins, telling Lucy she's doing well, and how she's inherited her grandmother's knack for baking. 'You didn't get that from your mum,' she'll say with a wink, and Lucy will laugh. Zac will feel left out and try even harder to prove that he's better than his sister. 'But you've got the artistic flair,' she'll say, 'the impossible thing to learn. You definitely get that from your mum.' Sarah heard her say that once, when she walked in on them making a batch of brownies.

And she realises she has made an awful mistake in bringing her dad here. What was she thinking? She should pick up their coats and go home.

But then the girl is back with the menus, and her dad is taking one.

'G-garlic bread,' he says.

He grips his arm, as if to hold it down in place.

'Is your arm okay, Dad? Is it hurting?'

'No,' he says, and he touches it again. Perhaps he is

nervous and has guessed who is coming. She told him she had organised a surprise guest. She looks around, but there is no sign of Elaine.

All week she has filled every minute with movement. Whenever she stops, it rushes in on her – the image of Luke sitting on the floor looking up at her. Then of Kate smoking and laughing on their sofa. The strange thing is, she doesn't blame Kate. It really isn't about her at all.

The girl appears again, with a small pad and a biro.

'We're just waiting for one other person,' Sarah says. 'Can you give us a few more minutes?'

The girl goes off. She is probably home from university or saving up to go travelling. Sarah never did go travelling – she was married and pregnant so soon after she graduated. She used to imagine their life, when the children were older, visiting Ha Long Bay in Vietnam, seeing the ancient sites in Machu Picchu, the lava lakes in Ethiopia – she has read so much about these places, filing them away like postcards she has already written. She didn't even tell Luke that she wanted to go to those places, realises she has never imagined being there with him – more an ideal of a couple in her head that she one day hoped they would become.

Elaine opens the door and Sarah sees her first. Her grey hair is thin and short and has been blown about in the wind, standing up in wisps. She seems smaller, despite the wider waistline. Although still the same heavy make-up, the same garish clip-on earrings. The wind takes the door from Elaine's hand, and it bangs against the side. A waiter goes over to help. Elaine smiles and pats her hair as she looks around the restaurant. She sees Sarah waving and walks towards the table, pulling at the collar of her coat, patting at her hair.

'Look, Dad,' Sarah says. 'It's Elaine.'

He turns around and says something that sounds like, 'Christ, no.'

Sarah gets up, stands waiting as Elaine approaches.

'It's so wonderful to see you,' Sarah says, pecking the air next to Elaine's cheek.

Elaine takes off her coat and folds it over her arm.

'Dad's so pleased you could make it. Aren't you, Dad?'

'It's good to see you, Colin,' Elaine says quietly. She pats her hair.

'Yeah,' he manages to say. He looks at Elaine briefly and then looks down at his lap, wringing his hands the way he does when he struggles with his words.

'I thought it would be nice for you to have a proper chat,' Sarah says, feeling a need to explain.

'Is Derek not here yet?' Elaine asks. 'Ian Dunlop and his wife? Will there be enough space for them? Shouldn't we move to a bigger table?'

Elaine looks around, sizing up the other tables. She is curt, defensive. Not at all how Sarah remembers her being.

'Ian and the others couldn't make it. I thought I said . . .'

'No, you didn't. I thought it was a reunion. That's what you said. Your dad wanted a reunion of his old crowd from the council.'

'Yes, I know. Such a shame they couldn't make it,' Sarah says. The lie could almost be real. 'But I didn't want to cancel completely, to let Dad down. Not after I'd said there was a surprise.'

'Oh well, never mind,' Elaine says, putting her folded coat over the back of the chair and settling herself next to Sarah. 'I expect something came up with their grand-children and Derek has a lot on with his golf matches. He

282

won the club trophy last year.' Elaine directs this across the table, at her dad, but he is still looking at the menu.

'We'd better get you another menu,' Sarah says, craning to look for the girl.

The strained politeness continues over the meal, with Elaine chattering about Derek – his grandchildren, his golfing practice, where he plans to go on holiday this year and how pleasant Southwold can be out of season. 'The hotel found out he was a recent widower,' Elaine says, 'so they gave him a complimentary breakfast.' By the end of the meal, Sarah knows more about Derek than she could ever wish to.

Throughout all this, Sarah's dad doesn't say a word.

When the coffees arrive, Elaine talks about the old days at the council offices. Her dad perks up then.

'Tha-that time with the letter. Ffhmm ppl the woman saying potholes and men.'

'Oh yes,' Elaine says, laughing. She turns to Sarah and explains that some of the letters they used to get were hilarious. A woman complaining about a huge pothole in front of her driveway. "I've had so many men trying to sort out my hole," the woman wrote in a long two-page letter. Or the ones they got about cones in inappropriate places. 'We were in stitches, weren't we, Colin?'

They both laugh – her dad actually laughs. Sarah sees her opportunity and says she needs to make a quick phone call. They are still laughing as she extracts herself from the table.

Outside, she pretends to dial a number and holds her phone up to her ear. She thought about phoning one of her friends, to hear a comforting voice, but her battery is dead. She stands in front of the window, pretending to talk into her phone before walking off in the direction of the estate agent's. The wind blasts in her face.

Stopping at the estate agent's, she stares at the photo of the cottage again. If she had been enough, she thinks, Luke would have been happy. She wants to know why he couldn't be happy with her. Self-blame is common, she has read, for the wives of addicts. And even though she understands this, even though he admitted that he is entirely to blame, still the thought will not leave her: he would have been faithful if she was enough.

An old couple walk past, the woman's arm looped around the man's. The woman tells him that he spent too long in the other shop and now they've run out of time. The man says they've got plenty of time if only she'd stop complaining for a minute. They continue grumbling at each other. Sarah is about to turn back to the restaurant when the man laughs and takes the woman's hand. He kisses it, saying something Sarah doesn't hear and then, 'You know I'd do anything for you my dear. Anything.' He gives a little bow, and the woman gives him a playful shove. 'Give over,' she says, and they link arms again, carrying on down the street. Sarah watches until they are gone.

When she returns to the restaurant, Elaine isn't there, although her coat is still folded over the chair.

'Did they bring the bill yet?' Sarah says. She feels out of breath.

Her dad shrugs and fumbles to open a little biscuit in a plastic wrapper. Elaine comes back from the ladies, patting at her hair.

'We didn't know how long you'd be,' Elaine says. 'And we asked for the bill, but Colin realised he didn't have his wallet. He said he didn't even know he was coming out for a meal.'

This is said like an accusation.

'Oh, he did,' Sarah says, giving a wide smile. 'I said we were going to your favourite restaurant, Dad. I did tell you that.'

'D-did you?' he says. 'I don't know.'

Elaine folds a flowery silk square into a triangle and wraps it around her neck. The girl comes over and Sarah pays the bill.

'It was a lovely meal,' Elaine says, when the girl has gone. She looks at Sarah's dad as she says this and then turns back to Sarah. 'Although the pasta wasn't home-made. You can tell, can't you, has that different texture. And my cannelloni was one of those bought-in things. Heated up in a microwave. Mr De Luca would turn in his grave.'

'All the-they want is p-pizza,' her dad says, and Elaine laughs.

Her dad gets up from the table and holds onto the chair.

'It was lovely to see you,' Elaine says.

'Yes, lovely,' he says. When he speaks, his words are clear. Sarah has rarely heard him speak so well.

They make their way to the door. Outside, it is still windy, and Sarah's hair is immediately blown about.

'Ooh,' Elaine says, and Sarah sees her dad take hold of Elaine's arm.

'We can give you a lift,' Sarah says, holding her key in the air and unlocking the car at a distance. 'The car's just here.'

'It's okay. Don't go out of your way. There's a bus due in twenty minutes.'

'No, don't be silly. It's so windy. You can't stand in this.'

Elaine agrees and Sarah watches her dad get into the back to sit with her. Sarah turns the radio on and tries not to listen to their conversation, even though she can hear Elaine's voice the whole time. She is telling her dad about a man who has moved into the flat below, who has a different car every few months, has people knocking on the door all hours. Elaine thinks he must sell drugs or something and has called the police, although nothing seems to have been done about it.

'It's hot in here, isn't it?' Elaine says loudly. 'So hot.' In the rear-view mirror, Sarah can see Elaine pulling her silk scarf out from under her coat. 'Phew!' she says.

'Sorry,' Sarah shouts. 'The children always moan about being cold.'

When they arrive at Elaine's address, Sarah turns off the ignition. The flats are on a new development, the other side of town. Three small blocks, all identical, three storeys high. Sarah can see pots and clothes airers on some of the balconies. Elaine told her over the phone that she'd moved here a few years ago and has a flat on the top floor. She wonders why Elaine never married. How lonely she must be.

'Bye then,' Elaine says, and she is out of the car before Sarah can unclip her seat belt.

Sarah lets down the window.

'Bye. Nice to see you,' Sarah shouts. Elaine goes up to the main door of the nearest block. It is a relief to see her disappear.

'Why don't you come and sit in the front, Dad,' she says.

'Door stuck,' her dad says. He rattles the handle and gets agitated. 'S-stuck.'

'Okay, okay, hold on,' she says and gets out to open it from the outside.

As her dad steps from the car, she sees Elaine's scarf in the footwell.

'I'll take it up to her,' she says, waving the scarf. 'You get in. I won't be a minute.'

She runs up the stairs to the third floor, deciding quickly which of the three doors to knock on. There is a waft of flowery air freshener as Elaine opens the door.

'I made a lucky guess with the flat,' Sarah says, breathing heavily. She holds up the scarf. 'You dropped it in the car.'

'Oh, thank you,' Elaine says. 'I didn't even notice.' She touches her neck and smiles. Sarah sees her teeth, small and squared off. Elaine hadn't smiled at her once when they were in the restaurant.

'Anyway, thanks for coming,' Sarah says.

Elaine pats her hair again. 'I felt like I was on a blind date. With a chaperone.' She smiles but says this in the same accusing tone as earlier.

'I thought it would be nice for Dad, that's all. It's a pity the others—'

'Felt like a set-up, you know. Orchestrated, so it was just me and him.'

'Oh no, not at all. The others, they didn't let me know until . . .' Her heart thumps loudly.

Elaine gives a blank stare. Sarah knows she should say thank you and leave, doesn't need to stay and make any further conversation, but she finds herself saying, 'I thought it would be nice for you to see each other. You don't know what it's like, how they are every time I visit, seeing them both . . .' There is a lump in her throat. It appears out of nowhere. She turns away, holding her breath, blinking quickly. A tear falls onto her cheek.

'Oh now, don't get upset. Why don't you come in a minute?'

'No, no, I'm fine. Dad's in the car. He's waiting.'

'Just come in. I'll get you a tissue.'

Elaine leaves the door open and goes off. Sarah steps inside and pushes the door to. The tiny hallway has a small table with a vase of fabric flowers, and one of those reed diffusers with sticks. The smell is so overpowering, she can almost taste it.

'Here you are,' Elaine says, holding out a couple of tissues.

Sarah takes them and dabs at her eyes.

'It's all very difficult, I'm sure. Seeing your dad like he is.'

'He's okay,' Sarah says. 'He's getting better. And his speech is improving all the time. I just want him to be happy. I just want both of them to be happy.'

'I'm sure you do.'

'They made a terrible mistake.' It comes out as barely a whisper.

Sarah once asked her dad why he did it. It was in a rare moment when she felt he would be honest. He said Elaine brought him joy, he couldn't really explain. This woman – standing here – brought her dad joy. Sarah wonders how her mum can bear it.

'I'm sorry. I shouldn't have asked you to meet him. I don't know what I was thinking.' Sarah reaches for the edge of the door.

'It was all over such a long time ago, you know,' Elaine

says quickly, and Sarah sees the struggle in her face. 'He would never have left your mum. Never. And there were all the other women – some men are just like that, aren't they? – but he would never have left. As soon as I knew he had a family . . . Well, I said I couldn't see him any more.'

Sarah feels the space shift, as if they are on a moving walkway.

'Women? I thought it was just you. I thought you were seeing each other for years. I thought—'

Elaine frowns and crosses her arms. 'I don't know who told you that. Your poor mum. People say things behind your back, but they never think to say anything to your face. How was I supposed to know?'

'What other women?'

Elaine shakes her head. 'It's all in the past now.'

Sarah nods although she wants to say, *No, no it isn't*.

'Some men can't help it . . . look at all the celebrities. And the French. It's all perfectly normal over there.' Elaine purses her lips and seems pleased with herself, as if she has said something reassuring.

'I must go,' Sarah says. She cannot stand there any longer. Her legs feel numb.

'Yes, all right, dear. You take care.'

The air freshener smell is cloying, unbearable. She fumbles for the door.

'Bye, dear. And thanks for the lunch.'

Sarah is already halfway down the first flight of stairs.

Back at the bungalow, they are greeted by Janet, who is visibly furious.

'Where on earth have you been?' she says. 'You've been

289

gone hours. I've been worried to death. Why didn't you answer your phone?'

'Sorry,' Sarah says. 'My phone was out of charge.' She remains in the hall, cannot move while her mum is looking at her. She feels sick.

Her dad is already making his way into the conservatory, and he sits down in his place on the sofa. Sarah can see him through the door of the living room. There are the sounds of the television.

'Are Zac and Lucy okay?' she says.

Janet jerks her head towards the living room. 'They've had a lovely time making rock cakes. I said they could watch something. They've been very good.' Her tone doesn't match her words. She runs her fingers across her string of pearls, stares at the carpet.

They stand in an uncomfortable silence until Janet says, 'You know, you could have called.'

'Sorry,' Sarah says. 'I thought I said I was taking Dad out for lunch. We were going to meet up with Derek. You know Derek? But he cancelled at the last minute.'

Janet goes off into the kitchen. Sarah pokes her head around the living room door. Zac and Lucy are on the sofa staring at the TV. Sarah goes to the kitchen, where Janet is making a lot of noise. She takes mugs from the mug tree and slams them onto the worktop.

Sarah stands next to the oven. She clears her throat to speak but doesn't know what to say. She feels so guilty about Elaine, about everything. All those times when she hated her mum, the way she was with her dad. She thought he had been the one who was suffering.

Her mum bangs a cupboard door. 'It just would've been nice if you'd let me know you'd be late. I thought you were only going out to the park.' She rearranges the mugs in a line next to the kettle. 'I was worried sick. Tried phoning and phoning but it kept going through to your answerphone. I thought he'd had another stroke, that you'd been rushed off to hospital. Any minute now, I thought, I'll get that call. The one I keep dreading.'

'I'm really sorry,' Sarah says. 'My battery died. And I thought you'd appreciate the break . . .'

'You don't think I do nice things for him? Try to get him up and about? Try to get him to stop moping.'

Sarah swallows back the lump. 'I know. That's why I come over as much as I can.'

Janet flicks the switch on the kettle, and it rumbles in the background.

'We could all have gone out for lunch. All together.'

Sarah goes to speak, but she can't find the words. She watches her mum splash milk into the mugs. A teaspoon of sugar in one, half in another. The kettle clicks off. Janet pours steaming water into the mugs.

'Oh, look what I've done,' she says. 'I meant to make a pot and I've put the bags in the mugs.' She starts to fish them out with a teaspoon.

'It's fine Mum, really. Don't fuss. It doesn't matter.'

'Oh dear,' her mum says. 'Oh dear.' And she falters, tries to clutch the edge of the worktop. Her breathing is heavy.

'Mum? What's wrong? Come and sit down, leave all that.' She takes her mum's arm and leads her into the hall, down the corridor and into the bedroom at the back.

'Here, sit on the bed.' Sarah takes a tissue from the box on the dressing table.

She hasn't been in her parents' bedroom since her dad

first came out of hospital. Dressing gowns hanging side by side on the door. The familiar smell of laundry liquid, warm and clean. She wants to take her mum's dressing gown and bury her face in it, wrap it around her body. Sorry, she wants to say, I'm so sorry.

Her mum gives a sudden snort, puts the tissue, now screwed up, to her mouth.

'It's too much sometimes.' Her words are muffled. 'And to know that it'll never get any better.'

Sarah sits on the bed, her hands in her lap. They've never been tactile, never the sort of mother and daughter to hug. She pats her mum's arm instead.

'Oh Mum, don't say that. Dad's speech was so much better over lunch. And his walking.'

Janet looks straight ahead, staring into the middle distance as if she is recalling a specific memory.

'We had plans you know. For his retirement. He said he'd do anything I wanted. And I always wanted to live by the sea.'

'I know.'

Her mum wipes her nose and sniffs, rolls the tissue into a ball in her hand.

'Here,' Sarah says, getting up. Her mum puts the balled-up tissue onto the bed and takes another one.

All Sarah can think about, as she sits back down, is the look on her dad's face as he took Elaine's arm to keep her steady in the wind.

'How could you ever forgive him?' Sarah says quietly. She waits.

Her mum sits up straight. Perhaps she didn't hear.

'I know lots of people divorce,' her mum says suddenly, inhaling sharply. 'That friend of yours from school, and the Kendalls from down the road. But it still wasn't like it is now, with everyone getting divorced and remarried like it's perfectly normal. I grew up believing you got married and stayed with that person for ever.' She clears her throat. 'I suppose I didn't want to admit what was happening. He's just flirting, I kept telling myself. He was a good-looking man.'

'But you knew?'

'Of course I did.'

Her mum looks over to the side, to the dressing table, where photos of Sarah and her brothers are lined up. When she turns back, her eyes search Sarah's face, a desperate bid to find something.

Her mum twists the tissue into a tight spiral. 'I told myself that as soon as you were married, I'd leave. I had it all planned out. But then you told me what you'd seen.'

'I don't understand.'

'I couldn't leave then, could I? And your dad promised it was over.' She shakes her head.

There is a large frame on Janet's dressing table, with a photo of Sarah in a taffeta dress. Sarah hasn't noticed before how the photo is placed in the middle, with smaller photos of her brothers on either side.

Janet takes a deep breath and blows it out. 'I had to protect you and your brothers,' she says. 'You hear what divorce does to children.' She doesn't look up at Sarah as she speaks but concentrates on the flattened bit of tissue. 'If I was honest, I couldn't face the fact that he'd be gone. I wanted him to love me like he did at the start. Perhaps I wanted to make him stay so I could punish him for ever . . . oh, I don't know. That was years ago. We put it all behind us.' She looks up at the ceiling before going over to the dressing table. She checks herself in the mirror and wipes under her eyes.

Sarah can see it all. Not her mother, but someone else, the real person underneath. Someone who's had to hide her pain for so long.

'I didn't know,' Sarah says. She's the one to cry now. 'Oh Mum,' she says. 'I'm sorry, I didn't know.'

Her mum comes back to the bed and pulls Sarah into a hug, wraps her arms around and squeezes her tight. 'Come on now, don't get all upset,' she says.

Her mum pushes her hair away from her face and it feels wonderful to be held like that. Sarah remembers a moment then – being in the car, sitting on the back seat with her mum. She must have been young, maybe seven or eight. It was a blue Ford Sierra with a plastic turtle dangling from the mirror. Her uncle's car, and he was driving them home from a family party. Her mum had danced all night. Her dad hadn't been there, and her mum had been happy. It felt so good when her mum was happy, and she had wished it would always feel that way. They sat in the back, and she nestled into her mum's posh fur coat. It was as soft as a kitten and Sarah had stroked her mum's arm, and her mum had stroked her hair. They sang Christmas songs. Yes, it was a week before Christmas, she remembers now, and her dad had gone away with work. Only, now she knows that it probably wasn't work at all.

Sarah sits up. She clasps her hands together, touches her wedding ring. It spins easily on her finger. It could slip right off. She's already put her engagement ring in its box, put it away in a drawer.

'Luke's left. I told him to leave,' she says.

Her mum doesn't say anything, just nods.

'I don't want him to come back.'

She has said it. All week she's imagined saying it out loud. She takes the ring off and looks at it. On the inside, their initials are engraved in a looping font. The date of their wedding. The letters and numbers catch in the light. She lets it rest in her palm and then puts it in her pocket.

Her mum gives a gentle smile and says in a soft voice, 'Come on, let's go and get that cup of tea.'

34

The rear end of the car swings out, making the box of Macallan slide around in the passenger footwell. Luke is on his way to meet Daniel. He adjusts the steering wheel and keeps his foot pressed down. A winding road with a hairpin bend. It requires concentration, especially as he hasn't driven it for many years. The last time he was here, he took the other road, the one that goes past the main entrance to the house.

Last night at the hotel, Luke lay in bed and thought about what he was going to do. He had been living out of his suitcase for two weeks and Sarah had made it quite clear she didn't want to talk to him. He needed to find a way to move forward. He felt a strange duality of calm and rage. Instead of thinking about the way in which he could break through Sarah's barriers, he kept seeing visions of the past long gone. The barn, the house.

When Daniel messaged him this morning, asking to meet, Luke knew what needed to be done. Not that Daniel is anything to do with the reason he is here, but it seemed linked in his mind somehow, as if it was one and the same thing. He suggested they meet at the pub in the village.

Luke keeps his speed steady at sixty-five and continues along a straight section of road. He can hear his father's voice in his head: *What's the limit point? If you can't see, you need to slow down.* His father was a good driver, passed his advanced driving test. He took Luke out at weekends sometimes, taught him about the line of the road, how to take bends by turning the wheel as little as possible. *You're too reckless, Luke,* he used to say. Seb, on the other hand, was told he was a natural.

Luke opens the window to let some air in. The place his father used to call *the tunnel of trees* is coming up. It is a cloudless afternoon and the sunshine filters through the leaves. Rays of light come across the road like a sheet.

His father drove this road every weekday to the station; every weekend to take Luke's mother to the delicatessen in town, calling into the wine shop, where they would pick up a bottle or two of something special. A road he knew better than any. Which is why it never made sense to Luke, how his father had lost control of the car that day, how he had taken the bend too fast. March the sixth was cold, and there was ice on the road, but even so. What happened to make his father forget? Luke was away at university when it happened, was probably still in bed that morning. He will never know what they were thinking about in those seconds before hitting the tree. He likes to imagine they saw it all for what it was, in that moment before the bang.

Sarah's face comes to him then. The way she looked at him last week, when he was at the house collecting the rest of his things. She didn't even ask which hotel he was staying at, or where she could reach him. It was the instant he knew he'd lost her as well.

Luke eases his foot off the accelerator. Here it is – the tree. There used to be a pale scar where the branch had broken off, but now it is just like all the others. Nothing to show, nothing to see. He carries on.

The road joins the old Roman road and goes past the row of cottages where the farm workers once used to live. The front doors are painted different colours, free from their previous uniform of dark red. The gardens are properly sectioned off with picket fences and new walls that stand out against the old brick. Different people, different houses. Everything is altered.

In the pub car park, there are only two other vehicles. Luke parks by the far wall and goes inside. A couple sit at a table in the corner, an older man sits on a bar stool with a pint, his head buried in a newspaper. The rest of the place is empty. The man behind the bar stands wiping a glass with a cloth. He nods at Luke.

'Heatwave coming, they say, but they're always saying that.'

'I'll have a pint,' Luke says, pointing to one of the taps, 'and a double of your best single malt.'

The man puts down the glass and cloth, grumbles, then says, 'Just got Bell's, but I might have something else.' He turns and rummages along a row of clinking bottles. 'Here we are,' he says, holding up one with a label Luke doesn't recognise. Not that it matters. He hadn't known what he was drinking that night he was here with Seb.

The man pours a measure into a tumbler and then another.

Luke takes his ale and whisky and sits at a table in the window. Now that he is here, it is hard to keep himself steady. A lorry goes by, making the windows shudder.

It was Luke's eighteenth birthday when Seb brought him here. They had sat at a similar table to this one, in the window. They drank pints and cheap whisky chasers. Seb was more serious that night, told Luke he was *a man now*. He behaved as if he was imparting some kind of powerful wisdom, but it wasn't anything he hadn't said before. *Just remember nobody else really cares about you, so do the things that make you happy.*

Luke swallows the whisky in one swig, letting it spread across his chest, and slams the glass down. He's been running towards this point for a long time.

Through the window, the sky is becoming overcast. He drinks his pint and checks his watch. Daniel is late. He continues to wait, though he doesn't know why — he already knows what Daniel will say — decides that he doesn't need this distraction. Why did he suggest it? What was he thinking? He had this notion that it would somehow assist in the poetic justice of what he is about to do. As if the bond with Daniel could override the mess of it all. That everything would be righted by their meeting. How moronic that suddenly seems. Everyone has deserted him, and he is alone. He has accepted that. He is here to put an end to the past and start anew.

Luke stands. He is resolute now and wants to get on with it. He gives an upward nod to the barman as he goes out. The man nods back.

In the car park, Luke takes his rucksack from the passenger seat and checks the small pocket for the lighter. The air has cooled, and it will be sunset in an hour or so. He doesn't have a torch, but he feels confident he knows the way in the dark. Anyway, he won't want to draw any attention to himself by waving a light around. He considers whether he should park somewhere else but decides it will be less conspicuous here.

He zips the box of Macallan inside the bag. As he closes the passenger door, a car rolls up in the next-door space. It is Daniel.

'Didn't think you were coming,' Luke says, as Daniel gets out.

'I came off at the wrong junction.' Daniel walks round and stands in front of Luke's car.

They eye each other, silently, before Luke puts the rucksack over his shoulder.

'I waited, but I've got to go now,' he says and starts to walk towards the road, not looking at Daniel as he passes.

'Why the hell did you get me down here?' Daniel calls out.

Luke stops. 'I wasn't the one who wanted to meet.' He half turns, wants to make it clear that he isn't going to stay and talk.

'You've never been able to face up to the things you've done.' Daniel doesn't look at Luke directly but fixes his gaze on the rucksack.

Luke didn't expect it to feel so painful.

'Well? What have you got to say?' Daniel juts out his chin.

Luke thinks, but where would he begin? It is all too late for that.

Another car pulls up to park. Luke keeps heading for the road and crosses over, walks along the narrow pavement towards the woods.

After a few minutes, he can hear Daniel coming up behind.

'Do you know . . .' Daniel says between breaths, 'I

300

actually thought . . . we could have a civil conversation.'

Luke keeps walking. 'You'll have a heart attack, running like that.'

'Oh, fuck off,' Daniel shouts. He comes in front, full of aggression, blocking the way. His face is red, his eyes narrowed. Luke wonders if he's got it in him to really let go. All those times when they had been out drinking and Daniel always made sure they got home. All the times when Daniel had hidden the bags of drugs, cleaned the mess in the house. All the times he covered for him. A faithful friend. And now look what Luke has done. He's really done it this time. The question is, will Daniel still try and clear up the mess, or will he give him the beating he deserves?

A car drives past, a blast of music. Then nothing. Silence.

'What do you want?' Luke says. For a moment he thinks Daniel will give up and walk away. He watches him weigh things up, deciding whether to continue.

'I want to know why?' Daniel says. 'That's all. Just why?' He searches Luke's face, seems unable to comprehend.

This is why, Luke wants to say. *Don't you see?* He puts his head down and continues to walk. The overgrown hedgerow scrapes his jacket sleeve.

Daniel runs alongside him and makes a dash to block the path again. 'For fuck's sake stop,' he shouts, holding up both hands.

Luke is suddenly aware of how straightforward Daniel is, how he has always been so rational. Things are simple for Daniel, black and white. Reasons, solutions. Luke keeps hold of the rucksack. He could put it on properly and run. It would be easy to leave Daniel behind.

'The light's fading,' Luke says. 'I have to go.'

'Where are you going?'

'Look – actually, it doesn't matter. I'm leaving tomorrow. I'm giving the place a last farewell.'

'Leaving?'

'It's the best thing.'

Luke pushes past, but he doesn't run, just walks on at a steady pace. After a few steps he can hear Daniel following again. They continue, one behind the other until they reach the fallen concrete post with the broken public footpath sign. Luke goes through the opening at the end of the hedge. He doesn't know why he's letting Daniel follow, but now he's here, there is something inevitable about it. Something necessary. They don't speak and make their way, as if they had both agreed to be silent.

They go through the wood. Crunching twigs, snagging thorns. There is a well-trodden path created by dog walkers and they are soon at the edge of the trees looking down the field.

'Where are you going? To the house?' Daniel asks. Luke doesn't bother to reply, keeps going in a straight line across the field.

As they approach the barn, Luke can see the bolt to the main door is rusted but unlocked. He pulls it and the door opens. Inside, there is a large hole in the roof. A shallow puddle has collected underneath. Luke looks up at the dimming sky. He doesn't know what he expected to see, but perhaps if something was here, it would have felt more dramatic. There is nothing to climb to reach the rafters as he had imagined. No bales of hay, no tractor. Just an empty shell. Empty, with a familiar smell that makes him think of late nights with bags of sweets, trying his first cigarette. Seb had laughed when he choked, the smoke hitting his lungs.

'Who owns this place now?' Daniel says. 'I don't think you should be here.' He walks back and forth, his hands in his jeans pockets, his shoulders up to his ears. He isn't wearing a jacket, only a button-down shirt.

Luke puts his rucksack down on a dry patch of floor and sits next to it, takes out the bottle of Macallan. He rips through the plastic tear strip and prises the cork with a pop, takes a large swig. It brings a satisfying burn. He holds the bottle out.

'Let's get this over and done with, shall we?' he says.

Daniel walks towards him but doesn't sit down.

'Go on, have some,' Luke says, but Daniel remains standing, staring across at the puddle in the middle of the floor.

Luke drinks some more. He takes out his lighter, gives the lid a flick and the flame appears with a snap of his fingers – he learned that trick at school after hours of practising. He looks at the bottle. Where should he pour it? The floor is too damp and there is nothing to light apart from the rotten walls. It's a pointless waste of time. Not at all how he imagined it would be. Perhaps he should drink the whole bottle instead, go and drive himself into a tree – the same tree his father drove into. Now that would be an ironic end to it all, wouldn't it? Seb would love that. A proper tragedy.

He takes out a cigarette and sucks it through the flame before clicking the lid shut.

'Ha,' he says aloud, and then takes a long drag on the cigarette. 'You know I was going to burn this shithole down.' He blows the smoke up at the hole in the roof.

'Do the house first and then here. This was the best and worst place of my life.'

He's feeling the alcohol now and takes another swig. It is odd, sitting here, in the empty space, Daniel standing over him.

'Why did you do it?' Daniel says.

Luke laughs, knows he shouldn't. 'Why do we do anything?' he says.

Daniel lets out an angry grunt, mutters something under his breath and Luke holds his hands up in mock surrender. 'All right, all right.'

Daniel walks to the other side of the barn and disappears into the shadows.

'You shouldn't have anything to do with me,' Luke shouts. 'I'm a hopeless case. A fucking train wreck. I thought you knew that when you met me.'

When Daniel comes at him, it is a surprise. The pain is sudden. *Bang*. A hard slam into his back, then across his side. The crack of wood, splintering. Luke drops his cigarette and leaps to his feet, brings his arms up over his face. Daniel has a remaining chunk of wood, and he comes at Luke again, shouting something about Kate, his eyes filled with fury.

'Nothing happened, for fuck's sake.' Luke makes a grab for the wood. A sharp piece drives into his hand and he instinctively pulls away. Pain in his hand, but then another whack across his shoulder. It pushes him off his feet and before he can save himself, he is falling onto the concrete. Then nothing.

When he opens his eyes, Daniel is crouching next to him, gripping his arm, giving him a shake.

'Can you hear me?' Daniel is saying. 'How many fingers am I holding up?'

Luke finds himself leaning up against the inside of the barn door. His vision is blurry. He waves Daniel away.

'It's all right,' he says. 'I'm all right. I need a drink.'

Daniel goes off and comes back with the bottle and the rucksack.

'Here,' he says. 'Do you have any water? I think you should have some water.'

'I'm fine.'

'You're bleeding.'

Luke goes to touch his head, where there is a bruised feeling above his eyebrow.

'No,' Daniel says. 'Your hand.'

His palm is sticky. It is still bleeding, and the wound is sore, throbbing.

'You'll need to have that looked at. Check there isn't any wood in it.'

'Leave it. For God's sake, I'm okay.'

Daniel sits down and lets out a long sigh. Luke doesn't move. They sit in silence for a while.

'Nothing happened,' Luke says, when it feels right to say something. 'I was just messing with her head. I forgot who she was.'

'You forgot?' Daniel scoffs. 'She obviously forgot as well.'

Luke takes hold of the bottle, has some and holds it out for Daniel, who takes it and has a swig. The liquid slaps and sloshes, like water up the side of a moored boat.

'Did you fuck her?' Daniel says, taking another swig.

'No. I told you nothing happened.'

'That's not true though, is it. She told me you kissed her. And I saw the email. I haven't seen the photo, but I can imagine.'

'Everyone's seen that email.'

'Well?'

'I messaged her, like you asked. About her dress, just like you said. And it carried on. She told me things weren't good. That she's trying to write a book and she wants to get a proper job at the university. She said you never ask about—'

'Of course I do. I ask her all the time.'

'It doesn't matter, does it? She isn't happy and she's worried.'

'We're all worried. That's life.'

Daniel drinks some more and wipes the back of his hand across his mouth. 'Did she come on to you?' He pauses and then says: 'Did she want to fuck you?'

It is both a discomfort and a pleasure to see Daniel in such pain – there is an awful connection in sharing this ordeal.

'She was upset about her book. I said I'd meet her for a drink, to cheer her up. And we got drunk. Like I said, I was just messing with her. Said I wanted to see what she looked like, and she sent me a photo.'

Daniel jumps up, still holding the bottle. 'And the whole time you were doing this, kissing my wife, feeling her up under the tree – yes, she told me about that, and how she'd tried to push you away . . . did you even consider what that would do to me?'

He throws the bottle into the black void, and it smashes.

'Fuck, Daniel. That was an eighty-quid bottle.'

Luke pushes himself up to stand. His head feels heavy, his body bruised. His hand is still throbbing.

'Look,' he says. 'I'm sorry. Is that what you want me to say?'

Daniel comes over, brings his face close. Their noses almost touch. Luke doesn't move until Daniel pushes him away.

'I want you to be honest for once!' Daniel hisses.

'Okay,' Luke says, stumbling. He touches his finger to his forehead, where the pain is pressing on his eye. 'So, as I said, I sent her a message. *You* asked me to do it in the first place. And we met in the park, and I got her drunk. I kissed her and put my hand in her knickers . . .' He stops.

Luke looks up at the hole in the roof. Birds are flying over, and he can hear their song coming from the trees. A noisy chorus, a jarring outburst of sounds. So loud. Jubilant even.

Daniel coughs and spits on the floor. Luke can see his pain in all its terrible purity. That's it, he wants to say. That's how I feel all the time. *Do you feel it now?*

'Why her?' Daniel says. He lowers his eyes, his voice barely a croak.

Luke shrugs. 'I enjoy making women do things. Is that what you want to hear, that I'm a monster?'

Daniel is silent.

'If you want to know if your wife was unfaithful, then no, she wasn't. And if you want to know if I'm to blame, then yes, I am. I'm not anyone you want to be around. I'll be gone soon, anyway.'

The birds continue. Chattering, calling out in clashing unison.

'Where are you going?' Daniel says.

'I don't know. Singapore maybe, the Middle East. Somewhere far away. I've sold my share of the fund to Geoff, so Sarah needn't worry. I'll make sure she's okay.'

'And what about the kids?'

307

Luke sees his children's faces – he hasn't been able to think about them for fear of breaking entirely. He sees them on the day they were born, holding them in his hands. So tiny. Lucy's first tooth falling out, putting a shiny pound coin under her pillow. Zac's first steps. His son.

'They'll be better off without me,' he says quickly.

'I don't expect they will. What does Sarah want?'

'I'm sure she's relieved to be rid of me.'

He feels dizzy, can just about keep his surroundings in focus. The air is stifling. Why can't he tell Daniel what he really wants? That he can't live without Sarah and his children, that he needs her. He won't survive without her.

That's what Seb had said to him, that last day. He said Luke would fall in love and end up with someone else. *I can't live without you.*

'We should be going,' Luke says.

'So that's it?'

'Yeah, that's it.' He forces himself over to the other side of the barn and picks up his rucksack, swings it onto his shoulder.

Daniel follows him outside and they set off, back the way they came, across the field. The sun has gone below the horizon. In the grainy light, they walk side by side through the long grass, their steps keeping time.

'You'll be okay, you and Kate,' Luke says. He knows it is important for him to tell Daniel this. 'You two always figure it out. She loves you.'

Daniel doesn't reply, but after a while says, 'Let me know when you decide where you're going. And don't go off without talking to Sarah.'

Luke could pretend that means everything is fixed. That

Daniel is still the same friend, that Sarah is going to forgive him, that he still has a family and a home.

'I will,' he says.

They are at the top of the field. Daniel stops to take a breath and Luke looks down towards the barn. He can barely see it in the nightfall. Perhaps he should've set light to it after all. They could be standing here watching it, aflame.

Daniel doesn't move, seems to sense that Luke needs to stay. He always did know when Luke needed to feel the weight of the quiet.

After a while, Luke says, 'We used to run from the house and come out here in our pyjamas. Felt like the middle of the night but it probably wasn't that late.'

'Your brother?' Daniel says.

'He'd come into my room, wake me up. We'd go over the lawn and through the walled garden. We'd stand about there.' Luke points. 'The dare was to see how long we could stay before we got scared. It's pitch black out here at night. I was always the winner. We'd run back to the house, screaming and barking like foxes.'

Luke sees them there in the middle of the field, two young boys, standing in the dark. Him and his big brother. And he realises how most of his life has been spent trying to find the purity of that time again. A time where he didn't feel like he was broken, that he was to blame for what Seb did to him.

'What—' Daniel goes to speak, but Luke interrupts. He needs to say it aloud.

'He used to get into bed with me,' he says, not looking at Daniel but continuing to look across the darkening field. 'I was about ten when it started, and he only held

309

me at first. Kissed me. I thought that's what brothers did.'

Luke closes his eyes, the relief of it. The futile belief that he needed to hold onto the grotesque images in his head. The things he allowed his brother to do. Maybe it was because whenever he let Seb do that to him, he felt a kind of release too.

'I don't know what to—'

'It's okay,' Luke says. 'I don't need you to say anything.'

They stand in silence for a few more minutes until Luke is ready to leave. He takes a final look, knows he will never come back again. It is done. He steps in front of Daniel, and they make their way through the trees.

Afterwards

A ripple of applause quietens as the host of the event takes the stand. She thanks the author for reading the excerpt from her latest book, *Anatomy of a Marriage,* and points to the stack of signed hardbacks on the counter, saying copies will be available for purchase. The audience, mostly comprised of university staff and students, are a little fidgety. They have been standing for too long and want to get on with things. There is a pub nearby where most of them will go as soon as they can.

The host continues. She tells a well-rehearsed anecdote about the time Elizabeth Taylor visited the bookshop back in the 1980s and bought a novel called *Bride.* The older members of the audience snigger. The students look confused. One of them writes down *Elizabeth Taylor, Bride,* then scribbles it out when someone else whispers, 'Not *that* Elizabeth Taylor.'

'But I'm sure if she were alive today,' the host says, 'she would most certainly be buying a copy of this fascinating book . . .'

Kate, who is standing to one side, facing the audience, gives a genial smile. Her first book, *Why Do We Stray?,*

311

sold well, and she is hoping for similar success with this second one. She scans the listening faces – the usual crowd from her department, a few eager first-years, and some other people she doesn't know. She can't see Florence. Perhaps she couldn't make it after all. Kate thought about messaging earlier, reminding her that her dad wasn't back from his business trip until next week, and it would be nice to have someone from the family present. Maisie hates coming to these things. But Kate didn't message in the end, didn't want to come across as needy. It was one thing having her daughter study at the same university where she works, but she doesn't want to be too overbearing. Flo must have her own life. At least Sarah is here.

The host gives a few closing words, mentions again the special discount that is available for tonight only. More applause and people disperse.

Stepping away from the front, Kate sees Sarah heading towards the wine table. *I won't be long,* Kate mouths. Sarah nods, *Okay,* making a drinking gesture with her hand. Kate goes off to mingle, thanking people for coming; writes some personalised messages in their books. This is the best part, she thinks.

Sarah stands in the queue for wine, hoping she doesn't have to wait too long. She has spotted a coffee table book about the history of Moroccan tiles and wants to buy it. Along with a signed copy of Kate's, of course. She is proud of her friend, has been telling everyone to buy it.

After the divorce, Miranda and the others had dropped Sarah altogether. It was interesting when they started contacting her again, a few years ago, after she had been featured in the *Sunday Times* magazine for doing the interior décor of a famous actress's summer house. Sarah took enormous pleasure in telling Miranda that she couldn't help with any refurbishments because she was fully booked for the next twelve months, at least.

Sarah picks up a glass of white and heads towards the art and design section. She avoids the gaze of a man who tried to chat her up earlier. He had suggested they meet for dinner to discuss renovation plans for his flat in Fulham. A possible client. Only, she knows his sort too well. He had his shirt undone so it showed off a bit of his chest hair and he made a point of telling her he was single. No thank you.

The wine is sour. Sarah drinks it quickly and finds the book she is looking for. A heavy hardback with a glossy jacket, beautiful photographs of coloured mosaic tiles. Perfect inspiration for her new client's bathroom.

The event winds to a close.

Kate says her goodbyes to the shop staff and ushers Sarah onto the pavement. They link arms, walking slowly towards the pub on the corner, where everyone else has already headed.

'That was great,' Sarah says. 'You're so confident up there.'

'I just hope it sells. There's not as much sex in this one.'

'Yes, but nobody knows that until they read it, do they?'

They are approaching the door to the bar and Kate finds herself stalling. 'Can't we just skip it? I could say you were taken ill or something, and I needed to get you home.'

'Of course. I don't mind, whatever,' Sarah says. 'This is your night.'

'I just want to have a wander. My last train isn't for ages.'

'You can always stay at mine, you know.'

Kate nods, although she knows she won't. Sarah has moved back to the house where she used to live with Luke. Her second divorce is finalised now, and her other house has been sold. Sarah told Kate she was considering selling this one, but then decided it was the perfect place for her business. She has set up her office in the basement – fabric swatches and colour charts – where the old guest bedroom and Luke's study used to be. Kate didn't say anything when Sarah told her that.

They unlink arms and Sarah readjusts her handbag. She wishes Kate wouldn't walk so fast. Her new shoes are pinching. She hopes Kate does stay over and wonders if there are enough eggs for breakfast – she could make them brunch, and then they could go to the Tate. They haven't done that for ages. It would be nice to have someone to stay. Zac and Lucy have only been coming home during the holidays. Last summer, Lucy didn't come back at all – she went travelling around Europe for two whole months. She is graduating soon, and it won't be long before she has moved out for good. The house is so big without them. Although she would never admit it to anyone other than Kate. She wants to be seen to be strong and independent. Especially now, given what she is considering.

'Shall we get something to eat?' Sarah says. Her shoes are really rubbing.

'Sure,' Kate says. 'There's a great place on the other side of Bloomsbury Square.'

They cross over the road, talking as they walk.

'Guess what?' Sarah says. She's been desperate to tell Kate all day. 'He called me again last night, and we were on the phone for over an hour.'

'I hope he was doing the talking as well. Not just you?'

'He said he's needed time to process things properly.'

'What, ten years?!'

They both laugh.

'But seriously, he's different now.'

'You need to be careful,' Kate says with a serious tone. 'Daniel said he seemed content the last time he saw him. But has he really changed? And without actually getting any proper help?'

'I don't know.' Sarah feels a chill. She wanted to tell Kate so badly, even though she knew what her response would be. She reminds herself she mustn't do anything rash. If she could only remember exactly what Luke had said, Kate would understand — something about finding slugs by his bed and how he couldn't sleep for worrying about where they'd come from and if his cottage was damp, and when he got up in the morning, tired from not having slept, he realised the slugs were a cover for his real worries, how he'd wasted so much time being abroad and now he was back he wanted more than anything to be with her, making a real home and growing old and — oh, it was something like that, although the slug part, she thinks, doesn't sound as romantic now. He told it so much better.

She thinks she wants to say yes.

'Daniel's meeting him next week, did I tell you?' Kate says.

'He really is different, you know.'

'Just be careful. Remember what you said after Marcus.'

'I know, I know.'

They reach the square and Sarah stops at a bench. She takes off her shoes and rubs the back of her heels, frowning. Kate sits next to her. She can tell that Sarah's anxiety isn't about her shoes. She has known for some time that Sarah is considering being with Luke again.

'We're nearly there,' Kate says, pointing across to the restaurant. 'Can you make it? I'm not sure I could carry you.'

Sarah laughs. 'Would you hate me? I mean, if we got back together.'

'It's just that everything would be different, wouldn't it?'

'Nothing would change,' Sarah says. 'I promise.'

Kate wants to tell her friend she is being naive, that nothing will be the same if she gets back with Luke. Sarah should be moving forward, not retreading old ground. But mostly, she is afraid of what might happen. What will she say when she sees Luke again? What will it be like if they all go out again, the four of them? She can't imagine Daniel wanting to do that.

They are at the restaurant now and the man at the desk asks if they have booked. He shows them to a free table in the corner, where Kate decides she won't say another word about Luke and only talk about fun things. After all, it was such a long time ago. They are all so much wiser now.

Sarah takes a seat and slips her feet out of her shoes. She decides to tell Kate that she is going to be sensible, that she will take things slowly with Luke. The notion of being happy and in love, like it was before, is so alluring, yet she needs to be sure she is not imagining it because she is afraid of being alone. It is too easy to go along with the idea of how something could be, rather than how it is.

They smile at one another and talk about what they are going to eat, laugh about the Elizabeth Taylor anecdote.

More people arrive at the restaurant. A couple are seated at the table next to them. Behind, there is a group of four. The lighting is exactly right for conversations to flow – not too bright for them to feel self-conscious, but soft enough to create a soothing sense of companionable intimacy. This is nice, they both think at the same time. Certain it must remain like this, always.

* * *

The manager of the pub surveys the bar. It is a particularly busy night, not unusual for a Friday, especially at the start of summer. He is thinking about the season ahead and any changes he might need to make to the rota. Two of the students he usually employs for the holiday period have told him they are moving away, and he is wondering whether he should place an advert with a proper agency, rather than doing the usual posts on social media. The pub has gained quite a reputation over the past few years, and he wants to make sure he employs the right calibre of person.

He is also feeling troubled because the owner of the pub is back – he is here tonight having dinner with a friend. Back for good, apparently. Living in the cottage he bought nearby. Their working relationship has been very formal up to now, with Mr Linton keeping a healthy distance. Living overseas, only returning for short stays and a traditional monthly visit in August. He worked in finance, somewhere in the Middle East – Dubai, was it? Or perhaps Bahrain. The man senses Mr Linton is rather a socialite, so he can't imagine him being anywhere like Saudi Arabia. Far too strict. The man hopes the pub won't be altered.

Over at table twenty-seven, Luke catches the eye of the manager and nods. He will tell the man later how pleased he is with turnover. He also wants to offer him reassurance. Just because he is back permanently, he won't be interfering. Not in the running of it, at least. The pub is his investment – perhaps more of a hobby. He saw it for sale one year, in a run-down state, and thought why the hell not. Property development is something he is considering now.

The area is good, too. One of those quaint rural places outside the commuter belt. Londoners come out this way when they are seeking a new life. Giving up the rat race is quite the thing nowadays. Luke is hoping Sarah can be persuaded.

He turns back to the table and tops up Daniel's glass.

'No more for me,' Daniel says, putting his hand over it.

'I thought you were going to crash at the cottage,' Luke says. 'I've bought a nice bottle of port for us later.'

'Have to do it another time, I'm afraid. I promised Kate I'd get back. You know how it is. Especially now the girls aren't around. She's feeling it, I think.'

'Of course, of course. Sarah's the same.'

Luke tops up his own glass and thinks about whether he should make his next move with Sarah before or after Lucy's graduation ceremony. Their phone call the other night was encouraging. He can feel she is on the verge of saying yes.

Daniel cuts into his steak. He wishes he'd ordered the truffle and parmesan chips instead of the salad, but he is trying to lose a few pounds. Kate says they need to be careful now they are in their mid-fifties. That's when it happens, she told him, the real downward slide. He didn't like to say they had probably already passed that point.

'Still running?' Daniel asks. 'I don't expect there's a gym around here, is there?'

'There's one at the hotel, but it isn't very big. I'm thinking of building a studio in the garden. A home gym.'

Daniel nods. 'I did a fifteen-mile ride out to Petworth the other week. A lovely route. You should get a bike.'

They chat about heart rates, fat burning, anaerobic training. Daniel doesn't exercise as much as he should, but whenever he meets up with Luke, he finds himself exaggerating his routine. Life abroad seems to have suited his friend – he is in much better shape than Daniel is. Still has a full head of hair. Daniel wonders how often they will meet up, now he has returned.

Luke looks over to the bar, where a woman is staring at him. She is sitting on a bar stool next to her friend. Both of them keep glancing around in a way that signals to Luke they are single. Divorced, probably in their forties.

He looks back at his food. It has been years since he's had a fall – he calls it that, because it is just like falling from a great height. And yes, the out-of-control sensation is exhilarating, but now he is able to abstain since he knows it ultimately ends in a painful smack on the ground. He hasn't succumbed to the lure of it for so long. When he thinks about what he used to do, it's as if he is thinking about another person entirely. He made a pact – only meaningful sex, meaningful relationships. Impossible at first, especially in those early years after the divorce, but then he reached a turning point. It was during one of his usual weekends – one woman on a Friday night, another on a Saturday – that he felt an awful hollowness. A desolation he hadn't ever felt during sex before. An ending. Yet

319

it was also a beginning. He realised the only woman he ever wants is Sarah. He is ashamed of what he did to her.

He is going to get her back.

'Did you say you'd put an offer in on that place in Broad Oak?', Daniel says.

'Hmm, no . . . I mean, yes. The big house, you mean?'

Daniel wonders why their conversation is so slow. Luke seems distracted, although it is probably also tiredness on Daniel's part. He has had a busy few weeks. A conference and then a work trip to Germany, meeting new clients, all the while trying to make sure Kate was supported. He felt bad not being there for her book launch last week, but she assured him he didn't miss anything. Sarah took her out for dinner.

'How many flats will there be?' Daniel says.

'Four, maybe five. I'm meeting with the architect soon,' Luke says.

'And that's what you've decided to do?'

'Not so much decided, more an opportunity. And why not?'

'The key to success, hey? Diversification.'

'Yes indeed,' Luke says.

They both give a weary sigh.

'Sorry, it's been a long week,' Daniel says, yawning.

'We could've done it another time.'

'No, it's good to catch up.'

Daniel isn't sure why he couldn't postpone for another time. Perhaps he is still in denial about Luke being back for good. He isn't sure how he feels about it. After Luke left the country, all those years ago, Daniel was able to reach an internal resolution. Now, things are being stirred up. A part of him can never forgive Luke for what he did.

Luke swigs his wine. 'I might rent the cottage out in due course,' he says. 'Add it to the portfolio. Or maybe keep it and buy something else. I can't decide.' He takes his final forkful. The duck is delicious tonight. He gives a cursory glance around the pub and notices the woman at the bar again. She is still looking over at him.

'Will you be moving back to London?' Daniel asks. 'Is that what Sarah wants?'

'It would be good for us to be somewhere new. Sarah would love it here. But don't say anything, will you? She might not want me back!' Luke laughs, expecting Daniel to give him encouragement, to tell him of course Sarah wants to be with him. He could ask Daniel outright, but that would be too crass.

Daniel yawns. He seems tired and out of sorts, Luke thinks, not his usual jolly self.

'I'll get the bill.' Luke puts his napkin on the table, gestures for Daniel to remain seated. 'No, it's on me tonight, old friend.'

In the car park, Luke sees Daniel off. He stands at the front of the pub and surveys the surroundings. It is only nine thirty, still light. The perfect kind of evening, the sun starting to set, casting long shadows. He will give Sarah a call when he gets home, tell her how peaceful it is here, how beautiful. She messaged him earlier, saying she was going to stay in and watch a film. I wish I could join you, he wrote. It took her two hours to reply, but he knew she would. Me too, she wrote.

First, he will have another drink. Then he won't be disturbing Sarah halfway through her film.

At the bar, he orders a pint.

'Oh, sorry.' A woman bumps into him. 'Didn't see you there.'

She is the woman who has been catching his eye all night.

'No worries,' he says.

She sits down and twists herself around on the bar stool. He notices her friend has gone and she is alone.

'I saw you eating,' she says. 'Is the food any good?'

'It's excellent. You should come for a meal sometime.'

'Maybe I will.'

She looks right at him. Her hand is next to his on the bar top. She crosses and uncrosses her legs. Presses her lips together as if she is blotting her lipstick.

'Are you local?' she asks.

'Just moved here. I've been working in the Middle East.'

She rests her hand in her lap. Her legs are bronzed and bare, as if she's been on holiday.

'Oh, I love Dubai,' she says. 'We went there a few years ago when my kids were younger. They loved the water park.'

He tells her what it was like to live out there and she says she's always wanted to move abroad. Somewhere hot. She smiles. He knows she wants him, and he smiles back. It is impossible to ignore, an old reflex trying to slip back into place.

When the barman calls last orders, she says she had better be going. She only meant to pop out for a quick one.

'Since the divorce,' she says, 'I try not to get into the habit of staying in all the time. The children are older now and, you know how it is, you need to force yourself to go out.'

322

'I'll walk you to your car,' he says.

'A real gentleman,' she says. 'Not many of them around.'

He resists the urge to brush against her. His hand is on fire.

When they are in the car park, she says it was nice to meet him. 'Maybe see you again. I'll probably be here next Friday.' She gives him a lingering look before getting into her car.

He watches her drive away. It is dark now, and he waits until the lights of her car are completely gone. Then he runs. Past the church and down the lane, past the post box and the sign for the farm shop. Keeps going, even when his lungs are burning, even when his legs are about to give out. By the time he reaches the cottage, he has to rest for a few minutes against the stone wall, gasping and sweaty.

He follows the path round to the side, through the wooden gate and into the garden, fumbling for his mobile as he goes. He cannot allow this panic to overtake.

I love you, he writes, as he stands on the patio. I miss you

His hands are shaking. He puts his mobile back in his pocket and walks towards the pond. Stops in the middle of the lawn and looks up. Sarah will adore it here. They will be so happy.

The bright moon is shining down, staining everything silver blue. Trees are silhouetted against the night sky.

A raspy bark of a fox in the distance breaks his concentration. A yelp.

He turns and goes back across the lawn.

323

Acknowledgements

This novel would not have been possible without the care and attention of so many brilliant people. Thanks especially to my agent, Sophie Lambert, who is the best mentor I could wish for. To my amazing editor, Francesca Main, who welcomed me to Phoenix Books and gave such incredibly wise advice. The wider team at Orion, including Lucinda McNeile, Charlotte Abrams-Simpson, Ellen Turner and Katie Moss, and Anne O'Brien who copy-edited the manuscript. Thanks to Alex Peake-Tomkinson for insightful thoughts on a very early draft; Dr Thaddeus Birchard at the Marylebone Centre, who helped me understand the psychology of sex addiction; the 2018 and 2019 cohorts and teachers of the UEA Creative Writing Prose Fiction MA, too many to mention; Maya Lubinsky for giving me the courage to delete what didn't work; Beth Wright for her invaluable feedback and careful reading; Pat McHugh and the South Side Writers for the ongoing support and laughs. To my parents for their unwavering belief in my abilities. My sons for understanding when I needed to write, helping with the dinners, and doing the washing-up without being asked. To Karen M, for being a friend through all of life's ups and downs; Debbie, for always being my champion. Finally, to Dale, for reading so many drafts, all of them approached with enthusiasm and honesty – *Everything We Are* would not exist without you.

Questions for Book Clubs

1. Which character was your favourite and why? Did your opinion of the characters alter over the course of the novel?

2. Why do you think the author chose to tell the story from four perspectives?

3. What surprised you most about the novel?

4. Do you think Daniel could have handled the revelations about his wife in a different way?

5. Daniel and Luke have known each other for many years. What did you make of their friendship and how do you think their shared history affected the way they handled the conflict between them?

6. How did Kate's background and childhood influence the decisions she made about her marriage? Luke's past also had a significant impact on his later relationships – how did that affect your understanding of his actions?

7. A big theme of the novel is morality in marriage. Did the book resonate with your view of love and long-term relationships?

8. Sarah faced significant challenges in her relationship with Luke. What would you do in her situation, and do you think she made the right decision in the end?

9. Luke experiences several forms of addiction in the novel. Which do you feel is ultimately the most destructive, and how optimistic do you feel about his future?